CW00865333

First Published in the United Kingdom in 2021.

Copyright © 2021 by Deborah Stone

First paperback edition December 2021
Deborah Stone asserts the moral right to be identified as the author of this work.

Book design by Deborah Stone

ISBN: 9798781372775

Me and My Shadow

By Deborah Stone

Part I

Chapter 1

'When my sister was born, I stopped walking for a whole year.'

The doctor glanced up from her notepad, her head slightly tilted to the left. 'Why did you stop walking?'

'How the hell would I know? I was four years old.' I bent forwards, studying my bleeding cuticles.

Silence. When I looked up again, Dr Blake was still staring at me, unblinking, like some doe-eyed dog waiting for me to toss her a biscuit.

'Well, can you expand on it at all? Was it a physical problem, or do you think it was triggered by something else possibly?'

'I've already told you, I don't know. Maybe my legs were tired.' I chuckled at my own witticism.

The doctor scribbled something on her pad with her shiny, black Montblanc ink pen. She was perched across from me in a plush green velour armchair, which matched mine exactly. We were separated only by a sparkling glass coffee table, which was supported by an intricate maze of crazy spiral legs. Behind her was an infeasibly large oak desk, meticulously tidy and virtually empty, aside from a leather penholder and a blotter, pristine without a trace of ink. Behind the desk, the wall was peppered with certificates. Dr C. Blake, Doctor of Psychiatry from this university, that university, another universe. I returned my gaze to Dr Blake, who was as immaculate as her surroundings, with her perfectly tailored navy trouser suit topped by a perfectly tied, creamy pussy-bow at the neck of her blouse. Her feet were encased in spiky red stilettos. I liked the shoes. They were sharp, edgy.

Dr Blake uncrossed her slender legs and recrossed them to the other side. Her silky ash-blonde ponytail swayed slightly as she moved. 'So, what did your parents do when you refused to walk?' asked her perfectly painted red pout.

I made no reply.

'Rachel, please tell me, how did they respond?' She leant forward slightly in her chair, caressing her notebook to her chest.

'They got frustrated and they became angry with me,' I sulked, pulling at a piece of raw skin on my thumb.

'How did their frustration manifest itself exactly?' Dr Blake enquired, leaning towards me.

'They told me to get up and walk – and when I refused, they just shouted at me. They shouted a lot,' I muttered.

The doctor did not even flinch. 'And how did you respond?'

'I screamed back, louder and then, even louder. But however much I yelled they didn't seem to hear me.' My ears rang as if my mother was still shouting at me.

'That must have been enormously difficult for you. How did that make you feel?'

I lifted my head and stared the doctor straight in the eye, yanking my matted, filthy fringe from my face.

'I felt like they didn't want me. I knew that they only had eyes for my little, precious baby sister, and that I could effectively go hang. I paused. 'But I got them to pay attention eventually.'

'And how did you achieve that?'

I smiled and pulled up the sleeves of my faded sweat top over my elbows, revealing a network of scars. 'I think you already know the answer to that, don't you, Doctor?'

I was deposited with monotonous regularity at Dr Blake's office. The heavy door clanging shut behind me made me jump every time, even though I should have been used to it by now. Often, I seemed to wake up and be in her office even before my day had begun. I wondered how much longer this probing into my psyche would go on and to what purpose. It seemed to me that it must be money for old rope for Dr Blake. She got to sit in her comfy armchair all day long, and listen to me tell her shaggy dog stories, for which I assumed she was paid a small fortune and I got…well, I had no idea what was in it for me. I did not want to come here. I was forced to attend.

We sat in uncompanionable silence. Dr Blake was patient, like a lion prepared to stalk its prey camouflaged in the long grass for hours on end, because the lure of the eventual kill was too delicious to forego. Eventually, she pounced.

'Let's explore what actually happened when your sister was born, shall we? What's your very first memory of her?' Dr Blake was settled in her familiar place opposite me, my psychiatric opponent.

I sighed. 'Depends on what you mean, doesn't it? Would that be when I first heard about her, or when I first fixed my eyes on the scrawny little runt?' I ran my fingers through my hair and located a decent knot to work on.

'Well, shall we begin with when you first became aware of Catherine?'

'I don't really remember my mother being pregnant.' The tangle in my hair was very dense and immensely satisfying. I pulled at it between my thumb and forefinger. 'I just remember that one day, my mother wasn't there anymore. Or my father, except briefly early doors.'

'What do you mean?' asked Dr Blake, looking up from her notebook.

'I mean that one morning when I woke up, my mother was replaced by her mum instead - my grumpy old

3

grandma - and no one really explained to me what the hell was going on.'

'And how did that make you feel?'

'Christ, you ask some stupid questions.' I hoicked my knees up to my chest and pulled at the plastic peeling off the bottom of my trainer. 'I don't really know how I felt, did I? I was only four, as I keep reminding you. If I look at in retrospect with the eyes of an adult, I am guessing that I was shit scared. My mother had always been there - and suddenly she wasn't.'

'So where was she?'

'I think you know all this anyway, but if it helps you get through our allotted time, I'll fill you in. My idiot sister was born prematurely, meaning that my mother spent three months living at the hospital staring at her adoringly through a plastic incubator - in case her darling baby pegged it - while I was left at home alone to fend for myself.'

'Where's Mummy? I want my Mummy.' I stamped my hands and feet onto the hard, cold kitchen floor, my face bloated with crying.

My grandmother on my mother's side was peeling carrots at the sink. I hated carrots. 'She's not here, Rachel. She's at the hospital. I've told you a thousand times that she has to stay there to look after your baby sister. Now stop all your nonsense this instant,' she huffed. My grandmother put down her knife and hauled me up from the floor, wrenching my shoulder in the process, so I kicked her in the side.

'You little madam. Right, I've had just about enough of you.' She scooped me up, tucking me under her arm. My grandmother was small, yet wiry and surprisingly strong. She carried me upstairs, oblivious to my screaming and wriggling, where she plonked me onto my bed. 'You can stay there until you calm down and decide to apologise.' The door slammed behind me, imprisoning me on my Barbie duvet.

'I want Mummy! I want my Mummy! Where is my Mummy?' I bellowed. 'I just want my Mummy.'

Weeks passed. I could barely remember what my mother's face looked like anymore and kept having to refresh my memory from the photos of her which were dotted about the house. Then one day, when I was convinced that she had run away and abandoned me for good, my grandmother made an announcement.

'Your mummy will be home in a minute,' she soothed, as we waited by the window in the front room. It had a good view of the road, and I was balancing on the cushions of the cream leather settee – which was strictly forbidden – so that I could peer through the net curtains. I was watching for my parents' car to turn into the drive. Every time I heard the vroom of a vehicle, I perked up like a baby chick waiting for the mother bird to fly in with much-needed sustenance, only to be disappointed every time an unrecognisable car sped past.

'Now listen to me carefully, Rachel. When Mummy and Daddy do arrive home with your baby sister, they will be very tired. You mustn't bother them too much,' my grandmother instructed me.

'Here they are!' I screamed, as my parents' red Ford Cortina turned onto the drive. 'Mummy's here...and Daddy's here too.' I raced to the front door, straining for the latch, but I could not quite reach it.

'Mind out of the way, Rachel,' boomed my grandmother, shoving me deftly to one side with her knee whilst opening the door. My mother stood there, stooped, car seat in hand, nestled inside of which was a wizened, yellow gnome sporting a silly white hat. 'Rachel, darling, say hello to your new sister. This is Catherine.'

I ignored the gross bundle of wrinkles. 'Hello, Mummy,' I roared, running to hug her. 'You came back!'

'Let your mother get inside the house first, there's a good girl, Rachel,' instructed my father, who was following on behind with copious heavy bags. 'Let us get our breath back.'

I kept tight hold of the hem of my mother's coat as she tottered into the lounge. She eased the car seat onto the floor by the sofa before undoing the buttons on her coat. Sinking onto the seat, she sighed. 'Ah, it's good to be back.'

The shrunken object in the car seat farted with a volume which belied its size.

'Ooh, did you hear that, Mummy? It made a smell,' I laughed.

'It's she, not it, Rachel, and Catherine can't help it. She's just a tiny, little baby. She's not a big girl like you. She doesn't know any better yet.' My mother leant down and unclipped the car seat, lifting the minute parcel out of it and raising its bottom to her nose. 'I think someone needs a new nappy,' she smiled, placing the baby in the crook of her arm, and leaning down to kiss her forehead. 'Rachel, mind out of the way while I go and change your sister. Go and help your Grandma to get tea ready.'

'But I want to come with you, Mummy. Can I help you - please?'

'Rachel, please don't whine, darling. I will be back down soon. You have got to behave like a big, grown-up girl now, because I need to look after your baby sister. We have all got to look after her now, as she has already been through a lot in her short life. Can you help me to do that?' my mother asked, her tone flat, her eyes deep-set within sunken, black rings.

'No,' I sulked. I reached forward and took a swipe at the baby but missed as my mother moved Catherine instinctively out of reach.

With her free arm, my mother smacked me hard on the leg. 'Don't you ever try to hit your sister again, do you hear me, Rachel? Now go to your room and don't come out again until I tell you to.'

I stood rigid in front of her, my leg smarting and tears coursing down my face.

'Rachel. I'm not going to tell you again. Get out of my sight,' yelled my mother. The baby awoke in her arms and began to wail.

I ran.

Chapter 2

It was a black shift dress today for Dr Blake, set off with a simple gold chain and killer, silver metal stilettos on her black court shoes. The only splash of colour was the deep ruby red of her lips. She had a tiny smudge of lipstick on her front teeth, but I did not bring attention to it. I smiled at this imperfection, knowing how much it would upset her when she finally rechecked her face in the mirror.

'Morning, Rachel. How are you today?' enquired Dr Blake, settling herself into her chair. She motioned for me to take my usual seat opposite her. I mooched over and flung myself into the seat, sighing.

'You look tired, Rachel. Are you sleeping OK?'

'It's hard to sleep with so much noise going on all night. It's like living in a zoo. When I do manage to nod off eventually, there is always some strange animal screech that wakes me up at some point in the early hours.'

'That must be difficult for you,' Dr Blake nodded, noting something in her book. She flicked over the last few pages of her scribble. I sat in silence, watching her.

'I'd like to pick up on where we left off last time, if that's alright with you, Rachel?'

'Whatever,' I mumbled, yawning.

'So, quite clearly, things changed once Catherine arrived back at home?'

I stared at her. She waited. I shifted in my chair and slung my leg over the arm.

'You could say that, yes.' I rolled my eyes. 'I think it would be fair to say that I can definitely divide my life into BC and AC.'

'BC and AC?' Dr Blake repeated. 'What do you mean by that, Rachel?'

'Well, I would have thought it was obvious for a woman of your superior intellect, Doctor, but if I must explain… BC is before Catherine and AC – well, AC is – can you guess?'

Dr Blake laughed. 'Yes, I can, thank you, Rachel. But given how young you were when Catherine arrived, and that the majority of your life has been lived in AC, as you term it, it seems odd to divide your life like that. Do you agree?'

'Well, clearly I don't agree, or I would not have described it like that, now would I?' I picked at the skin on my arm. 'Everything changed from the minute Catherine set foot in the house. My mother, for one thing, became a completely different person.'

'In what way was she different?' Dr Blake asked, leaning across to reach her coffee mug. She sipped silently.

'I suppose that before Catherine - in my so-called BC era – I remember my mother being happy and fun and playing with me, but afterwards…' I trailed off, staring at the floor.

'And afterwards?' coaxed Dr Blake.

'Afterwards, she, I…' I gulped back the tears which were inexplicably welling up, hurting my throat. I swallowed hard. 'Afterwards, she never had any time for me. She was constantly knackered and only ever seemed to have enough energy to help Catherine. I hated her for it.'

'Do you think your mother might have been unwell after Catherine's birth?' asked Dr Blake.

I pulled at a loose thread on my sleeve, but it was stuck fast. 'I think now, looking back on it, she was probably depressed. Catherine was extremely demanding, because she was premature and a total pain in the arse - and my father was always at work, so Mum had no one to help her out, and I…'

'And you?'

'Well, I guess I didn't help too much either. I just wanted everything to go back to how it had been before.'

It was my sixth birthday, and I was beside myself with excitement. I woke up early that morning and skipped into my parents' bedroom.

'Mummy! Daddy! It's my birthday!' I shouted, tugging at the duvet cover on my mother's side of the bed.

'Mmm,' my mother replied, rolling away from me.

I patted her on the shoulder and, receiving no response, clambered in behind her and kissed her hair. 'Mummy,' I stage whispered. 'It's my birthday.'

'Rachel, it's five o'clock in the morning. It's not your birthday yet. I've been up all night with your little sister, and I am very tired. Go away and come back at seven-thirty.'

In reply, I summoned all my strength and wrenched the duvet off my mother, hoping she would turn over and tickle me. She did indeed turn over, but instead of playing our tickling game of old, she shoved me hard off the bed. As I fell, I caught my arm on the side table.

'Ow,' I cried, rubbing my arm and bursting into tears.

'Rachel, go back to bed as your mother asked,' my father bellowed from his side of the bed. 'Now!'

I got up slowly and left the room, but I did not go back to bed. Rather, I tiptoed down to the kitchen, sobbing to myself with every creaking step. In the half-light, I could see the outline of the box which contained my beautiful birthday cake. My mother had let me have a quick peek at it yesterday after she had collected it from the shop.

It was fuchsia pink with a cute Barbie doll stencilled in icing on the top. *Happy 6th Birthday Rachel* was piped at Barbie's tiny feet. I opened the kitchen drawer and located the rolling pin, which my mother used to use to batch make apple pies for the freezer. I carried it over to the table where my cake sat patiently, waiting for the candles to be duly lit and extinguished at my party later that day. I pulled a chair out from under the table and hoisted myself onto the seat. Then I stood upon it, wobbling slightly as I held the rolling pin in my other hand. I raised the rolling pin high above my head and brought it down with a thwack onto the lid of the cake box. The centre of the box caved inwards. I thumped it several more times, so that pink icing oozed out of the edges of the box and splattered right across the table. Then I threw the rolling pin onto the floor and did as I was told. I went back to bed.

Chapter 3

'I remember that my parents took me to see a doctor once, who told them that I was a polar bear, or something like that. I'm guessing that in those days, they didn't know how to help me with that.'

'A polar bear?' queried Dr Blake.

'Yes, I'm fairly sure that's what he said. How weird is that, right?'

Chapter 4

Doors banged shut in my wake and yet again, I was back in the inquisition chair. It was rather like appearing on *Mastermind*, as I sat across from my questioner. All that was missing was the spotlight.

'And your specialised subject today is?'

'How my family fucked me up.'

'OK, Rachel, you have two minutes on how your family fucked you up, starting now…'

'Can I ask you to think back to a specific bad memory you might have from your childhood? I don't mean an ongoing issue, necessarily, but just a moment in time, when you were aged anywhere between six to ten years old. Is there any particular incident which stands out for you?'

Blood. I could see blood.

'Rachel, can you hear me? Dr Blake queried.

I was squatting on the seat of my designated armchair, my hands over my ears and my head between my knees.

'Rachel, could you raise your head so that you can listen to me, please?' It was more of an instruction than a question.

I lifted my forehead slightly and peeped out through the gap in my arms. Dr Blake, cool as crystal, peered back at me.

'The glasses are new,' I commented, raising my head out of its shell a little further.

'I need them for reading sometimes when my eyes are tired.' She removed her glasses and rubbed her left eye.

'You've been far too swotty, Doc - too much reading of the small print in your medical textbooks.'

'You may well be right,' smiled Dr Blake. 'Now, to come back to my original question, can you think of anything from when you were that age which you still remember as a bad moment?' She replaced her glasses and stared expectantly at her notebook, her Montblanc poised.

'You want me to tell you another story, do you?'

'If you like, yes please, Rachel.'

I closed my eyes. Glass. Blood.

Catherine and I had both received dolls for Christmas, but not just any old dolls. These ones wee'd and cried after you poured water into their mouths. You could press a button on the back of their heads for tears, or on their belly button if you wanted them to wee.

One afternoon, when my mother was asleep as she often was these days, and my father was out at work, Catherine and I decided to feed our dolls and instruct them to excrete from both ends. We located a glass bowl in the kitchen, and I filled it up carefully in the sink. I could reach the taps, whereas Catherine was still too short, being only around five at this time. I carried the Pyrex bowl over to the kitchen table and we both began to fill the requisite pipettes with water to hydrate our dolls. Catherine's doll, Daisy, had long blonde hair to match her own and mine, Gilly, was a brunette like me. Once the dolls began to regurgitate water from their mouths, we knew that they were full. They were now ready to emit other bodily fluids.

'Daisy is very sad today, Rachel,' Catherine told me.

Catherine called me Wachel, as she was unable to say her Rs until she was a teenager, but apparently that was just cute, according to my parents.

'Why?' I asked.

'She wanted to have ice cream for lunch, but she wasn't allowed to, 'cos she hadn't eaten her spaghetti first.'

'Well, that serves her right, doesn't' it? She's a very, very bad doll,' I replied, and I slapped Daisy on the leg.

'Ow, that hurt,' replied Catherine, pressing Daisy's head. Lo and behold, tears trickled down Daisy's face.

'And Gilly really needs a wee, 'cos she drank so much apple juice this morning that she can't stop peeing,' I laughed, pressing Gilly's tummy button. I held my hand out underneath Gilly, but she remained dry. I pressed again, but nothing happened.

'Maybe Gilly wants to cry instead,' suggested Catherine, wiping away Daisy's tears with a piece of kitchen roll. 'Maybe she didn't get any ice cream either.'

I thought this might be a possibility, so I pressed Gilly's head instead, but no droplets appeared on her cheeks either.

'She probably needs another drink,' Catherine diagnosed.

'Perhaps,' I replied, force-feeding Gilly another large pipette of water, which ran straight out of her mouth and down her dress. I pressed her head one more time. No reaction. I pressed her stomach. No urination. I banged her head on the side of the sink. I pummelled her stomach with my fist. Nothing.

'You'll hurt her, Rachel,' said Catherine.

'She's a stupid doll. She's broken,' I replied, slamming Gilly onto the black and white chequered lino. 'Give Daisy to me and I'll try her.'

'No, Daisy is my doll, and she wants to be with me,' Catherine retorted, hugging the doll close to her chest, and cradling her head.

I lunged for Daisy, wrenching her from Catherine's weaker grasp. I noted the wet patch the doll had left behind on Catherine's T-shirt.

'Give her back, Rachel. She is my dolly. Give her back to me right now!' Catherine stamped her feet, jumping up to grasp her doll.

I held Daisy out of reach of Catherine and started to pour another pipette of water down her throat.

'I want Daisy,' cried Catherine. 'Give me her now, Rachel.'

I merely laughed and began to fill another pipette. Unable to reach Daisy, Catherine grabbed the glass dish containing the water. It slid off the side of the sink and smashed onto my foot. Sockless as I was, a sharp shard of glass pierced my skin - and suddenly everything went red.

My mother raced in 'What the hell is going on? I can't leave you alone for two minutes without all hell breaking loose, can I? What's wrong with you?' She stopped suddenly. 'Rachel, are you alright? Stay where you are. Don't move, there's glass everywhere and you're bleeding. Catherine, go over to the other side of the kitchen table - and stay there. I don't want you cutting yourself as well.'

My mother scooped me up and sat me on the draining board. I was trying to be brave, but I was crying now, and I was scared, because my whole foot was covered in blood. My mother ran the tap and soaked some kitchen roll under the water. She began to clean my foot.

'This is an awfully bad cut, Rachel. Try to keep still while I clean it. Now, hold this for a moment,' she instructed, placing a large wad of kitchen roll over the cut. She left me wobbling on the draining board while she fetched the first aid kit. When she returned, she soaked iodine onto a cotton pad and placed it over the wound. I howled. 'Stay still, Rachel, for Christ's sake.' Eventually, my foot was bandaged up and Mum carried me into the sitting room, depositing me on the sofa. After this, she carried Catherine in as well, before mopping and hoovering up the glass instructing us every few seconds not to move. Catherine and I sat side by side.

'Are you OK?' whispered Catherine.

'No, I'm not,' I sobbed. 'It hurts - and it's all your fault.'

'It's not my fault, it's yours.' Catherine retorted.

My mother marched back into the room and pulled up the poof. She plonked her bottom onto it and faced the two of us.

'Christ almighty, will you two stop bloody bickering? You're giving me a damned headache. Now, exactly what happened?'

'Catherine pulled the dish off the table, and it cut my foot,' I whimpered.

'But that was only 'cos Rachel took Daisy, 'cos Gilly wouldn't cry or wee, and then Rachel banged Gilly, and then she took Daisy instead. I wanted Daisy back and Rachel wouldn't give her to me, so I tried to take the water away.'

My mother turned slightly to face me head on. 'Is this true?'

'No, it was Catherine. She dropped the bowl on purpose.'

'No I didn't.'

'Yes, you did,' I replied, poking Catherine.

'Stop it now,' my mother shouted. 'Rachel, this is clearly your fault. You are not allowed to use the glass bowl unless I am there, and you cannot just snatch away Catherine's doll because yours does not work. It is unbelievably bad behaviour, and frankly, you have got what you deserve. And it could have been so much

17

worse. You could have cut Catherine as well. You have been very irresponsible. You can go to bed without any supper and no bedtime story - and then perhaps you'll think about what you've done.'

'What about Catherine?' I moaned. 'She started it.'

'She's much younger than you, and you need to set a good example, Rachel. How many times do I have to tell you that you need to look after your little sister? It's time for Catherine's bath now anyway, so you can go to your room, and I'll sort Catherine out. I'm extremely disappointed in you, Rachel.'

'What about Gilly?' I mumbled.

'Gilly is confiscated until further notice. Now go.'

I got up from the sofa and hobbled gingerly to the door.

'Right now, Rachel, I mean it,' snapped my mother.

I trudged slowly up the stairs, my foot throbbing, and when I got to the turn in the staircase, I looked back to see Catherine cradling Daisy. Gilly had been placed on the top of the bookcase, where no one could help her.

Chapter 5

'And good days? Do you remember any good days with your mother after Catherine became part of the family?' asked Dr Blake.

Tenerife when I was around eight or nine years old. The sun was so scalding that I could not walk on the sand without my plastic sandals, so we had to sprint to the water's edge with them still on our feet. Mummy and me. We held hands as we galloped towards the waves. I could swim now, but I was not allowed to go into the sea by myself. The cold water soothed my burning toes. I glanced back and I could see my father sitting on the deckchair reading his book. There was a small hump wrapped up in a beach towel sleeping on another chair under the umbrella, which was Catherine.

'Come on, Rachel, let's take the plunge,' my mother called, pulling me into the froth. We strode out, the water shocking our nether regions. I shivered and Mummy pulled me up onto her hip, dancing around and around. Eventually, she let go and I swam a few strokes - Mummy staying right beside me - before I put my feet back down again – just to check that I could – and splashed her. She splashed me back.

'Ooh, you little monster,' she teased and splashed me some more. The saltwater stung my eyes.

'I left my goggles behind on the deckchair,' I laughed, wiping the salt away.

'Salt is good for you, Rachel. You'll get a delicious tan from the sea water.'

My mother glowed, already bronzed, and more relaxed than I had seen her since, well, certainly since she had delivered Catherine. Catherine - the innocuous antichrist under the towel - who had dominated our lives ever since she had arrived before her time. She was constantly ill, or 'under the weather', as Mummy like to call it. Chest infections, asthma, tonsilitis, pharyngitis – she had a permanent appointment at the doctor's surgery. She needed to be allowed to eat whatever she chose – whenever she felt like it– because she was sickly. She needed to be helped to dress, and to undress, to make sure she was warm enough or cool enough. She needed an extra bedtime story to help her sleep. She needed, and she needed, and she needed, and my mother gave, and gave, and gave, as if somehow, she felt guilty for creating a premature child, constantly striving to protect her.

'Let's have an underwater tea party,' I shouted over the waves.

'You'll have to teach me the rules,' giggled my mother.

'There are no rules,' I smiled. 'We just go under the water, and I protond to serve you tea, and you pretend to eat it.'

'What's on the menu today?' asked my mother.

I considered for a moment. 'Tuna sandwiches and chocolate cake with chocolate oozing out of the middle of it.'

'Mmm, delicious,' replied my mother, rubbing her tummy. 'And what have you got to drink, besides sea water?'

'We don't serve sea water in the Underwater Café, but we do serve hot chocolate or milk shakes. What would you like to order?'

I flattened my palm, steadying myself again the undulating seabed, ready to scribble down her requests with my other hand.

'I'll have everything, with extra oozy chocolate' she declared. 'A full afternoon tea for me, please.'

'Excellent, madam. That will be £4 please.'

My mother handed over the imaginary payment coin by coin, and I pocketed it into my swimsuit.

'Now, if you'd like to join me underwater, I will serve.'

And we dived down under the water and enjoyed our tea. And this was a good day. An excellent day. The very best day.

Chapter 6

Another night of sleep morphed straight into yet another morning in Dr Blake's office, as if, on waking, my uncomfortable single bed transformed itself into the far more luxurious armchair in her office. I was slouched across it today, with my head resting on one arm and my legs dangling over the other.

'Are you comfortable, Rachel?' enquired Dr Blake, settling herself in the opposite chair, neat and trim in black tailored trousers and a tan sweater, which buttoned to the left of her neck. I could never have worn it, as I hated anything that made me feel claustrophobic.

'Quite comfy, thanks, Doctor. So, what do you want to talk about today? More gossip about my shitty little life?'

'Well, firstly, no life is merely shitty, Rachel. Bad things happen, obviously, but they do not negate everything about you. Good accompanies bad and so on.' She sipped her coffee. It was a cappuccino with a perfect froth on top.

'Ying and yang. ebb and flow, up and down, good and evil– I get it. How can we recognise one without the other? That old crappy argument that poncey philosophers have wrangled over for centuries.'

'Well, Rachel, it's certainly an interesting debate. How do you think that we can differentiate between good and bad?'

Her notebook was open, pen poised. I thought I had better say something worth writing down.

'Well, it's the great unanswerable question, isn't it, Doctor? Who gets to decide on the correct societal moral code? What is deemed to be generally acceptable? Why do such definitions vary by society? The concept of what is morally acceptable and unacceptable even differs amongst parents - and even amongst children, as you well know.'

'Was that the situation in your case, do you think?' Dr Blake paused, the lid of her pen hovering close to her lips.

'Have you been listening to a bloody word I've said in here? Of course, that was the case with me. Catherine could do no wrong, and I was bloody Satan.' I picked at one of the scars on my left arm. It bled a little and I smeared it across my skin.

'Is that a new cut?' Dr Blake asked, nodding towards the livid line on my forearm.

I shrugged and dug at it a little more. The pain pleased me.

'When did you start hurting yourself? Are you able to explain why you cut yourself? Did it start while you still lived at home, or later on?'

I wrenched my sleeve back down. 'I started doing it at school.'

'What happened when you were at school to make you begin to self-harm?'

'I had a good friend, Lucy and I, she, well we, went through a difficult time.'

'Would it help to talk about it?' Dr Blake asked, leaning back in her chair.

'We can talk about it, sure, but whether it will help or not is really rather moot.'

I met Lucy on our first day of senior school when we were both aged eleven. We were next to each other in the alphabet, which is how we found ourselves thrown together originally. Our desks were at the back of the sewing room, as our first-year class teacher was the head of needlework. We bonded further because neither of us were any good at sewing and we were constantly criticised for our bungled cross stitch and inability to thread a sewing machine. To this day, I have no idea how to do it.

Lucy and I remained in the same class throughout the first few years of school, right up until the year we were due to take our 'O' Levels. Lucy was extremely attractive, with long, strawberry blonde hair which cascaded down to her waist in undulating waves. She was as thin as a poker until she was fourteen, when she suddenly sprouted curves which were the envy of everyone, both male and female. The boys at school regularly crashed into walls as she passed by. Some people said she should quit school and become a model, but Lucy was so unassuming and modest. Her true beauty lay in the fact that she never thought that she was anything particularly special.

Our birthdays fell three weeks apart, and we agreed to hold a joint sixteenth party. Eventually, I persuaded my parents to hold it at our house, as it was bigger than Lucy's house, although my mother and father were not keen.

'How many people will be there?' asked my mother.

'How will you stop all the gate crashers?' my father questioned. 'The last thing we need is a load of local louts tipping up because they hear there's some shindig going on.'

'Who the hell uses the word 'shindig' anymore?' I laughed.

'Don't be rude to your father, Rachel,' my mother scolded. 'You really don't understand when not to say something, do you?'

'Evidently not, 'I quipped. 'Look, it's just a few friends, that's all. I'll keep it to twenty if that helps,' I suggested.

'Will there be boys?' My father glared at me.

'Well, yes, some, I suppose.'

My parents passed a meaningful look between them.

'In that case, we will obviously be around the party, circulating,' my father stated. 'We won't get in the way, but we will supervise, you know, oversee things.'

I groaned aloud.

'And there will be strictly no alcohol, and no one can go upstairs,' my mother added.

'What if they need the loo?' I asked.

'We have a downstairs toilet, Rachel. That will have to do.'

'I guess you could invite a couple of friends over too,' I suggested, thinking that it might distract my parents from permanently patrolling the party.

'We will think about it,' they agreed.

Lucy and I spent ages planning the guest list, although it was essentially all the usual people from school. The party was in late April, but the weather was unseasonably warm, so we decided we could use the garden and keep the adults indoors. On the day, we set up fairy lights and lanterns and as dusk approached, it all looked rather pretty. Alcohol was banned in theory, but Lucy and I emptied out a few of the large lemonade bottles my father had purchased and refilled them with gin and tonic. Everyone at school was advised to ask for the lemonade when they arrived.

The first hour or so of the party was excruciating. My mother and father patrolled the grounds like Alsatians, offering my friends mountains of mushroom vol-au-vents and cheese and pineapple on sticks. Conversation was stilted, although everyone mysteriously began to relax after their second glass of lemonade. Thankfully, my parents had eventually decided to ask a few friends over, and once they had established that we were a

25

teetotal, relatively well-behaved group of teenagers, they retired indoors to drink themselves stupid on G&Ts.

The only person who was still prowling around was Catherine. She was dolled up in a new pair of white jeans and a pink, frilly top, bouncing around among my friends like Tigger on speed. After a while, everyone grew bored of talking to her, and she sulked away in the corner of the garden, watching the proceedings from a distance with her beady little eyes. I very much hoped she would get fed up soon and go to bed.

Sometime later, Lucy rushed over to me and pulled at my sleeve.

'Rach, come here,' she begged. Her face was red and blotchy.

'What's up, Luce? Have you been crying?'

Lucy promptly burst into tears. I put my arm around her. 'Let's go up to my room for a minute.'

We headed upstairs, past my parents who never noticed, as they were guffawing over something or other in the front room. We went into my room, and I closed the door.

'What's the matter, Lucy? Tell me,' I urged her.

'I, oh my god, Rach, what have I done?' Lucy sobbed, her chest heaving.

'What have you done?' I asked, hoping that she had not broken something, or thrown up on the dining room rug.

'I was in the downstairs loo with Ross, and your sister walked in.' She pulled a tissue from her sleeve and blew hard.

'And? What were you doing with Ross?'

'I was giving him a blow job. Christ, I don't know what I was thinking – but I was – am – a bit pissed, and we started kissing and then he asked me, and I said no and then he kept asking me and it seemed like the easiest thing to do to get out of the situation without being called a prick tease and…oh, Christ. What have I done?' Lucy dissolved again.

'Don't worry, Luce. Catherine won't understand even if has she actually seen anything – which she probably hasn't. I'll talk to her later. Don't panic. No one will ever know.'

Lucy attempted to smile and blew her nose again. We waited a few more minutes until she had composed herself and then we returned to the party and had another drink.

The next day was a Sunday. I slept in late. In fact, the whole family slept well past eleven, and then I was forced to help my mum and dad clear up after last night. Catherine had gone on a playdate and a sleepover at a friend's house, so I did not get a chance to talk to her.

When I arrived at school on Monday, the whole class was buzzing with news from the party. Apparently, Catherine had seen Lucy having sex with Ross. Ross was too chuffed with his new status as someone who had actually had sex – supposedly – to contradict the story, although he swore blind that he had not told anyone when I confronted him and called him out as a bastard.

'It's that sister of yours, Rachel. She's the one going around telling everyone, not me. Sort it out with her,' he laughed.

Lucy and I hid in the cloakroom at break and lunchtime. Her face was swollen from crying. On her locker, someone had scribbled the word 'slag' in indelible marker pen.

'Shit, what am I going to do? What if my parents find out? I'm totally screwed,' she sobbed.

'How will they ever find out?' I answered, but I knew that they would, because she had a younger brother in

Catherine's year, and he was bound to carry the hot news home with him.

I travelled on a different bus home from school than Catherine, who was usually let out fifteen minutes earlier than I was. When I reached home, I marched straight up to her room and slammed the door shut.

'You little bitch. Why did you have to spread rumours all over school about Lucy?' I screamed.

'They are not rumours - they are actual fact, Rachel,' Catherine replied, her smug little face smiling up at me from where she lay on her bed.

'You've told everyone they were having sex!'

Well, they were, sort of.'

'Yes, sort of, but not actually. There's a difference, Catherine, and it matters.'

'Whatever she was doing, it was gross and she's a slut. If she didn't want to me tell, she shouldn't have done it,' Catherine retorted.

'You really are a stupid little cow, you know that?' I shouted, jumping on the bed and thwacking Catherine on the arm. She screamed out in pain.

'What the hell is going on in here?' my mother screeched, steaming in through the bedroom door. .'What are you two fighting about this time?'

'Nothing,' I replied - because there was no way I could tell my mother.

'Rachel thumped me,' moaned Catherine.

'Rachel, what the hell is wrong with you?' my mother shouted. 'Stop attacking your little sister and go and get on with your homework.'

I rose from Catherine's bed and made for the door. As I moved towards it, Catherine gave me the finger behind my mother's back.

The next day, Lucy did not appear in school. I called her house when I got home, but her mother told me that Lucy felt unwell and could not come to the phone at the moment. Much later that evening, rang me back.

'I can't talk for long, Rach,' she whispered, 'but Luke told Mum and Dad about the rumours at school, and they've gone completely mental. Even they are calling me a whore.'

'Oh, Lucy, I'm so sorry. I wish there was something I could do,' I murmured down the phone.

'It's not your fault, Rach, it's mine. I was a total idiot and I'm so ashamed of myself. I wish I could undo it all, but...' She paused. 'Look, I've got to go now, sorry' she whispered. 'See you.'

'See you,' I replied, but all I could hear was the dial tone.

Chapter 7

'Lucy hung herself?' Dr Blake looked stunned.

'Yes, Doctor, she hung herself.'

Chapter 8

I am no physicist, but when I think of myself and Catherine, I imagine two nuclear particles, fizzing with energy, circling each other, attracted yet repelled by each other. Occasionally, we collide with dangerous consequences, ranging from the mild to the totally catastrophic.

'Did you receive any counselling after Lucy died?' Dr Blake was in a cream pencil skirt with a red silk shirt tucked into it, which clung around the top of her cleavage.

For novelty, I was wearing a clean sweat top, devoid of holes, but that would not last long.

'Counselling?' I laughed. 'Don't be ridiculous. Unless you count talking to myself – and I wasn't much help, I can tell you. No, it was all very much swept under the carpet. The whole episode was an embarrassment for all concerned. Lucy's parents obviously did not want to discuss the root cause of the suicide. They buried her deep under the ground and moved away from the area with her brother as fast as they possibly could. We never saw or heard from them again.'

'And your family?'

'Oh, my family simply dismissed Lucy as a 'troubled young woman' and told me that it was just as well that she had not managed to influence me, given that girls could easily encourage others into communal suicide, or other such nonsense. I was better off out of it, etc, etc.'

'And Catherine?' Dr Blake asked, looking intently at her notebook.

'Catherine? Oh, she wasn't vaguely affected by it. She had no sense of the causality. In fact, she had no concept that she was, in reality, the catalyst for the whole affair. And I could not even begin to discuss what really happened at the party with my parents, because I could never have had any kind of conversation with either of them about sex. Consequently, I could not tell them about Catherine's involvement in the aftermath either, so she got off scot-free. Yet again.'

'But Catherine was incredibly young, wasn't she? She probably didn't really understand the consequences of her own actions.'

'I don't really know what to believe about it what actually happened anymore.' I shrugged and scratched at my arm. 'I try not to think about it.'

'And you?'

'And me what?'

'How did Lucy's death affect you?'

'Look, we've talked about this. I started to cut myself. After Lucy died, I felt so desperately lonely all the time. There was no one I could talk to about my feelings, no one to tell how much I was grieving. My father was always out at work, and he was tired and bad-tempered when he got back. My mother frequently took herself off to bed in the afternoon, often not waking up until the following day, and when she was awake, she was confrontational. There was only Catherine left. She was twelve and I was sixteen. We had absolutely nothing in common, and even more importantly, I absolutely loathed her. I blamed her. I could not forgive her. All I wanted to do was escape.'

Chapter 9

Dr Blake seemed to be completely obsessed with talking about my family. I wished sometimes she would just give it a rest, but no. Here she went again.

'So, Rachel, what was your family motto?', the doctor asked me, picking up her pen.

'My family what? Would you like to see my coat of arms as well, madam? Let me think. Maybe it was ignorantia lex non excusat. That would have been perfect, in fact.'

'Ignorance of the law is no excuse. An interesting choice of maxim.'

'Highly apt, though, don't you think, Doc? I think the shield would show two lawyers stabbing each other.'

'That's not really what I meant, Rachel. Every family has a motto – a moral code if you will. It's the mantra our families, and especially our parents, teach us to live by. Things such as, 'you can only do your best' or 'never a lender or a borrower be.' Do you know that quote?'

'I'm not dumb, Doctor. I had a decent education just like you. It's that Polonius bloke from *Hamlet*, the one who got it up the arse.'

'Yes, that's right, but he was actually stabbed through the arras.'

'It sounds even more painful when you put it like that,' I snorted.

Dr Blake made a short note in her book and sighed.

'To be serious for a moment, Rachel, try to think about what yours was. What were you brought up to adhere to? What was it that you strove towards?'

I was sweet seventeen and within sight of being released from home into the wild. Yet my view of where I should escape to was somewhat different to that of my parents.

'Rachel, you aim for a proper profession. You're more than bright enough. You could be a lawyer or a doctor,' my mother carped, stirring the chicken soup on the hob. She skimmed a layer of fat off the top and began to stir again with slow, rhythmic motions.

'I hate science, so becoming a doctor is a non-starter, and the law is so boring – and I'd never suit the wig.' I yanked the lid off the biscuit tin and removed a handful of chocolate digestives.

'Rachel, we are eating in just under an hour. Put those back. You need to lose that tummy of yours, and all those biscuits are not going to help!'

I slammed the lid back onto the tin, without replacing the biscuits. I bit into three biscuits in one go, crumbs tumbling from my lips all over the countertop.

'Rachel!' my mother huffed. 'Look, all I'm trying to say is that, with your brains, you could really make something of yourself. All this art nonsense you're wittering on about will get you absolutely nowhere. You can't make any money painting. It's not a proper job.' My mother lifted the spoon to her lips and blew before tasting her soup. She added some more salt, sipped again and then ground in some pepper.

'I like art. I thought I might study art history, and then maybe work in a gallery. It's what I enjoy.' I finished off the biscuits and considered reopening the tin, but my confidence failed me. I scratched my arm.

'Life isn't all about enjoyment, Rachel. It would be lovely if it were, but it's really all about hard work and earning enough money to live well. How about accountancy instead?'

'I'd rather cut off my own leg,' I replied, picking up a spatula from the tabletop and pretending to saw away at my knee.

My mother turned the gas down on the hob to allow the soup to simmer and placed the lid on top of the saucepan. Wiping her hands with a tea towel, she sighed. 'Rachel, you may not believe it now, but your father and I are only thinking of you and your future. We don't want you to make the wrong choices now, only to regret them for the rest of your life.' She began to chop carrots vigorously with a sharp knife. I loved the way it sliced through the hard orange root cleanly, again and again, and again. I always wondered if my mother would chop her own finger off, but she never did.

'That's exactly it. I don't want to make the wrong choices and all of the options you suggest would be horrendous for me. I don't want to be chained to a desk twenty-four hours a day fiddling about with mundane, robotic tasks. I want to be creative - ideally in art, but maybe something more generally in the arts. Maybe drama school would be a laugh.'

'Well, you're a drama queen, that's for sure,' Catherine sniped, strolling into the kitchen. She was still wearing her school uniform, socks pulled up just so, and her blouse uncreased as if she had just put it on. 'What's for dinner?' She raised the saucepan lid and peered inside. 'Yum. Chicken soup, my favourite.'

'*Yum. Chicken soup, my favourite,*' I mimicked. 'You are such a little creep, you know that?'

'Takes one to know one,' Catherine retorted.

'Quit it, you two. Rachel, set the table for dinner, please,' my mother asked, her voice slightly raised.

'Why can't she do it?'

'Because I've got to finish my biology homework,' Catherine replied.

'Do it later, lazy.'

'She's not lazy, Rachel, and you know how tired Catherine gets, plus she's not as old as you. So, just get on with it, will you, and set the table as you've been asked.'

Catherine stuck her tongue out at me as she sidled out of the kitchen and I lunged for her, but she slammed the door too quickly for me. I would catch her later.

'So, if we had to summarise, your motto might be 'get a profession to do well in life,' Dr Blake noted down with a smug smile.

'Or, in my case, if we are being strictly accurate here, it would be 'don't get a profession and be a no-hoper for the rest of your life'.' I wiped my nose on my sleeve.

'Well, that's quite a negative way to look at it, isn't it, Rachel? Do you not think that perhaps your parents were just trying to help you realise your true potential, and to make sure that you could live well in the future when they might not have been around to help you?'

'No, I think they had a traditional, rather bourgeois concept of career choices, and were unable to think outside the box. It did not help that Catherine was so intent on doing exactly what they told her to do. She was always Little Miss Bleedin' Miss Goody Two Shoes.'

'And what did they suggest she did??'

'They wanted her to become a doctor, just like you, and that's exactly what she did. I bet you were like her – dead set on getting a proper qualification. Your parents must have been so proud of you.'

Dr Blake recrossed her long legs. 'This isn't about me, Rachel.' She paused. 'But it looks like you stood up for what you believed in, Rachel. That's good, isn't it? It demonstrates strength of character, don't you think?' She leaned forward slightly, staring at me.

'I think it was far more like bloody-mindedness. You know, the typical teenage thing of doing exactly the opposite of what is suggested by your parents.' I finally tore off the pesky piece of skin from a scab that I had been picking at. I rolled it into a ball and ate it.

'So, do you regret not following your parents' advice now that you reflect with the benefit of hindsight?'

'No, I don't think so. Maybe. Sometimes. Not really. I mean, who would have wanted me anyway? I never excelled at anything, I never did anything my parents approved of, or that they were immensely proud of. I couldn't have become any of those professional things even if I'd wanted to.'

'But why not? You're clearly bright enough, so that wasn't the issue. So, what was the problem? What was holding you back?' Dr Blake twisted the clasp of her necklace, so that it was tucked neatly behind her neck once more.

'My parents were only ever interested in Catherine and what she achieved. She got away with murder. No household chores, no punishments when she misbehaved, no real responsibility. She was the chosen one. I could have become a High Court judge, or the world's leading brain surgeon, and no one would have given a flying fuck. In fact, the motto for me was essentially 'You'll never be good enough, so don't even bother trying.'

'How did you eventually resolve the issue of what you should do?

'I suppose you could say we compromised.'

'In what way?'

'Well, I agreed to go to university, but not to read Law or Medicine. I chose English in the end. Arty and a bit useless, but not as hopeless in the eyes of my parents as actual Art.'

'And did your parents accept your choice?' Dr Blake shifted in her chair.

'They didn't have much option. I submitted my choices without consulting them.' I began to suck the hem of my sleeve. It tasted of detergent.

'And where did you go?'

'I went to Durham in the freezing North.'

'An excellent university. You must have been pleased.' She smiled.

'But it was not as good as Cambridge, eh, Dr Blake? Your alma mater, I believe.' I pointed at the certificates on the wall. 'You topped me there.'

'You and I are not in competition with each other here, Rachel,' Dr Blake commented, scribbling away.

'But that is exactly where you are wrong - and you know that as well as I do, don't you?'

Dr Blake's cheeks flushed slightly, but she did not look up.

'So can you tell me about Durham, Rachel. Did you enjoy your time there?'

'Well, that's quite a long answer, Doc. How long have you got?'

'I'll give you as much time as it takes to work this through. I've got eternity, Rachel, as you well know.'

Chapter 10

Growing up in Manchester, I had grown up used to the perennial damp. Living and studying in Durham, however, I never managed to cope with the penetrating cold. During the second half of the Michaelmas term and most of Epiphany, I was forced to wear all my clothes all at once in an attempt to stay warm, bowling along the streets like a bloated Michelin tyre. It was the only way I survived.

Where Durham did have a monumental advantage over Manchester was that it was intensely beautiful. Instead of the centre of town resembling a large public toilet, which masqueraded as the Arndale Centre in Manchester, I now lived in a college aloft the highest hill in Durham City. Granted, the college I lived in was built in the 1960s and was not, therefore, the most glorious construction, being built mostly from concrete. The view of the city, regardless of the season, always left me breathless - as did the steeply undulating hills I was forced to climb up to and from town several times a day. The cathedral dominated - a stunning masterpiece of Norman architecture. Sitting in there was possibly the coldest place of all. Even matriculating in October had been intensely chilly on my rear end.

I was so excited to get away from home finally. I really believed the hype that university would be the best time of my life. In theory at least, university provided me with a one-off opportunity to get up and go to bed when I wanted, to over-indulge, to live in squalor if I so wished, to spend all my waking –and some sleeping - hours with my friends and to enjoy zero responsibility away from my critical parents. All of this was true. Yet what I had not grasped was that university life would also be enormously challenging, and that it would often be tough to make the right choices coming straight out of school, when I was underconfident, somewhat bewildered and unsure of myself.

From the outset, university was not quite what I expected. The disappointments began on day one when I met my new roommate. Before I arrived at Durham, the college had sent me a questionnaire to complete, so that they could match me up with the most suitable roommate. This is why a reasonably social Jewish girl from Manchester ended up twinned with an ultra-religious Catholic girl, who liked to knit, pray, and go to bed by 8.30 p.m. Bernadette Grey had arrived in our room before me and appropriated much of the limited floor space with her numerous battered boxes. Our shared room was long and thin, with a sink by the door, and two beds arranged side by side, separated only by a small aisle. Behind them were two desks arranged in the same fashion. Bernadette's parents had already left when I arrived, and she was sitting cross-legged on her bed reading the Bible and fingering her rosary beads.

I struggled through the door with an overly large suitcase and plonked it noisily onto the floor. Bernadette stared at me over her holy book, clearly annoyed at the interruption to her devotions.

'Hi, I'm Rachel,' I announced. 'You must be my roommate.'

Bernadette did not reply. She merely surveyed me from underneath a parted curtain of brown, lank hair and returned to her studies.

'What's your name?' I persevered.

'Bernadette,' she sighed, bringing her bible down onto her lap with a thump, ungodly in its severity.

'And where are you from?' I asked as brightly as I could, given that I could feel my mood sinking like a stone.

'Leeds.' Bernadette raised her book and turned onto her side with her back facing towards me. It was one of the longest conversations we ever held.

Later that night, after I had attended the corridor party of our floor until the early hours and Bernadette had not, I managed to put myself to bed in the pitch black, so as not to wake her. Half an hour later, I was awoken by Bernadette turning on the overhead light and rummaging under her bed. She retrieved a large biscuit tin, from which she proceeded to stuff her face for the next hour, before rising to brush her teeth and go back to bed - but only after she had knelt and said her prayers. I hoped that she was just nervous on her first night away and that things would settle down. They did not.

Bernadette was an extremely early riser - up at seven for a lengthy prayer, before she donned her twinset and tweed skirt to welcome in her coven of fellow religious maniacs, who would arrive for a breakfast prayer meeting. All of this was conducted while I desperately tried to sleep with my pillow rammed over my head. Bernadette would then work – she was reading Theology – until midday, when I would usually surface from my cocoon. We would then go our separate ways until teatime, after which Bernadette would invite her knitting circle over to purl until her 8.30 curfew. During this window of time, I would work at my desk listening to my Walkman in a vain attempt to drown out the noise of the offensive clacking. Bernadette then turned in for the night, while I headed out to one of the college bars. Halfway into the first term, we both complained to the college authorities— quite independently – that our room share arrangement had broken down completely due to irreconcilable differences. It took until the third term for the college to grant us a decree absolute and to find us separate rooms.

One of the things Bernadette abhorred most was men - or boys, if I am being strictly accurate - as none of my fellow students could really be deemed to have evolved into real men at this point. She either did not like them, or she was frightened of them –who knew – but she certainly acted as if they were unclean, and in many cases, she was quite right. However, I seemed to attract a reasonable amount of male attention, and this did not please Bernadette. I must admit, it came as something of a shock to me. I had not been out with anyone at home and after what happened to Lucy, I had been wary of the opposite sex myself.

Well, I suppose that there had been a couple of interested parties when I was doing A-Levels, but I never reciprocated their attention. One had been a forty-five-year-old man, with dyed blonde hair and trendy jackets. He was introduced to me at a family funeral and became bizarrely obsessed with me, sending daily bouquets of roses, and bombarding me with dinner invitations. My mother adored having so many fresh flowers in the house, moaning to my father that he never, ever sent her any. Meanwhile, my father rampaged up and down the house, muttering darkly about paedophilia and lecturing me on keeping my legs crossed. My other admirer was the boyfriend of a good friend and neighbour of mine, who suddenly decided that he was in love with me, rather than with my friend. He called me constantly on the telephone to beg me for a date, while I explained politely that I could not do that to Naomi – even if I had actually wanted to. After a few weeks, he gave up and slunk back to my friend.

The boys at university struggled to control their unleashed urges. During Fresher's Week, and for most of the rest of that first term, even I was never short of a male partner to accompany me to a gig, or down to the bar, or to sit next to me on the floor in the long corridor outside our rooms, where we all convened after the bar closed, sharing a bottle of whatever came to hand. It was fun, but it also required some skill at fending off the over-amorous individuals, or the odd one who believed they had truly fallen in love, despite knowing me for all of five minutes. One boy, Vince, lived further along my corridor, and did not take it well when I refused to be his girlfriend.

He was large, spotty, and extremely loud - lovely as a friend, but not as any more than that. I tried to let him down gently, but he was as obtuse as rhino hide, so in the end, I had to make it clearer. As a result, over the next few weeks I often returned to my room to find a variety of unpleasant messages scribbled on the white board on the front of my door.

One evening in mid-November, I was in my favourite college bar in Durham Castle, which was in the under-croft, complete with original stone arches and floors long steeped in spilled beer. A group of us were drinking around a wooden table, peeling the tops off beer mats and stuffing down packets of cheese and onion crisps. I suddenly became aware of a guy to my left. I turned my head and he smiled at me. I nodded back, and this was the only invitation he needed to drag over a chair.

'Hi, I'm Tim,' he shouted over the din.

'Hi. I'm Rachel,' I replied, pulling the sleeves of my top down over my fingertips to hide my most recent cuts.

'I've seen you in here before, haven't I, but you're not at this college,' Tim commented, smiling.

'Given that this college is all-male, I don't think so, unless they've changed the rules. I'm a usurper from up the hill,' I giggled.

'You girls are always invading our bar, thank goodness,' Tim laughed, draining his pint. 'It's a terrible hardship for us, I can tell you. Can I get you another drink?'

'Well, I should really be heading back soon,' I hesitated.

'One more won't do you any harm. What are you drinking?'

'Oh, alright then. I'll have a vodka and tonic, please.'

'I'll be right back. Don't let anyone take my seat,' Tim ordered me with a grin, sauntering towards the bar. He appeared to know everyone, slapping various people on the back as he passed, stopping to provide short sound bites, his dark curly hair jiggling as he threw his head back to laugh at their ripostes. I dropped my bag onto his vacated seat and chatted to my friends until he returned.

Tim and I ended up talking for much longer than I realised, until the bar had almost emptied out. Truthfully, I am not sure that I spoke that much, as Tim was highly entertaining and clearly skilled at monopolising the conversation. I laughed a great deal, more in fact than I could remember doing for quite some time.

'Look, it's been great to meet you, but I really must get back. I've got an early seminar tomorrow, and I've not quite finished the work for it yet,' I stuttered, slurring slightly after the extra vodkas. I rose from my seat and shrugged on my coat, wrapping my scarf tightly around my neck in preparation for the windy trek back.

'Let me walk you home,' Tim offered. 'I'll just nip to my room and get my jacket.'

'There's really no need, thank you. I'm fine.'

'I insist. Just wait a sec.' Tim grabbed my arm and squeezed it slightly too hard.

'Look, it's OK. I'm walking back with my friends. They said they'd wait outside for me. I'm sure I will see you around. Thanks for the drink.'

Tim's dark eyebrows knitted together for a moment. 'Alright, I'll see you soon.' He paused. 'I'm certain of it.'

Half an hour later, I was back in my room, attempting to restore my circulation after the frosty walk back. I realised that had been smiling to myself most of the way home. I had enjoyed meeting Tim and being the focus of his attention. In need of something warming and non-alcoholic, I fumbled my way in the dark over to the sink to find the kettle, so as not to disturb Bernadette more than was necessary. I felt around for a teabag and threw it into a mug, hoping it was vaguely clean. The kettle boiled and I was just pouring the water onto the bag - which took some hopeful guesswork in the gloom to avoid scalding myself - when there was a sharp rapping on the door. It was probably my lovelorn friend from down the corridor, popping in to tell me once again why I was such a cow to have rejected him. The rapid knocking came again, and Bernadette turned over in bed, huffing loudly. I moved over to the door and inched it open.

'Go away, Vince… Oh, it's you.'

'Hi, just thought I'd come up and see if you got back OK.' Tim was standing in the corridor.

I opened the door a little more and slunk outside.

'What are you doing here? Obviously, I got back OK. I walk back at night all the time, and I wasn't on my own anyway.' I was suddenly extremely tired, and all I really wanted to do was to drink my tea and go to bed.

'I know, I just wanted to be sure you'd made it back safely, that's all.' He smiled and held out a packet of chocolate digestive biscuits. 'I thought you might be hungry - if you've still got work to do.'

'Thanks,' I whispered, taking the packet from his outstretched hand. I was never one to turn down free food.

'If you invite me in, we can share them,' Tim suggested, grinning.

'My roommate's asleep, sorry. Look, it's genuinely kind of you, but I really need to finish up my work and get some sleep.'

'No problem. I'll see you tomorrow.' Tim grinned.

'Yes, maybe. Night.' I edged back into my room and closed the door softly. I moved over to my desk and switched on the reading light. Glancing back towards the door, I could see that someone was still standing outside.

For the whole of the next week, I kept coincidentally bumping into Tim. As I trudged back up to college, he would be loitering outside my lecture halls on New Elvet. Or I would meet him slowly sauntering over Prebends Bridge, pretending to admire the energetic weir which tumbled constantly in front of the spectacular Cathedral,

'Hi, Rachel, fancy seeing you here,' Tim shouted, jogging over towards me as I walked across Palace Green from the library towards the end of that week. 'Look, do you fancy coming over to my college for a formal dinner tomorrow night? Ben is bringing Caroline, so you girls could come down together. How about it?' He smiled and I smiled back.

'Yes, that would be great, thank you.'

'Lovely. I'll see you then,' smiled Tim, walking away from me backward. 'See you then.'

'What time?'

'6.30 for drinks in my room. See you later.' He turned to walk away, looking pleased with himself. 'Oh, I almost forgot. I got you a little something to keep you your energy going up that hill.' He rummaged in his bag and handed me a Kit Kat.

'Trying to fatten me up?' I giggled.

'Oh, you could never be fat. You're lovely just as you are.'

My cheeks flared with heat, despite the coldness of the day. 'Flatterer,' I called, turning to wend my way back down Saddler Street.

I ambled back to college, excited about being asked out by someone who appeared to be so popular, and who seemed to like me as well. It felt good.

Caroline was a friend who live further along my corridor in college. She and I usually hung out together at dinners and in the bar afterwards. Actual formal dinners happened a couple of times a term at our college, where we were treated to a more sumptuous menu than normal, in return for wearing dresses and gowns. Gowns were a pain to wear at dinner, as the sleeves kept dangling into the food. We never washed them, so by the end of the year, they were a decent map of the fodder we had consumed. Formal dinners at the male colleges were more frequent, but they were a treat to attend. The dining rooms were far grander and tended to be smaller and more intimate than the ones in the more modern colleges, where try as they might, it always felt like you were eating in a large barn.

At six fifteen the following evening, dolled up in the dresses we reserved purely for formal college functions – in actual fact, the only dresses we possessed at university, given that the rest of the time we lived in jeans – Caroline and I tottered down the hill and along the pebble-stoned streets to Durham Castle. Our black gowns were stuffed into our bags. The college Tim belonged to was called University, but was housed in Durham Castle, so everyone simply called it Castle. It was still strictly men only, as were the rest of the colleges in town, women being relegated to the surrounding hill colleges as lesser beings. Some of these hill colleges were all-female and a couple were mixed. Mine was a hybrid - it had been all girls until the year I went up, at which point men were introduced. We liked to joke that we only got the wimps and strays - those who were not able to get into the more prestigious boys' colleges in town. The boys in our college begged to disagree.

We duly arrived at Tim's room fashionably late, and were greeted by Ben and Tim, looking very dapper in their suits. Tim had bought a bottle of Blue Nun for the occasion, and we drank all of it in the half hour before going to dinner. The Great Hall shimmered in the candlelight, as we tucked into our three-course meal, totally oblivious to the sheer splendour and history of our surroundings. The noise was deafening, as a hundred odd students clattered cutlery and banged glasses onto the table throughout the meal. The acoustics were not that great for easy conversation, and I shouted myself hoarse trying to speak over the general din. Finally, after a couple of hours of asking 'What?', 'Who?' and 'When?', we retired to the bar, where we found a quieter corner table for the four of us to chat. I sat sandwiched between Ben and Tim, with Caroline wedged on the other side against a pillar. We devoured several packets of crisps and salted peanuts, even though we had only finished eating less than an hour before. I felt so fat that I was sure I was going to be able to roll back up the hill later on.

Ben was a rower, blonde, extremely handsome, and as broad as he was tall. His reputation as a womaniser preceded him, but he was charming with it. It was easy to fall for his patter.

'So, Rachel, tell me all about Manchester. Are all the girls there as cute as you?' enquired Ben, leaning in closely, our knees touching.

'Oh, the streets are paved with them, Ben. It's all the rain, you know. It's good for the complexion,' I giggled, enjoying his attention.

Tim stretched his arm around my shoulders, pulling me towards him. 'Yes, she is beautiful, isn't she?' I shrugged him off and moved to the edge of my chair away from him. I found Tim slightly disconcerting and a little too sure of himself. We had only just met, yet he was acting as if he owned me.

Caroline, who had been quite quiet for the past half an hour or so, suddenly grabbed her scarf. 'Rachel,' she scowled, ' I think we'd better head back, don't you? It's pretty late and I've got a seminar first thing in the morning.'

'Oh, OK, sure,' I replied, grateful to her for her timely intervention. I retrieved my bag from under my seat. 'Can we just grab our coats from your room please, Tim?'

'Don't you both want to come back for coffee before you go?' asked Tim.

'No,' answered Caroline, a little too sharply, I felt. 'We need to go. It's later than I realised. Come on, Rachel.'

Having retrieved our coats from a sulking Tim, who had clearly hoped that the evening might result in something a little more interesting than us heading home, we wove our way a little tipsily over Prebends Bridge, the moonlight highlighting the tumbling weir in the distance. 'I love this bridge, don't you, Caroline? Sometimes I just stand here looking at the view for ages.'

Caroline did not answer for a moment. 'I don't think you were all that nice to Tim this evening, Rachel.'

'What do you mean?' I responded, turning to face her.

'Well, he obviously really likes you - and you seemed rather offhand with him. You seemed somewhat keener on Ben.'

'Well, I didn't mean to be,' I stuttered.' I thought we were all having such a good time together. Everyone got on really well as a group, I thought. And I'm not sure how interested I am in Tim if I'm being honest.' I stared into the river, feeling slightly queasy.

'Yes, well that's as maybe, but I didn't get much of a chance to talk to Ben, and I really quite like him, you know.'

'Yes, I can see why.' I smiled into the dark water. I had enjoyed Ben's flirting with me. It felt odd to be flattered by both boys.

'Ben invited me tonight, not you,' Caroline retorted. 'You were Tim's date. You should have paid Tim more attention, and Ben a little less.'

'I didn't really see it as a date. I thought we were all just mates, that's all. I didn't mean to tread on your turf.' I muttered, feeling duly warned. 'Come on. I've got some Bailey's in my room, and we can finish the bottle off when we get back, if you like.'

The next morning, I emerged from breakfast to find Tim was perched on the top of the steps outside my college. I stopped short, uneasy about precisely what he was doing there.

'Hi, Rachel. The view is amazing from up here, isn't it…and not bad looking in your direction either. Look, I did not get a chance to say goodnight properly last night, so I thought I would pop up to see you. What was up with Caroline? She seemed rather grumpy, didn't you think?'

'Oh, I think she was just a little tired, and she's under the cosh with her essays this week. Anyway, I need to get going. I've got to get to a lecture by nine,' I ventured, turning away from him

'Going to offer me a morning coffee?'

'I don't think I can. There is a prayer meeting going on in my room. Besides, my lecture is in twenty minutes and I'm already running late'

'A what?'

'A lecture,' I repeated, glancing back at him. 'It's when a boring man stands in front of a large group of students and talks at them for an hour. Surely you've been to at least one?'

'I was referring to the prayer meeting.'

'Ah. Well, that is an awfully long story. Look, I need to grab my stuff and get into town.'

'I'll wait for you, and we can walk down together,' Tim answered.

'OK,' I replied, although I felt rather rattled as I returned to my room.

We walked quickly to Elvet, pausing briefly outside my lecture building. 'Good to see you. I need to dash,' I puffed, rummaging in my bag to check I had remembered to put a pen in it.

'What time are you free again?' Tim asked.

'Oh, in a couple of hours, but then I'm going to work in the library, as I've got another seminar later and I don't want to walk back up the bloody hill in between. I'm far too lazy!'

'Come and use my room. You can work there anytime. Really, it's no problem - and I can provide free cups of tea and plenty of biscuits.'

I hesitated. 'Maybe. I'll pop in if I don't go to the library.'

'I'll count on it.' Tim gave me an odd half salute and sauntered off in the direction of Elvet Bridge, his jacket slung over his shoulder.

I pushed open the heavy door into the building without reply. Maybe he was just being friendly, and I had to admit that I was attracted to him. But something felt slightly off. Or was I just being paranoid? After all, none of us had been In Durham long.

I emerged brain-addled from a linguistics lecture on Chomsky, wondering what man in his right mind would try to reduce sentences to mathematical constructs and more importantly, why I needed to be subjected to such crazy ramblings so early in the day. I turned left and walked along towards Elvet Bridge, contemplating whether to stop for a hot chocolate on the way to the library. Chomsky may not have fired my interest in linguistics, but he certainly induced a sugar slump.

I felt a tap on my shoulder. I jumped, my heart racing.

'Going the long way back to my room?' enquired Tim, dancing in front of me.

'I, er, no, I was just going to buy a hot chocolate. I need a fix,' I stuttered.

'No need. I have hot chocolate chez moi, and look…' Tim raised the plastic bag he was holding in his left hand and opened it up for me to peer inside. 'Cream cakes. Let's go.' He grabbed my hand and I found myself propelled over the bridge, up the Bailey and inside Tim's room before I knew what had happened.

And so, the love bombardment began - and I lapped it up. Tim would turn up outside lectures, at college, in the bar – wherever I was, he found me – usually bearing a small gift of biscuits, cake, tea, a tiny teddy bear, a soppy card, a *Love Is*…book. He told me I was beautiful and laughed at my poor jokes. He was funny, charming, and attentive, and I started to relax a little with him. I began to work in his room as a matter of course – it was, after all, convenient, warm, and not all the way back up that wretched hill. I felt safe and wanted. Tim made me feel special.

'So, Rachel, tell me about your family,' Tim said one day, as we slouched on the algae-coloured nylon carpet on the floor of his room.

'Well, there's not that much to tell. I have one younger sister, Catherine. She is four years younger than me, and intensely irritating in the way that only fourteen-year-old girls can be. It wasn't helped by the fact that my parents allowed her to get away with murder. I always have to help around the house, work hard at school, be polite, do exactly as I'm told. Catherine doesn't have to do any of those things. She's the blessed child.'

'You're lucky to have her, though,' mused Tim.

I shrugged, unconvinced, and bit deeply into a fairy cake.

'So, what about you?' I enquired, licking buttercream off my fingers.

'Oh, I'm an only child. My father died when I was quite young, and my mother is ill and in hospital for long periods of time – mental issues, you know.'

'Oh, that must be awful for you,' I said, touching his arm.

'Yes, it has been at times.' Tim looked down and started to scratch at a piece of the nylon carpet, which had started to wear away.

'So, who do you live with?' I asked.

'I live on my own most of the time – in my mother's flat. It's great - really. I get to do my own thing. No- one tells me what to do.' He smiled.

'Isn't it a bit lonely?'

'Sometimes, but that's why it's great to have you around, Rachel. To have someone like you to talk to, you know. I haven't had much of that.' Tim shuffled over to me and kissed me gently on the lips. I did not pull away.

Tim and I spent almost all our time together now. I stayed over at Tim's several days a week. He constantly needed something from me - and I was happy to run errands for him on the way to his room when he was so immersed in his work. The only downside was that I saw my college friends less and less - and I missed them.

'There's a girls' only quiz night in our college bar this evening, which I'd quite like to go to. I haven't caught up with Caroline and the gang for ages.' I was sitting at the desk in Tim's room, desperately trying to grind out an essay on Henry James. Tim was lying prone on his bed, wearing only a T-shirt and a pair of threadbare Y-fronts, reading a tort textbook.

Tim frowned and lowered his book onto his lap. 'But I want you here, with me, tonight. I've got that essay to finish, and you know how I like to have you around, just in case I need to talk anything through.'

'Christ, Tim, surely you could manage on your own for just one night?' I snapped and turned back to the incomprehensible notes I had made in my lecture. Why did I find it so bloody hard to concentrate?

Tim was silent for a moment and then, without warning, he hurled his heavy hardback across the room towards me. It narrowly missed my head, but only because I ducked just in time.

'You bitch! I said, I need you here. And all you can think about is seeing your little witchy coven. Just goes to show how much you care about me!'

My hands were trembling, and a large ink blot spread across my work, where I had dropped my pen. I felt as if he had actually thumped me with the book and my heart was pounding. 'I'm sorry, Tim. Really. I didn't mean to upset you. I'll stay if it means that much to you.' But the truth was that I desperately wanted to leave. I was simply too frightened to do so.

I flinched as Tim leapt off the bed and walked towards me to retrieve his tome. 'I'm sorry to get so cross, Rachel, but I miss you – and I really need you. Just stay here tonight. Please.' He wrapped his arms around me, as I sat rigid in the desk chair. 'It's just that I love you so much, you know that don't you?'

I shivered and without turning to look at him, mumbled, 'Yes, I know that Tim.'

Chapter 11

'How did that make you feel, Rachel?'

'How the hell do you think I felt? I was bloody terrified, and shit scared. I thought I was in love with Tim and that he loved me, but his outburst really shocked me.' I shivered involuntarily and pulled the hood of my sweat top up over my head.

'He clearly frightened you.'

'Yes, he did, but I also knew that he had had an odd childhood with his mother being ill and that he needed me. And in a way, I wanted to be needed, because before this, no one really seemed to.'

'What do you mean?' queried Dr Blake, jotting something down on her pad.

'You know full well what I mean. At home, it was always all about Catherine. Either she was so frail as a small child that my parents only had enough energy to deal with her, or she was better behaved than me – which she absolutely wasn't. Or she did better at school. They just preferred Catherine.' I poked my face out of my hoodie and glanced at Dr Blake, scratching at my arm.

She smiled back. 'Maybe that was just your perception as the elder child. Older children often have to break barriers for the younger ones to walk straight through. So, you may have felt that she was favoured, when in fact the relationship was merely different.'

'You know that's not true, so stop with the schlock family dynamics babble, will you? It's a load of crap and you know it. It's incredible that you would even go there after everything we have talked about.'

Dr Blake said nothing for a moment or two. 'OK, so going back to Tim, he clearly made you feel wanted in a way that you hadn't done before,' she summarised.

'Yes, for a time, he did. I thought he loved me, and his neediness made me feel stronger. It was only as our relationship progressed that I began to realise how toxic it was – and by then, it was too late to do anything to change it.'

Chapter 12

A week later, Tim and I were in *Klute*, sticky from dancing to the extra-long version of Soft Cell's of *Tainted Love* on the overcrowded floor. *Klute* was the only nightclub in Durham, and it was disgusting. It stank of stale beer and the sweat of the thousands of bodies that had passed through its unhallowed walls. However, as there was no alternative, it was packed every night and was the place to be seen – sad as that was.

Ben and Caroline, now firmly a couple, were draped across the bar, so Tim and I fought our way through the throng to join them,

'Hey, you guys,' called Ben. 'What are you drinking?'

'I'll have a vodka and tonic, please,' I shouted over the din.

'Beer for me, mate. Thanks,' called Tim.

'You've been keeping yourselves to yourselves for quite a while, haven't you?' Ben laughed. I've not seen you for ages, Rachel. I've missed you,' he laughed, reeling me in for a peck on the cheek.

Tim tugged me back towards him and clamped his arm around my shoulders. With a smutty grin, he replied, 'Well, you know, I've been keeping Rachel pretty busy.'

Caroline raised her eyebrows at me, and I shrugged.

'You know, Ben,' Tim continued,' When I first saw Rachel's tits, I was so disappointed. Somehow, I just thought they would be more impressive, bigger, you know? But beggars can't be choosers, as they say.' He reached for his pint, which had just been delivered onto the soaking shelf of the bar and took a deep swig

Ben flushed scarlet, and suddenly an extreme wave of nausea overtook me.

'I never told you that, did I, babe?' Tim asked, turning to me, and giving my shoulders a hard squeeze.

I wriggled free. 'I just need to go to the loo,' I whispered and hurtled across the bar, locking myself into one of the filthy cubicles, and wishing I could flush myself away.

When I finally plucked up the nerve to return to the bar, Tim had disappeared.

'Tim said to tell you he'd gone back to college. Early lecture, or something. Do you want to walk back with me?' asked Caroline, with a sympathetic smile.

We meandered our way slowly along the riverbank in awkward silence, the trees trailing their leaves into the silent water. Once back at my college, I said a quick goodnight to Caroline before I snuck into my darkened room. I undressed, removing my bra only when I had pulled on my pyjamas, lulled by the gentle sound of Bernadette snoring like a walrus with the flu. A full moon streamed through the window, highlighting her lumpy body. I stood in the moonlight and pulled at the top of my pyjama top, peeping down at my pathetic chest. Then I jumped into bed, pulling the duvet up over my head, so that I would not wake Bernadette with my sobbing.

I worked in my room for the next two days. The weather was miserable anyway, and I did not have any lectures I really needed to attend, so I stayed where I was, drinking tea and stuffing my face with chocolate biscuits. I only left the room for the library when the God Squad arrived for their daily bible bashing séance and to buy more snacks at my college bar.

On the Thursday evening, Caroline popped her head round the door. 'Coming to supper, Rachel?' she called brightly.

I hesitated for a moment but thought better of it. At some point, I needed to leave the room, so it might as well be now.

'Sure, just hold on a second while I find my shoes.' I located one under my desk, but the other one was more elusive. I eventually found it under Bernadette's bed next to her not-so-secret biscuit tin. I must have kicked it there in the dark the other night.

Caroline and I queued up with our trays for tonight's culinary extravaganza – macaroni cheese and a banana. To be fair, college food was not too bad in general, but there was never enough of it, which is why the bar sold boxfuls of crisps, nuts, and chocolate. Caroline and I ate quickly and then retired to the JCR to watch *Top of the Pops* and to share a large Twix. We secured the highly sought-after prime position right in front of the television, as we were about twenty minutes earlier than the usual crowd.

'By the way, Rachel, I hope you don't mind me saying this, but I didn't think what Tim said about you the other night in Klute was very pleasant.'

'No. No, it wasn't. But I don't think he really meant it,' I answered, crossing my arms over my chest. 'You don't really know him like I do, Caroline, but he's not usually unkind like that.' I fiddled with the sleeves of my jumper, pulling them out of shape. 'I think he'd just had a bit too much to drink.'

'Well, I'm just saying. I know guys talk like that behind our backs, but it was a bit much to say it in front of us. I wouldn't put up with that kind of comment from Ben.'

I am sure you wouldn't, I thought to myself. Caroline was a brittle Liverpudlian, who never thought twice about voicing her opinion on most topics to almost anyone she met, even when they really did not want to hear it. She was not really one to criticise Tim, given her own forthrightness. Equally, I really did not understand why I was defending Tim's behaviour, when deep down, I knew that Caroline was absolutely right.

'Well, you should straighten him out, Rachel. Don't let him treat you like a doormat. It's a disgrace,' Caroline continued, snapping the last piece of Twix in half, and offering me mine.

At that moment, *Tops of the Pops* began blasting out its familiar theme tune, and we fell silent, distracted as The Smiths took to the stage with *What Difference Does It Make?*

The next morning, after I had emerged from an incomprehensible lecture on Middle English verse, I walked round to Castle to see Tim. Caroline had strengthened my resolve and I had decided to tell Tim exactly how much he had embarrassed me the other night - and to ask him never to do it again. I knocked on his door.

'Yeah,' came a shout from within.

I poked my head round the doorframe.

'Hey, Tim. How are you doing?' I breezed.

'Where've you been?' he barked.

'Working up in college. I didn't have much on down here, so I stayed up there for a bit. I got quite a lot done, actually.'

'And now it suits you to work here today, does it?' He glared at me from his chair, the harsh glow from his desk lamp ghoulishly lighting up one side of his face.

I came through the door and closed it. 'Is that a problem?' I snapped.

'*Is that a problem?*' Tim mimicked. 'No, why should it be a problem, Rachel? You just saunter in here, use this place when you feel like it, and sod what I want.'

'And what exactly do you want, Tim?' I countered, moving towards him.

Tim leaped up from his chair. Hissing like an irate cat, he shoved me hard in the chest. I fell backward onto the floor, hitting my head hard on the skirting board. Pain seared through the back of my head and, when I put my hand to it, I felt wetness. Tim made another move towards me, and I cowered away from him.

'Rachel, I'm so sorry. I didn't mean to do that - to hurt you, I mean.' He knelt down and placed his arms on mine, raising me up. 'Come and sit on the bed and let me look at your head.'

I allowed him to pull me up and he sat me on the edge of his bed. I was shaking uncontrollably and trying not to cry, but despite my best efforts, fat tears were rolling down my cheeks.

Tim went over to the sink and ran the corner of a tea towel under the cold tap. He came back and sat next to me on the bed. I flinched. 'Rachel, move your hand. Let me see your head.'

I lowered my arm and Tim dabbed gently at the cut. 'I'm so sorry, Rachel. It's not my fault. You must believe me. I'm not like this with anyone else. It's just that I love you so much, and sometimes, that feeling simply overwhelms me.' He kissed my face. 'I've missed you, that's all. I've missed you so much.'

I managed a half-smile.

'That's better. Here, let me make you a cup of tea. Why don't you lie down for a bit on the bed?'

Tim bent down, pulled off my boots and I curled into a ball on the bed, facing away from him.

'Have a rest, Rachel. That's it. Good girl. Just close your eyes,' Tim crooned

I lay there, my head throbbing. I did not close my eyes.

61

Chapter 13

Catherine was mooching around my room, emptying the contents of her overnight bag onto any available surface she could find. I had finally secured a place of my own, free from clicking needles and clacking rosary beads. It was tiny – I think they converted a broom cupboard to find me a room of my own – but it was mine, so I did not care. Catherine had come up to Durham on the train for the annual college ball, and was going to be partnered by Simon, a genial friend of Tim's, who was always happy to oblige - especially if there was a ball ticket and a pretty partner on offer. Catherine was super excited and ready to let her hair down. Her visit had not been my idea at all, but my parents wanted Catherine to see Durham as a possible backup plan to Cambridge.

'Of course, I won't need it,' Catherine crowed. 'I can't see Cambridge rejecting me. Mum and Dad seem convinced and so does school.'

'You'd be lucky to get a place here,' I sneered.

'You're such a loser, Rach,' she replied.

Catherine had decided that if she had to visit some dreary little place up north, she may as well do so when there was a party on. That was why I had been saddled with her at the ball. When I met her off the train, she was dressed for a festival rather than a university sightseeing trip. She was all legs and boobs as she burst onto the platform in skimpy shorts and a low-cut top. It came as a shock to me, seeing her as a woman rather than as the scraggy little girl with a pancake chest of old. Catherine was an extremely late developer, but when it had finally happened, she had rather overdone it. Everything overflowed as she sprang towards me.

'Here, hold this,' she commanded, handing me her suitcase.

'If you think I'm dragging that bloody heavy thing all the way back up the hills to college, you must be out of your sodding mind,' I replied in welcome.

'Can't we get a cab?' Catherine looked horrified at the thought of walking and the height of her heels suggested that it would be an impossibility anyway. I giggled at the thought of it.

'Only if you've come with cash. I'm broke.'

Catherine squeezed her hand with great difficulty into the pocket of her ridiculously tight shorts and pulled out a wad of notes. 'I tapped the folks up before I left, obvs,' she laughed.

We went to find a taxi.

'Mum wants you to call her when I arrive,' Catherine told me as we bumped along in the car.

'Why can't you call her?'

'I don't know. She wants you to ring. Who knows what goes through her tiny head?'

'I'll call later if the payphone is free.'

When we reached my room, Catherine meticulously unpacked her bag, hanging the suit carrier containing her gown on the back of the door.

'You've not got much wardrobe space, have you, Rach? This really is a dumpy, little place.'

'It's not the fucking Ritz, Catherine.' I picked up a pile of my own clothes, which were in a heap on my bed, and slung them onto the floor.

'So, I brought this to get us started,' Catherine announced, unwrapping a half bottle of vodka concealed inside one of her many jumpers. 'It's the only way I'm going to get through this visit.'

'How the hell did you get hold of that?' I asked.

'It was at the back of the cocktail cabinet in the lounge. They'll never notice because they never open it.'

I rolled my eyes and grabbed a couple of mugs. Catherine poured two generous portions.

'So, what's my date like tonight? Is he drop-dead gorgeous, captain of the rugby team, and hung like a donkey?' Catherine slurped her vodka and smiled.

'No, he's a just nice bloke, who plays hockey and has a girlfriend at home. He's doing me a favour partnering you tonight.'

'That's big of him – at least I hope so!' Catherine giggled.

'Don't be so juvenile!'

'Don't be so juvenile,' Catherine mimicked. 'And when do I get to meet your mystery man of yours? I can't quite believe you've bagged one. Mum and I were convinced you were a lesbian.'

I threw my hairbrush at her and sadly missed.

'Christ, Catherine, look at the time. It's almost six. We need to get changed, or we won't be ready in time.' I spluttered, banging my mug down on the floor. I plopped down onto the bed next to Catherine, so that I could wriggle out of my jeans without falling over and breaking my neck, as I was slightly squiffy already. 'The boys will be here in less than an hour.'

'What are those bruises on your legs?' Catherine asked, peering over the edge of her mug.

I jumped up quickly and pulled on my dressing gown, which was hanging over the back of the door. 'Oh, nothing. I fell over the other day coming out of college. It was stupid, really. I just tripped on the top of the stairs.' I picked my mug up off the carpet and drained the contents. 'I felt like a total tit.'

'Well, you are a total tit, Rachel, but you must have gone with one hell of a bang. Those bruises look awful. Maybe it's leukaemia. Maybe you'll be dead soon, and I'll be an only child. I may as well be.'

'Hilarious, Catherine. In your dreams! Look, you're not a bloody doctor yet, so leave off with the diagnosis, will you? Anyway, you won't see them under my long dress. Look, I'm going to shower quickly. Do you need one?'

'No, I already smell good enough,' replied Catherine. 'And don't forget to call Mum.'

'Blast, I forgot. I'll do that now quickly.'

I grabbed a couple of 10p pieces and ran down the corridor in my dressing gown. Miraculously, the payphone was free. I dialled and the phone rang.

'Hello, 4529. Who's speaking?'

'Hi, Mum, it's me, Rachel.'

'Rachel, hi, is your sister, OK?' my mother asked.

'Yes, why wouldn't she be?' I retorted.

'Well, she's young and it was a long journey. Is she tired? Has she eaten?'

I rolled my eyes, thinking of Catherine swilling vodka down her neck back in my room. 'She's absolutely fine. Look, Mum, the ball starts soon, and I'm not changed yet, so if that's it, I'll speak to you tomorrow.'

'Now, you listen to me, Rachel. You are in charge of your sister. If anything happens to her when she's in your care, you will answer to me for it. Do you understand?'

'Yes, Mother. Goodbye, Mother.' I slammed the receiver back onto its cradle.

And how are you, Rachel, I enquired of myself as I left the phone box. How's it going up there, darling? Enjoy the ball. I love you, sweetie.

The dining hall in college was a 1960's construction, which is to say that it was essentially non-descript, bordering on ugly. However, with the blinds closed, a few festive banners blu-tacked to the walls and a smattering of fairy lights strewn across the ceiling – and viewed through an alcoholic haze – it appeared almost attractive. Of course, the mere fact that the room was in total darkness, apart from the twinkling lights and the stage where the band was playing, helped the ambiance enormously.

Every year, each college in Durham held its own ball and you could invite a partner to accompany you. Tickets were not cheap, and while the wealthier students might be able to attend more than one, most people stuck with attending their own. There was a formal type of dinner and a great deal of entertainment, from bands playing to fairground stalls, to students masquerading as fortune-tellers stroking glass balls purchased from the local shops, so that you could cross their palms with silver. Copious amounts of alcohol flowed all evening and the event ended with breakfast in the wee hours.

Catherine was wearing a long black skirt in a shiny, metallic material with a slit up one side, which appeared to go all the way up to heaven, and a matching top with spaghetti straps. She wore no bra and every time she leaned forwards, she almost fell out of it. Simon, her date for the night, was mesmerised, as was every male who met her that evening.

'So that's Tim, is it? Catherine stage whispered, as they walked towards us, all dolled up in their tuxedos. 'Yuk. He's got really hairy hands. Is he a yeti, or some strange half-man, half-goat?'

'Fuck off, Catherine.'

'Language, big sis, language.'

I had suggested to Catherine that we stayed together as a four for the night, not because I wanted her anywhere near me, but because I felt some weird responsibility for her after the call with my mother. However, after the first couple of drinks at the bar, Catherine and Simon disappeared. I fretted about her whereabouts momentarily, but after a couple more drinks, I forgot all about her.

There was always a headline band at the ball and ours that year it was Sad Café. Tim stood behind me, arms draped around my waist, as we rocked gently to *Everyday Hurts*.

'I love this song,' I shouted up at Tim. 'Mind you, I think tomorrow my head is really going to hurt.' Tim laughed and kissed the top of it.

When the concert finished, we wandered out into the garden. The night was warm, and we lounged on the grass, drinking from the neck of a half empty bottle of wine that we had pilfered from an abandoned table. We chatted until it started to get light, and I felt happy and so close to Tim at that moment. Around five, we wandered back inside for breakfast. I surveyed the other party survivors as I nibbled queasily on my toast. Most of the boys had shed their jackets and bow ties hours ago. One appeared to have lost his kilt. Their white shirts were stained with red wine and, in the odd case, vomit. The girls, all of whom had resembled goddesses at the start of the evening, now slumped across the tables in their ball gowns, their mascara having made a mad run for it down their cheeks and their lipstick having deserted them long ago. Carefully coiffured hairstyles were now lopsided and mussed up. If an artist had painted the scene, he might have titled it *Dawn of a Thousand Hangovers*.

'I'd better go and find Catherine,' I mumbled into Tim's shoulder. 'There'll be all hell to pay if I can't find her and if she's not back on the right train tomorrow. I'll see you after I've dropped her at the station.'

I turned to kiss Tim, but he shoved me away roughly.

'So where am I going to sleep?' he barked.

'I assume back at your place. Catherine is in my room with me. You'll go back with Simon, won't you? Wherever he is.'

'I had assumed I could stay with you tonight. It's a pain to have to walk down the hill. I'm tired.' His eyebrows knitted together in the half light.

'It's not very practical, is it, Tim? Not with Catherine here. I'll see you tomorrow.' I stroked his arm.

Tim hugged me close, pulling my hair as he did so. 'You are an ungrateful bitch, you know that don't you, Rachel,' he whispered, his hot breath stinging my ear. He grabbed my wrist with both his hands, quickly twisting it and burning my skin. Then he leaped up from the breakfast table, grabbed his jacket and stomped away. I cried out in pain. I sat rubbing my wrist, hot tears trickling down my face and onto my gown, but no one seemed to notice me.

After a few minutes, I wiped my eyes on the back of my hand. I was tired and desperately needed to sleep. But where was Catherine? I scanned the dining room, but there was no sign of her. I walked back through the gardens, straining my eyes in the gloom to see if I could spot her, but she was nowhere to be seen. Sighing, I wondered whether she might have already gone back to my room. Removing my shoes, I wobbled my way along the corridor and stumbled through the door, throwing the light switch on as I did so. Catherine and Simon were fast asleep, stark naked and fully entwined, on top of my duvet.

Much later that day, Catherine and I trudged wearily from the college to the station, which were at polar ends of Durham. Neither of us could afford a taxi back there, having spent far more than we should have done at the ball. Progress was terribly slow, as we were both in terrible shape. My head felt as though someone was banging on the top of it with a frying pan with every step I took. 'I'm never drinking again,' I informed Catherine, between blows.

'I'm definitely having sex again,' giggled Catherine.

'I can't believe you did that – with Simon and in my bed. You're gross, Catherine.'

'Ah, chill out, Rachel. It wasn't my first time, and it definitely won't be my last. Simon was sweet and he deserved a treat. It was only fair after he did you a favour taking me to the ball, after all.'

'If Mum and Dad ever find out, they'll hate me even more than they do already.'

'Is that even possible? Ah, Rachel, don't worry. The only reason they would ever need to know is if I'm up the duff. Then it will definitely be all your fault.'

At that moment, the train mercifully chugged onto the platform. I shoved Catherine onto it and turned away without waving goodbye.

I headed back towards town, relieved that she was gone. It was a sparkling day, the bright sunlight searing my corneas as I walked back down the hill. At the bottom of the station steps, I paused momentarily - unsure whether I was going to be sick – before plodding extremely slowly towards The Bailey to visit Tim. I had no real desire to see him after the night before, but I knew that if I didn't go, things would only be worse by the time I did. I dawdled all the way along Saddler Street, taking the longest route around Palace Green, past the imposing Norman cathedral and the ancient library. Finally, I reached the cobbled pathway which led into the Castle and paused there for a long while, a small part of me wanting to go in, with a larger part wanting to go back to my room and hibernate under the duvet for several days.

I was startled out of my reverie by Simon, who appeared silently by my side – lanky, pasty, with significant stubble on his face. He looked just like I felt.

'Hey, Rachel,' Simon drawled. 'Thanks again for last night. I had a ball…ha! ha!'

I grimaced, which was about as much of a smile as I could muster. 'Sadly, I noticed that when I got back to my room last night.'

'Ah, sorry about that, Rachel. The moment somewhat overtook us.' Simon blushed scarlet.

'You mean Catherine overtook you.' I swayed slightly.

'Something like that, yes. She's a terrific girl. Are you OK?' Simon queried.

'Yes. No. I'm not sure. Slightly worse for wear, to say the least.' I smiled a half-smile.

'Are you coming in?' Simon gestured towards college.

'I guess so. I said I'd pop in to see Tim, but I just haven't quite summoned up the courage, I mean, the energy, yet.'

'Come on then. I'll walk in with you.'

I linked arms with Simon, and we supported each other as we wandered up the path and into the castle. When we reached Tim's door, Simon leaned down and planted an imperceptible peck on my cheek. 'Thanks again, Rachel.'

At that moment, Tim's door flew open. 'I thought I heard someone out here. Are you coming in, or what, Rachel?'

I nodded bye to Simon and crossed into Tim's room, the door thudding shut behind me.

'What the hell was that?' Tim screamed, his face right up to mine, red and steaming.

'What was what?' I replied, backing away from him towards the window.

'That. With Simon. So is that why you wanted me to ask him to the ball. For you, not for Catherine. I should have known, you unfaithful whore.' Tim edged closer until he was right in front of me again, his hands on my shoulders, pressing down hard.

'Tim, you're being ridiculous. I met Simon on the way in just now. He walked me to your room, because I was feeling rather groggy, that's all. And what's more, he bonked Catherine last night, so bang goes your theory.'

I grimaced, preparing myself for more shouting from Tim, but to my surprise, he released my shoulders and moved over to his desk. I took off my coat and sat down on his bed, resting the back of my head against the cool plaster wall.

'I don't know why you get so jealous, Tim. You know there's absolutely no need.'

'Well, at least someone had sex last night after shelling out all that money for that boring ball. Perhaps I'd have been better off taking your sister ad shagging her. I could have dumped you off with Simon.'

I ignored him, too jaded to rise to the bait.

Tim began to peel an apple, concentrating so that he could keep the skin in one piece. 'D'you want some?' he asked, cutting a slice, and holding it out towards me.

'No, I'm good, thanks. I don't think I could eat a thing for a least a week without throwing up. How's your head?

'My head? Oh, my head's absolutely fine, Rachel. I rarely feel the effects. I'm always in control.' He bit down hard on the apple and laughed.

I moved just in time. The knife he had thrown dented the wall just behind my head, before falling into the folds of his bedding.

Chapter 14

Dr Blake remained silent for quite a few minutes after I finished speaking, her pen poised over her notebook, yet the page was still blank.

'My goodness, Rachel, it must have been incredibly difficult for you to suffer such trauma over such a prolonged period of time. How did you feel at this stage about your relationship with Tim?' Dr Blake was leaning forward, sweeping away a stray hair over her left eye, which had miraculously escaped from her tight ponytail.

A single tear slipped from my eye, and I batted it away with my hand.

'How did I feel? How do you think? I felt like a sodding hamster, endlessly turning on my vicious wheel. The vista from the top was always good, it was always calm. Tim petted me and fed me titbits. Then my wheel would begin to turn, descending slowly clockwise, and as I fell, tensions rose. I was damned if I did anything, and I was definitely damned if I did not do exactly what was required. I was carped at and belittled in private and in public. My wheel then smacked hard to the floor in an explosion of ire. The tiniest incident meant that I felt the full force of gravity. Slap, push, punch, crack, bang, bite, whip, and whack. Random acts of violence, as I swayed and wallowed. There seemed to be no escape and yet then, on a sudden draught of air, I would begin to ascend once again. I was wafted upwards on a wave of reconciliation, apologies, gifts and grovels. I was implored to stay. It would kill him if I ever went away. I floated back to the summit in a momentary oasis of calm before the wheel began to turn once again.

I was utterly incapable of stepping off. Durham was a tiny claustrophobic cathedral city affording me nowhere to run. I could not reveal my secrets to anyone, because I was petrified by the inevitable repercussions. And it was not as if I had any real friends, who might play my knight in shining armour, striding in to defend my honour, or hold my hand in solidarity and lead me to safety. They probably thought we were a perfectly happy couple because we spent all our time together. And even if they had guessed that something was wrong, they could never have known for certain, so they would not have enquired - and even if they had, what could they have done and where would I have gone? Where the hell would I have gone?'

'It must have been a terrible predicament to be in, Rachel, and at such a young age. How did you resolve it?' Dr Blake pressed.

'I didn't, clearly. It had moved beyond a point where I felt I could solve it.'

And then, suddenly my finals were upon me. I remember that my mum and dad in an unusually thoughtful moment had sent me a good luck card, and rather oddly, so did the guy who had shown an interest in me in Manchester – you know, the one who had been my friend's boyfriend. He had bumped into my mum and asked how I was, and she must have mentioned it was my finals or something. It was all a bit weird. Anyway, his card arrived one morning. It had a small leprechaun perched on a shamrock wishing me good speed. I discovered the card waiting for me in my pigeonhole after I finished breakfast and I ripped open the envelope as I meandered my way slowly back to my room.

At that precise moment, Tim barged through the door unannounced. 'Rachel, you're here. Great. Look, I am really stressing about this human rights module, and I didn't catch a wink of sleep all last night. I had bloody nightmares about murdering someone. It was truly bizarre.' Tim slumped onto my bed, wiping his dirty boots on my duvet cover.

He did look tired. His bloodshot eyes appeared ghoulish with deep, dark hollows carved out underneath them.

'Look, Tim, you'll be OK. You fret and worry, and then you always do incredibly well. Try not to panic,' I soothed, hoping that he would leave quickly, so that I could get on with my own revision.

'It's easy for you to say, Rachel. It's not like I can just read a few novels and spout some critical bollocks about them. My stuff is difficult, and it has to be accurate - and I just don't know it.' He thumped his hand into my mattress and my faded old teddy bear jumped in alarm.

'Do you want a cup of tea?' I asked, realising that he was not going to leave any time soon. I moved over to the sink to fill the kettle.

'Yes, alright. Then I've got to go back to my room and crack on. I can't have you distracting me. I just needed some fresh air and some moral support, so I thought I'd come up to see you. It was a mistake, really. I can't afford the time and there's nothing you can say that helps anyway.'

'Well, if it's any consolation, I know how you feel. I'm totally overwhelmed and can't see how I'm going to plough through it all before the exams start on Monday.' I found a couple of pre-used tea bags and dangled them into hot water.

Tim stomped backwards and forwards across the floor like a caged tiger. 'That's right, Rachel. Make it all about yourself. You're a shit listener, you know that? You're just so bloody selfish.'

I bit my lip and ignored him. I did not want a fight today. I just did not have the time, or the energy. I walked over to the window behind my desk, raising the sash to retrieve the milk from the ledge, where I kept it cold in lieu of a fridge. I opened the top of the carton and sniffed it. 'I think this just about OK.'

I turned around and Tim was right behind me, at the edge of my desk. I glanced down at my good luck cards and shifted a file to conceal them, but I was too slow.

'What's this, Rachel? What the bloody hell is this?' Tim shouted, picking up the card from the boy at home and waving it in my face.

'It's just a good luck card from a friend,' I spluttered.

'A friend?' He read the inscription inside. 'Which streak of piss is he?'

'It was a long time ago, Tim. He's just a friend - never a boyfriend.'

'Well, I can't see any other cards from *friends*.' Tim seized my face in his right hand, pinching my chin.

'Mum bumped into him recently and she must have told him I had exams. I'm guessing,' I spluttered, spilling the milk down my jeans.' I haven't seen him in years.'

Tim released my chin and I rubbed it with my free hand. I walked slowly back towards the mugs with the remainder of the carton of milk. Tim was still holding the card, turning it over and over, before he suddenly ripped it into small pieces. He threw the shards up in the air and they rained down like confetti onto the carpet. Then he strode over to where I was standing at the sink.

'I won't stay for the tea, Rachel,' Tim hissed, taking a hot mug of tea off the side, and flinging it against the mirror. The boiling liquid splashed onto my forearm, and I cried out in pain.

'Ah, did that hurt, Rachel? Diddums. I'm sorry. Let me take a look,' Tim whispered, taking my arm. He raised it to his face, as if he were about to kiss it, but instead, he bit down hard on it. 'Better now?' He laughed into my face, grabbed his coat, and left, slamming the door behind him. I sank to the floor, surrounded by the remnants of good luck. I hated him, this man child who I thought had loved me. He was just another person in my life who wanted to hog the limelight and to grind me further into the dust. I hated myself for having been so pathetic for all this time, for knowing that I could not extricate myself.

The exams came and went. Somehow, I graduated with a fur-trimmed hood and gown, smiling in photographs surrounded my grimacing family. Tim was in them too, of course, ecstatic about his first-class degree, and bolstered even further by his offer of a job at one the leading Magic Circle law firms in London. Mum, Dad, and I packed up my room and I squished into the back of the car, knees around my chin all the way to Manchester, crammed in next to three years' worth of university detritus.

I did at least have a plan of sorts. I had been offered a job as an accountant at a reasonable firm in London, which was a shock to me, given that my Maths was average at best. It was a good job, with a decent salary and, most importantly, my parents were bloody delighted. I was obviously completely mortified about the prospect of being an abacus grinder, but I planned to live with some friends and if nothing else, it would be an adventure.

'So, you're going to get a proper profession after all,' laughed Catherine, prancing around the kitchen in her pyjamas. 'Thanks goodness you're finally making something of yourself,' she crowed, in perfect mimicry of my mother.

'Piss off, Catherine, and concentrate on your own life.'

'Don't worry, I will. When I'm a top consultant, you can do my accounts.'

I lobbed a wooden spoon in her general direction, but she ducked.

I got remarkably close to a few advertising jobs, attending several final interviews, but never quite landing the prize. So, I had been coming to terms with life on the audit trail when the phone rang one afternoon. It was the very last advertising agency that I had seen a month ago, calling to inform me that, due to winning several new pieces of business, they had decided that they would now employ three, rather than two, graduates. As I had been their third choice, they asked if I would still be interested to work with them as a trainee copywriter? I told them I would be there tomorrow if they needed me. We agreed to a September start.

I finally had a job that I was excited about and which I thought I might do well at. I had the chance to move to London, away from my family and away from Tim, who was going to be in Guildford for the year while he completed his Law conversion course. For the first time in a while, I felt as though I could breathe freely and that I could relax a little.

'So, it was a fresh start of sorts, Rachel?' Dr Blake smiled.

'It was certainly the beginning of another chapter, Doctor, even if it didn't quite go the way I anticipated. Am I right?' I asked, laughing.

'Let's pick up again next time,' suggested Dr Blake, snapping her notebook shut.

'Yes, let's do that Doc. Let's please keep gnawing away.'

Chapter 15

Back at home before moving to London, I was lying on my bed, safe in the knowledge that I was here and Tim was somewhere else, when my mother burst into my room.

'What the hell did you do to your sister when she came to Durham?' she yelled, slamming a carton of contraceptive pills onto my bed.

'Excuse me?' I replied, hoisting myself up onto my elbows. 'What are you talking about?'

'These. I'm talking about these,' my mother replied, picking up the packet back up again and waving them in front of my face.

'They're not mine,' I responded, feeling relieved that she had not found where I actually hid my own pills.

'I know that. They are Catherine's.'

'OK, so if they are Catherine's, why the hell are you screaming at me?'

'Because Catherine tells me that a boy – a friend of yours – forced himself on her in Durham. He deflowered her.' My mother was tomato red. I thought she might explode with embarrassment.

I burst out laughing. 'Deflowered?'

'This is not a laughing matter, Rachel. I told you to take care of her, but instead, you led her straight into vice.'

'Vice?' I tried not to laugh again, but failed. 'I think you'll find that your innocent little girl had already lost her virginity and that she actually seduced him. Hence the pills.'

'How dare you lie to me, Rachel. Don't you think I know my own children? Catherine was a virgin when she came to stay with you - and you have destroyed her innocence. You disgust me, and the sooner you leave this house the better.'

'Did you actually ask Catherine for the truth?'

'I did and she is completely distraught. She said the guy virtually raped her when you left her alone with him. She says you disappeared with your hairy lover boy, and she was left utterly defenceless. I wanted her to press charges, but she doesn't want to. She won't stop crying. I think she's going to need some serious counselling.' My mother put her head into her hands and rubbed her face. Her mascara was smudged over her cheeks as she re-emerged. 'I blame you and you alone for this, Rachel, and I will never forgive you. You've ruined her life.' My mother turned on her heel and left, attempting to slam the door, but it merely rocked against the frame and opened again.

I jumped up and stormed into Catherine's room.

'What the fuck, Catherine?'

She raised her eyebrows and smiled. 'Well, I had to tell them something, and you were the first thing that popped into my head. You'll get over it, Rach. You're moving out soon, and I've got to be here for at least another year, so it makes sense that you take the fall. They'll will get over it and the game of happy families will resume.'

'Bloody happy families? When has that ever been the case? You're a total bitch, Catherine, and I hate you. You're never staying with me, or even coming out with me again, anywhere, ever.'

If only I had been true to my word and stuck to that promise.

Chapter 16

'Sometimes, I just feel totally overwhelmed by anger. It's uncontrollable, such that I feel I can either hurt someone else or take it out on myself. That's when I grab the nail scissors and cut myself - sometimes just a little, other times a bit more.'

'How does that make you feel?' asked Dr Blake, flicking over another page of her notebook, scribbling away.

'It just means that I can feel, that's the point. Sometimes…sometimes I feel like I'm in complete despair and at other times, I feel utterly numb. When I cut, I like the sharpness of the pain. It makes me feel alive - if that makes any sense?' I glanced up at her quickly, and then down again at my ragged cuff. 'It brings me a feeling of complete release from all the shit, from everything that's happened and everything I've done. In that moment of agony, I feel so much better.'

'Yes, I understand how it might relieve such feelings. I get it…but did you ever try to talk to anyone about how you felt? Before you began speaking to me, I mean.' Dr Blake put her notebook down on her lap and folded her hands.

'Before it was too late, you mean? Talk to who, exactly? No one ever noticed anything about me. At home, they only bothered with me to tell me I should know better than to do whatever I was doing at the time. Or to let me know that I should have been cleverer like Catherine if I'd worked as hard as she did. Other than that, they had no time for me. I was the invisible child. At university, I never made any close friends, because I got caught up with Tim so early on and he monopolised me – as well as making feel like a worthless piece of shit. I despised myself for being so pathetically weak. So, no, Dr Blake, I never spoke to anyone – and no one ever asked me how I was either.' I glanced up at the ceiling.

There was an ugly, modern chandelier with three bright bulbs, which left sharp oval shapes on my retinas.

'Unless, of course, you count Richard,' I added.

Chapter 17

I first met Richard when he was being bawled out by my boss, the head of the creative department where I landed my first job as a junior copywriter. I could hear the violent tirade as I turned out of the lift onto the third floor. Roja was a six-foot four titan, tattooed from floor to ceiling. He had a penchant for wearing silk shirts unbuttoned to the naval to reveal his full inky story. Phenomenally talented, Roja – not the original Scunthorpe spelling– did not believe in taking work too seriously. He tended to wander into the agency around eleven, go for lunch around twelve thirty, return around three thirty and retire to the pub at six o'clock sharp. This regime rendered him remarkably productive, developing some of the most memorable advertising campaigns of all time, so the agency forgave all and every one of his eccentricities. And the clients adored Roja, as he made them feel somewhat daring and bohemian by association.

The account handlers, on the other hand, were absolutely terrified of Roja – and for good reason.

'Rachel, never take any shit from the suits,' Roja drawled in his strange Yorkshire by way of Los Angeles accent, when he briefed me on my first day. 'They are merely two-dimensional stick men in fancy suits. Without us, they would be nothing, nil, zero, kaput. So use that power, baby. Work it.'

The older, more gnarled stick people knew the precise amount of buttering up they needed to undertake to get good work out of Roja, which as a bare minimum would be a three-course lunch at a good restaurant – preferably Michelin-starred - to discuss the initial brief. He then required the buying of an expensive lunch following any presentation of concepts to the client - by way of a thank you for Roja's hard graft - and at least a case of Dom Perignon should the client approve the work. A weekend in a luxury hotel was not unheard of should Roja be required to attend a client meeting. He obviously needed to replenish his creative juices after such a traumatic experience as meeting with the common man.

The most difficult encounter for any account handler with Roja, however, was when they had to tell him that the client required some amendments to his vision, or worse, that the client did not approve of it at all. If the work Roja had proposed was judged to be 'not on brief', this would cause Krakatoan eruptions - much to the delight of the rest of the creative department.

Richard was on the receiving end of such an outburst that particular morning. I had just wandered back from the cheese shop round the corner from the agency. They made gigantic doorstop sandwiches crammed full of cheese and pickle – and crucially without any healthy additions, such as lettuce or tomato. As a lowly junior, I had to survive on such lunchtime fodder. It was not senior enough to be bribed to do my day job.

As I rounded the corner into the creative department, I could hear Roja screeching from his office at the far end of the corridor. The door was closed, so I could not actually see what was going on, but it was pretty much a one-way discourse, which ended with a heavy object being hurled against the door.

'Get out of my office, you turgid piece of shit, and don't ever darken my door again - unless it's to tell me that you're leaving,' Roja yelled.

His door opened and Richard appeared, his tie slightly askew. His handsome face was ashen, making his dark fringe appear even blacker against his skin. A bead of sweat meandered slowly from his forehead onto his cheek. He rushed along the corridor, eyes down - and careered straight into my sandwich. I dropped it and hunks of cheddar spattered onto the green nylon carpet.

'Gosh, I'm so sorry,' Richard sputtered, kneeling down to clear up the mess. His trouser leg was now smeared in brown pickle.

'Don't worry,' I muttered, staring in dismay at my ruined sandwich. I was starving and had used the last of my money to buy it. The cheese shop was good, but it was not cheap.

Richard stood up; the mangled sandwich returned in part to its greaseproof wrapper. He handed it back to me. 'I'm deeply sorry about your lunch. It's probably not that edible now.'

'And I'm really sorry about your trousers,' I laughed, looking down at the brown, greasy stain below his left knee. 'You've now got a dry-cleaning bill on top of the pasting you got from Roja.'

Richard glanced down at his leg. 'Yes, it's not been my finest hour, I must admit.'

He glanced up at me again and I was suddenly aware of how scruffy I looked. I was wearing a baggy black skirt and some mishappen, psychedelic shirt, which I had bought from a stall in Camden Market, thinking it made me look arty, when in fact it made me look more like a lumpy sack of potatoes. I scratched at the skin on my forearm and ran my hand through my hair.

'You've got cheese in your hair now,' giggled Richard.

I felt myself flush scarlet.

'Look, I haven't eaten yet, and I really need some food after that meeting, so how about I buy you another sandwich to say sorry?'

I smiled at his lopsided smile and felt a little dizzy. I could not recollect a time when I had ever spoken to someone quite so good-looking. 'Um, well, if you're sure, then yes. Yes, please.'

And it started from there, I suppose. We became firm friends, often nipping out together at lunchtime to grab something to eat and stopping off in the park for a short picnic if the weather permitted. Then, one day, out of the blue, Richard asked if I would like to go out with him that evening.

'Like out out?' I asked.

'Yes. I thought we could get dinner in Chinatown or somewhere. My treat.'

'OK. Why not.' My heart was pounding so hard that I was sure it must be visible.

'I'll meet you outside around eight. I won't finish writing my pitch document until then. Is that too late?'

'No, that's fine. I'll wait.' Of course I would wait.

I did wait for Richard, but in the pub, so I had had a couple of beers by the time I wandered back round to the front of the agency to meet Richard. He bounded down the steps like a frisky puppy dying to go for a walk.

'It's Friday!' he shouted, as he ran towards me.' Let's go and have some fun.' And he grabbed my hand and we headed off to Chinatown.

We lingered long over our meal in a corner booth of a slightly shabby restaurant, consuming vast amounts of crispy duck along with sweet and sour prawns. I did not mention anything to Richard about the fact that Tim was due to stay over the following night. I did not think it was fair and anyway, Richard and I were not a couple. This was a very chaste date, even if I smouldered with unrequited desire. I was, however, a woman of principle and was not going to two-time either man - even if in my imagination, I already had on several occasions.

I smiled tipsily at Richard. 'I've had a lovely evening, Richard, thank you. It's been an exhausting week at the agency. There just seems to be so much to learn and I'm not sure I'll ever get the hang of it.'

'Of course you will, Rachel. You've only been there for six months. They're not expecting you to run the place already, are they?' Richard smiled and held my hand. 'How could they not love you?'

I took another sip of wine to steady myself as Richard squeezed my hand tighter. 'And it's great that you're more settled in a proper flat now,' I mooned.

'Yes, it is, actually. You must come over and see the flat. It's not much, but it's home, as they say. I'm so pleased to be out of renting. What are you doing tomorrow?'

I gulped the last of my wine too quickly and choked my reply. 'I've got a friend from university staying tomorrow evening, but maybe next weekend might work.'

'Ok, perfect. I'll hold you to it.' And Richard kept a tight grip of my hand.

At that moment, a large, sweaty man, whose stomach bulged alarmingly below his red waistcoat, straining above his trousers, appeared at our table. He wielded a fraying wicker basket crammed full of red roses. 'Buy a rose for the beautiful lady, sir' he implored Richard, holding a single flower towards him. 'Just three pounds.'

Richard released my hand and handed over the money in return for a rose. The man thanked Richard profusely, spitting over the tablecloth as he did so, before moving on to spice up the romance at another table. Richard presented me with the rose. 'For the beautiful lady,' he announced.

I had to grip the edge of the tablecloth to restrain myself from kissing him.

The following afternoon, Tim arrived. When I opened the front door, he just stood there rigid, brandishing a dozen red roses in one hand and tickets to *Evita* in the other. Tim thrust the bouquet at me before he had stepped over the threshold, and I accepted it quickly. My mind was racing, as nestled in the kitchen was Richard's rose. I had the foresight not to leave it in my bedroom, but even so, Tim was always horribly suspicious.

'Hi Tim, come in. Why don't you take your bag up to my room? You can't miss it. Just keep going all the way to the top... and mind your head, as it's in the eaves. I'll just put these gorgeous roses in a vase, and I'll be up in a minute.'

For once, Tim did not argue and I raced into the kitchen, hastily searching for a vase. Richard's lonely stem was currently luxuriating in a chipped pint glass. I found a dusty water jug, which I filled under the tap, before removing the paper from the roses and cramming them into it. I knew I was supposed to bash the ends of the stems to help them to live longer, but there was no time for that. Then I grabbed Richard's rose and stuck it into the centre of Tim's bouquet. It was a slightly different red, but Tim would never notice.

'These flowers are so beautiful, thank you, Tim,' I blustered, joining him in my room. 'It's extremely sweet of you.' I plonked the jug down on my dressing table.

'Well, I wanted to make today a special occasion, you know.' He was staring at me oddly. 'I've got the whole day planned, Rachel. So, go and put on a nice dress and let's get out of here. I've booked tea at the Ritz, then we are off to the theatre, and I've sorted dinner afterwards. Come on then. Don't stand there gaping like some cod. Let's go.'

I felt slightly nauseous, as I stood with the wardrobe door open, attempting to choose a dress. To be honest, I only had two, so it should not have taken that long, but I hoped that the longer I dawdled, the less time I would have to spend out with Tim, pretending that I wanted to be with him.

'Get a move on, Rachel. I don't want to sit in this scrotty little room all day,' Tim moaned.

Disgust crawled over me as I repaired to the bathroom. The distance I had achieved from Tim over the last few months had crystallised for me - as if I had not known it already - that I could no longer be with him, and that I would have to break this perpetual cycle of love and violence today. I certainly was not going to have that conversation in my bedroom, however, without other people present. I needed a public forum for safety.

I donned my dress, slapped some blusher on my cheeks, glossed my lips and attempted to brush my hair, moving slowly.

'I'm good to go,' I announced, as I returned to the bedroom.

Tim did not glance at me. 'You know, Rachel, this is so weird. There are thirteen roses in this bunch. How strange is that?'

'Unlucky for some', I muttered.

Tim was being horribly attentive. We were clearly right at the pinnacle of the circle, in full heroine worship mode, but my absence from him over the last few months had hardened me. I was no longer in a small cathedral town with no friends and no other lifeline. My outlook on my life was shifting and I had begun to realise that I could be a person in my own right. And I was angry – at Tim for ruining my time at university, and at myself for submitting to his coercive behaviour. I felt the stirrings of some form of self-esteem, and I was not about to let go of that slender thread.

Over tea, I was struggling to concentrate.

'What's wrong with you, Rachel? You seem distracted,' Tim asked after the waiter had overladen the table with sandwiches and cakes. The sumptuous spread made me feel nauseous.

'Oh, I'm alright,' I spluttered.' 'I'm just a little tired from the new job. It's long hours and there's a lot to get used to.'

Tim waved my words away on the air.

'What's there to worry about? You've got to come up with a few cheesy slogans every now and again. It can't that stressful.' He stuffed a sandwich into his mouth and chewed noisily.

'Well, you're effectively still a student, Tim, so I don't think you can comment on the world of work as yet,' I snapped.

Tim was about to respond, but thought better of it, and munched another sandwich. I poured myself another cup of tea, splattering some of the dark liquid onto the pristine white tablecloth.

Tim wittered on about his course, only too happy to jabber on about it for hours, while my own mind flip-flopped around in blind panic. It no longer mattered what he said or how much he spoiled me. In my heart, I was already gone.

There's nothing more I can think of to say to you.

Evita was a delight. I already knew all the songs, of course, and Elaine Page was a marvel. For almost three hours, I almost forgot I was with Tim, as apart from the interval, we were not required to talk to each other. When the show ended, Tim insisted on whisking me off for a post- theatre meal at a small bistro around the corner.

'Tim, don't you think we've done enough today? I'm so full after eating all that afternoon tea earlier. Maybe we could just have a drink in the pub on the way home?' I suggested, thinking that the pub was almost on my doorstep, so that I could say what I had to say and run - quite literally.

'Don't be so bloody boring, Rachel. It's my evening, and we will do it my way.' Tim grabbed my hand and dragged me to the restaurant. He had spared no expense all day, and I did wonder how he had afforded it all, but that was not my problem. Yet somehow, I felt guilty. I should have told him how I felt when he arrived, or even before that, on the phone. At least we could have avoided this pantomime.

When Tim ordered champagne, I began to fidget. 'Tim, don't you think you've spent enough on me today?' I ventured. 'There's really no need for champagne as well. Honestly.' I fiddled with my serviette. 'Let's just go home. I don't feel very well'

'Nonsense, Rachel. Don't be so pathetic. I haven't seen you in weeks and anyway, there's so much to celebrate.'

The champagne arrived and Tim raised his glass up to mine for a toast. 'To us,' he whispered across the table. I drank my glass down in one without replying. I saw Tim fumble in his pocket and produce a small box. Suddenly, I thought I was going to vomit.

'Excuse me a minute,' I muttered and dashed off to the toilet. In the Ladies' loo. I splashed water onto my face and tried to breathe, but my breath would not come, and I was wheezing for air. He was about to propose, and I was about to refuse, and there was going to be some almighty scene. I ran the hot water in the sink until it was steaming and put my hand under the stream. The scorch felt good, and the pain sharpened my mind.

I pulled my sleeve down and emerged from the toilets. Tim was still seated at the booth, his back towards me. I could see him flicking the lid of the box, up and down, up and down. His shoulders were hunched as his patience was thinning. I strode quickly towards the door, not stopping to retrieve my coat. Once outside, I ran to the corner and hailed a black cab, sinking into the seat as I slammed the door. It would take me twenty minutes or so to get home. It would not take Tim much longer to realise I had deserted him.

When I reached my flat, I raced up to my room, grabbed Tim's bag and threw it out onto the front doorstep. Then I locked and bolted the door. My flatmate was away, and I was taking no chances. I ran up to my bedroom in the attic and slammed the door. My heart racing, I pulled my battered old armchair across from the window, so that it was wedged behind my door. It was heavy and both the effort of pulling it and my own terror made me sweat, heavy beads trickling down my back. There was no way that Tim could break in, but then again, he was capable of almost anything if he were angry enough – and I was frightened. I threw myself onto the chair and waited.

Less than an hour later, Tim began hammering on the front door.

'Rachel, come and open this fucking door,' he screamed, his voice climbing the stairs to my room. The intense banging continued, and I sat gripping the arms of the chair, praying that the front door would hold its own against the onslaught.

'Rachel, I promise that I will fucking kill you if you don't open this door right now,' Tim informed me and the entire street.

'Keep it down, mate, will you, or I'll call the police,' came a distant, unrecognisable voice.

In response, Tim kicked a dustbin over and hurled the lid at our ground floor window. I dropped to the floor and cowered, hoping that the window had not shattered, hoping that whichever neighbour had called out of his window would act on his threat to call the police.

Tim continued to holler and shout and bang. I sat shaking and sweating with fear.

'Rachel, you fucking bitch, I won't let you forget this ever. I'll be back and when I do come again, you won't be able to ignore me. I'll make your life a permanent bloody misery, you whore, until you give me the respect I deserve.'

Eventually, I heard his heavy footsteps receding and the night fell silent, except for the local dogs barking their indecipherable nocturnal messages to each other. Tim had given up, finally. Exhausted, I heaved a huge sigh and burst into violent tears.

Chapter 18

The following Saturday afternoon, I chugged up the Holloway Road to visit Richard at his place in Highgate. I was the proud owner of a rather clapped-out Nissan, which was pitted with a variety of small dents like old acne scars. It ran fine on the flat, but it seemed to suffer from angina when tackling hills. Richard had recently purchased a flat, with the help of a loan from some American friends of his parents, and he rented out the second bedroom to a friend from Oxford.

I parked by Waterlow Park and crossed the road to the entrance of the block. Richard lived on the very top floor, up a series of ragged, uneven stairs, so you had to concentrate on each individual one to avoid tripping over. I was more than slightly out of breath by the time I reached the fourth floor. I resolved to start doing some proper exercise soon – even though I knew I never would.

I rang the bell and waited. Nothing happened, so I rang again. Eventually, a few moments later, the door was opened by a noticeably short man, wearing an open dressing gown stained all over by various unidentifiable substances. Beneath the dressing gown, he wore crumpled, striped pyjamas, his portly stomach peeping out over the strained buttons. His feet were completely bare. His hair was thick, black, and standing on end, as if he had just had a close encounter with a Van der Graaf generator.

'Hello, Rachel.' he boomed. 'How are you? Come in, come in.'

'Thank you,' I mumbled.

'I'm Peter,' he boomed, suddenly grabbing me, and hugging me tightly. I hung there, awkward in his unexpected embrace. Eventually letting me go, he continued, 'It's so good to meet you. I've heard such a lot about you.'

'You have?' I glanced around the hallway for Richard. 'All good, I hope?'

'Oh, yes. Billy has talked about you incessantly. It's so great to meet you at last – it really is.' Peter seemed genuinely excited, and I was worried I might disappoint his clearly sky-high expectations.

'Billy?'

'Yes, Billy. Oh, sorry, you probably don't know him as Billy, but we all called him that at Oxford - because he was so bloody idle! Get it?'

I laughed without real conviction and stared at this strange man, who looked like a shorter, darker, grubbier version of Arthur Dent from *The Hitchhiker's Guide,* wondering if I had perhaps passed into a parallel universe.

'You must know Billy Idol?' Peter scratched inside his ear and then inspected his finger for debris.

'Yes, yes, of course I do. *White Weddings* is a brilliant song.'

Peter looked at me askance, as if he did not really agree.' Anyway, don't just stand there in the hall. Come in. Take a load off. Billy will be back in a minute.' Peter ushered me through a set of glass doors into a small square lounge, which housed nothing except a large television and two shabby brown armchairs.

'Thanks,' I muttered. 'Where is Billy, I mean Richard, anyway?'

'Oh, he's just popped up the road to buy some milk and a cake. He wants to impress you, I think. He was a bit annoyed, to be honest, because I finished up the last of the milk with a spot of sherry for breakfast. Nothing like it to get you going in the morning.' Peter paused. 'Can I get you anything in the meantime? I can offer you sherry, but sadly without the milk, or maybe you'd prefer tea or coffee?'

'No, I'm fine, thank you.'

'If you're hungry, there's a bit of last night's curry left in the oven.'

'No, I'm good, thanks, honestly.'

'Well, don't say I didn't offer. Right, well if you'll excuse me for a moment, I must get dressed. I make it a rule never to be in my pyjamas after two-thirty in the afternoon.'

'A good maxim,' I replied.

Peter shuffled off and the next moment, I heard a key turn in the door and Richard stumbled through it.

'Rachel's here,' called a voice from somewhere deep in the flat.

Richard staggered into the lounge, laden down with plastic shopping bags in each hand.

'Hi, Rachel. Sorry I wasn't here when you arrived. Have you been waiting long?' He walked over and kissed me on the cheek, banging one of the bags into my left leg.

'No, not at all, Billy.'

'Oh, Christ,' signed Richard. 'You know about that already, do you? It didn't take long for Peter to fill you in on my secrets.'

'I do indeed, Mr Idol. And I know all about his milk, sherry, and leftover curry habits. Is there anything else I should be made aware of?'

'No, I think those are more than enough revelations for one day, don't you? Tea?'

'Oh, yes, please,' called Peter, emerging from a room on the left. Clouds of white powder wafted behind him. 'Talc,' proclaimed Peter by way of explanation. 'Helps with the sweating.'

'More and more unnecessary intimate information revealed by the second,' groaned Richard.

The three of us shared a highly entertaining hour, drinking tea, eating cake, and generally taking the piss out of Richard. I was granted a grand tour of the flat, which consisted of Richard's bedroom, bathroom and kitchen all of which took less than three minutes. Peter's room was off-limits, as he had not tidied it since he moved in four months ago - and apparently, every surface was buried under a thick layer of talcum powder. His words, not mine.

'And then Billy decided to demonstrate that he could walk on water, but sadly he soon found that being completely blotto didn't mean that he had the gifts of Jesus, so he merely sank into the Cherwell and ruined his only dinner suit.' Peter guffawed with laughter as he told yet more stories, spitting tea all over the arm of his chair.

'Well, I do believe that's enough character assassination for one day,' announced Richard. 'What do you fancy doing now, Rachel?'

'Why don't we go into town and have a walk along the river? It's such a gorgeous day.'

'Sounds like a plan,' Richard agreed.

'I'll stay here, as I've got to catch up on some work,' Peter noted.

'I don't think you were invited, but thanks for letting us know,' Richard laughed.

We carried the mugs and plates into the kitchen and piled them in the sink. I started to run the water, but Peter told me to stop.

'No need, Rachel. I'll sort them out later.'

'Seriously?' questioned Richard.

'No, but you can do it when you get back. Rachel is our guest, after all.'

'Ah, I thought for a brief moment that you'd suffered a transformation, but I was clearly mistaken. See you later, Pete.'

'You too, Bill. Good to meet you, Rachel,' Peter roared and hugged me even harder than when I had arrived.

'Put her down,' laughed Richard, rolling his eyes at me.

The traffic driving into London was horrific, but Richard did not seem to mind. We chatted easily about everything and nothing, but in the back of my mind, I knew that I had to clear the air about the situation with Tim. As we idled at yet another set of temporary traffic lights, I decided to clarify my position.

'By the way, Richard, just to let you know, the guy I was going out with – well, I no longer am...going out with him, that is.'

Richard said nothing, but out of the corner of my eye, I noticed a small smile appear on his lips.

'I told him last weekend,' I explained.

'And how did that go?' Richard turned towards me, frowning.

'Well, to be honest, I'm not sure. He certainly wasn't too happy about it, but it could have been worse, I suppose.' I stared straight ahead through the windscreen, even though we were not moving. 'He's not the most understanding of people.'

'Well, that's nice and ambiguous,' Richard replied. 'Look, I don't know the ins and outs of what happened between you, but whatever they are, I'm glad he's gone.

I don't know why, as I know nothing about him, but I got the impression that he wasn't all that kind to you.'

'No, you could say that. One day, I'll tell you all about it.' I smiled at Richard, and he placed his hand over mine on the gearstick.

'Well, his loss is most definitely my gain and I promise you one thing, Rachel. I'll never hurt you. I mean that.'

My heart backflipped and I ground the gears badly as the lights turned to green. 'Thank you, Richard. I appreciate that, I really do. But just so you know, I'd never let that situation happen again anyway. I don't know why I let the whole thing continue as it was, But I hope I've learnt my lesson.' The lights changed and we shuffled forward.

'So why did you let it go on, do you think?'

'I suppose that I just didn't know how to end it and I was boxed in at Durham. It's such a small place – much smaller than Oxford where you were. And I had no one to tell, and even if I had told someone, they would not have been able to help me. More than that, I feared Tim. I needed to wait until we didn't live in such close proximity anymore. But I really regret it. I hear you talk about what an amazing time you had at university, and it makes me really jealous - and angry as well. I wasted all that precious time and for what?' I felt a hard lump form in my throat and tried to gulp it away.

Richard squeezed my hand a little tighter. 'Well, you're out of it now, Rachel and I'll look after you. You can forget about him. I just hope I never meet him, that's all.'

We spent a comfortable hour or so walking along the Embankment and just chatting away about everything and nothing. Then, out of nowhere, the heavens opened, and we got soaked as we ran back to the car for shelter, our afternoon stroll over. The drive home was shorter, as the traffic had thinned considerably, and we stopped off at the Odeon Holloway Road on a whim to watch the evening showing of *Ghostbusters.* The film was hilarious, but it was rendered far funnier by the fact that Richard and I sat on the front row of the balcony, where the seats had clearly come adrift from their moorings. Every time anyone shifted position, the whole row lurched forwards or backward like a rollercoaster. It was as if we had our very own ghoul controlling our viewing pleasure. In addition, about a third of the way through the film, as the seats seesawed back and forth, the box of Maltesers, which I had balanced precariously on the rail in front of us, toppled over, pelting the people below with chocolate balls. They may well have believed it was a special feature laid on by the Odeon, although the person who was hit on the head by the cardboard box was probably less than amused.

We laughed so hard during the film that any thought of canoodling through it did not enter our heads. We drove back to Highgate in high spirits and Richard invited me up for coffee.

'I don't like coffee - only tea,' I faltered.

Richard looked at me somewhat bemused. 'I'm sure I can find some tea for you, Rachel, or at least a teabag which can be resuscitated. I can't guarantee that Pete will have left us any milk. He might have made more of his sherry concoction, although that does appear to be a breakfast fixture, rather than an evening one, so we might be in luck.'

Richard duly made tea and even found a small amount of cake left from earlier, which we devoured between us. Then he opened a bottle of wine, and I had a small glass.

'Would you like another?' Richard asked. We were nestled together on the couch, Richard's arm around me and my head resting on his warm chest.

'I would, but I'm driving.'

'Why don't you stay over, Rachel? I promise that nothing will happen. Scout's honour.'

'Were you ever a scout?' I giggled, holding out my glass for a refill, my decision already made, even if I had not admitted it yet.

'No, but that's irrelevant. Look, I'll lend you a shirt and we can just cuddle. OK?' He topped up my wine a little more.

'Are you sure?' I faltered.

'Yes, trust me. I'll be as good as gold.'

I smiled, knowing full well that this would not be the case, but equally knowing that this was what I wanted.

We polished off the bottle and Richard dutifully found me a shirt to wear. He left me alone in his bedroom, while I changed into it. I left my knickers on and dived under the duvet quickly, because it was cold in the room, and I did not want to be found standing there when Richard came back. Richard knocked and entered, carrying two more glasses of wine. He was wearing his pyjamas. He placed one glass on each side of the bed and then slid under the covers beside me. We turned towards each other without touching.

'I'm sorry, this room is always cold. Are you chilly? Let me warm you up,' Richard offered.

I scooted over and nestled my head into his chest. I could hear his heart beating very quickly.

'I can tell that you are still alive,' I told him.

'I most certainly am,' exclaimed Richard, as he rolled me on to my back and kissed me gently. 'Is that OK?'

'Yes,' I breathed.

'Shall I do it again?''

I nodded. I felt nervous about embarking on another relationship so soon after the old one had finished, and yet this felt so completely different. Richard took time to find out about me, to ask about what I liked to do and how my day had been. He was kind and thoughtful and so different from Tim. And so, before I realised it, my shirt was happily unbuttoned, and I had discarded my knickers as we fumbled about and it was glorious, and right. During the night, and early the next morning, we tried again, less nervously.

'Tea?' Richard asked, sometime afternoon.

'Yes, that would be lovely, thank you,' I mumbled, reluctant to let Richard leave the bed. 'Without sherry though, please.'

He pulled on his pyjama bottoms and left the door ajar. I heard mutterings from the kitchen. Peter was obviously awake.

'Can you grab three mugs please,' I heard Richard boast to Peter.

'Three?'

'Yes, Rachel stayed over.'

'Good man!' I heard Peter shout, accompanied by what sounded like a high five. Richard appeared with two steaming cups of tea, surprisingly followed by Peter.

'Hi, Rachel. Great to see you again. Did you sleep well?'

I pulled the duvet up past my chin. 'Yes, fine, thank you.' My cheeks roared red.

'Want any breakfast? I've got some pizza in the oven from lunch yesterday?'

'No, I'm fine, thank you.' I glanced at Richard.

'Bye, Peter.' Richard slammed the door on him.

'See you later, Rachel,' Peter screamed through the door. 'Maybe we could do lunch?'

'He's an acquired taste, but has a heart of gold really,' Richard beamed, climbing back into bed. 'By the way, thank you.'

'Thank you for what?'

Richard brushed my hair back from my face. 'Oh, just for being here, for being you.'

I pulled his face towards me and kissed him.

'There's nowhere you really need to be for the rest of the day, is there?' Richard giggled.

'Let me consult my diary,' I answered, diving under the sheets.

I returned home much later that Sunday evening. My flatmate, Sarah, was seated at the kitchen table, wearing a pink onesie, and tucking into a steaming plate of chilli con carne.

'Do you want some?' she offered, waving her fork towards the stove, which looked like it had recently suffered a grenade attack.

'No, I'm good, thanks.'

I slumped down next to her at the table and rested my head on the plastic, floral cloth.

'So, you were out all night. Fess up, come one. Tell me everything.'

I gave Sarah a quick run-down of the previous day, doing my best to avoid any bedroom details, which was a genuine source of disappointment to her. 'His flatmate, Peter, is hysterical. You must meet him.'

'Is he hot?'

'God, no. You are impossible, you know that? But he is great fun. You would really like him. Anyway, I am totally knackered. I'm off to bed.'

'By the way, someone left a package for you yesterday. I've left it in your room.'

'Thank you. Night, night. See you in the morning.'

I trudged slowly upstairs, suddenly exhausted. Opening my bedroom door, I slung my bag onto the floor and collapsed onto my bed, knocking a box off the pillow as I did so. I sat up again and retrieved it from the floor. I was never one to be able to leave post unopened, even when it was obviously a bill. The box was extremely badly wrapped in newspaper and my name was scrawled on it in black marker pen in writing I did not recognise. I ripped off the paper and discovered a Clarks' shoebox, the lid sellotaped down. I peeled back the tape and removed the lid. Then I started to scream, shoving the box off my knee and back onto the floor.

Sarah bolted up the stairs and slammed through the door.

'Jesus, Rachel, what's the matter?'

'Look – look in the box,' I sobbed.

Sarah retrieved the box from the floor and peered inside. 'Christ, Rachel. Who the hell would send you that?'

Chapter 19

The box contained a dead, decomposing bird teaming with maggots.

At work, I felt increasingly uneasy. My line kept ringing, but as soon as I answered it, the caller hung up. Initially, I thought there was a fault on the phone, but Eric from Maintenance tested it more than once and said it was fine.

At least at work, I had company and therefore, there was safety in numbers. However, I began to dread going home at night. I had recently moved out of the rented house which I had shared with Sarah into a small flat of my own in Child's Hill. I loved it, because it was mine, and I could use the bathroom whenever I wanted to and could even walk around naked if I desired– which I never did, because I was always far too cold. But a couple of weeks after I moved in, weird, unpleasant letters and parcels began to arrive several times a week. I received a copy of the poetry anthology *Love is a Dog from Hell* by Charles Bukowski, accompanied by a cuddly Snoopy dog toy with its throat slashed. I was sent a dozen long-stemmed roses, painted black, their petals crushed inside their box. Another day, a white, lace wedding veil appeared, muddied, and torn. I received leaflets from the Samaritans asking if I was suicidal, and a variety of horrific photographs of lynchings. None of these things were ever accompanied by a note, but it was obvious who was behind them.

My nerves were shredded. I was frightened to walk down the street alone, even in broad daylight. I spent lunchtimes at my desk, arranging to meet Richard or Sarah, my old flatmate, at the end of the day to delay returning home. I was sure I was being followed at times, but I never saw him, only shadows taunting me and making me feel dizzy. I spent more and more of my time at Richard's flat rather than my own. I kept bursting into tears for no apparent reason and I was struggling to sleep. My dreams turned to nightmares most nights and they were violent. I awoke panting, drenched in sweat. Everyone begged me to go to the police, but I could not prove anything. All the postmarks were different and anyway, I had a feeling that reporting Tim would only make things worse. I was hoping that if I ignored him, eventually he would give up and go away. But, of course, Tim was not one to be ignored.

Richard and I were slouched on his sofa, my head resting on Richard's chest, drinking wine, and listening to Dire Straits' *Making Movies.* This was the only place I felt truly safe – in Richard's arms.

'I wish we could stay like this all the time,' I murmured.

'It might make it awkward to have a shower - and I suspect Roja might notice, even if you smuggled me into the creative department under your coat,' Richard laughed. 'But in all seriousness, Rachel,' Richard said, removing his arm and turning around to face me, 'this can't go on, can it? You're a nervous wreck - and things might escalate. At the moment, it's simply weird, creepy stuff Tim is sending, but what if he starts coming to see you? You already think he might be stalking you, and I wouldn't put it past him from what you've told me. What if he begins to threaten you? He could get violent. Let's face it, he's done it often enough before. Now you've rejected him, he could really hurt you. He doesn't like losing his control over you – or anything else, for that matter. You're frightened – and I'm frightened because I'm not sure what I can do to protect you unless we go to the police.'

I began to sob, and Richard folded me in his arms, my tears soaking his shirt.

'Rachel, you don't have to face this alone.' Richard hugged me tighter. 'I'm with you, but you have to trust me. Together, we can sort this out, Rachel. I love you and I don't want anything to happen to you. It would break my heart.'

'I don't know what to do, Richard,' I hiccupped. 'I just don't know if I can face going to the police. I can't prove Tim sent any of those things, or even that it's him calling me all the time. And then they'll want me to talk about what he was like in Durham – and then it will be his word against mine – and he can be pretty convincing, as we know. Oh, it's really hopeless.'

'Well, think about it. I'll come to the police station with you. Let me know what you want to do.'

'Thank you, Richard. I really love you. You know that, don't you?' I clung to him as if he were a life raft preventing me from sinking. I just prayed that he did not give up on me for constantly being an emotional wreck and decided he had had enough of me.

The strangest thing happened later that week. On Wednesday and then again on Thursday, the only calls I received at work were calls from clients or friends. No heavy breathing. No dialling tones. When I returned home, there were only bills waiting for me and the odd letter. Maybe Tim had gone away, or perhaps he was too busy to keep up his morbid mailbag. I could not believe it was any more than a ceasefire in his torture regime, but I was grateful for it.

I rendezvoused with Richard outside my office on the following Friday and we headed down to The Spaghetti House on Sicilian Avenue. It was a regular haunt of ours, given the generous portions of pasta and wine carafes at reasonable prices.

'You look a little better, Rachel,' Richard commented, as we took our seats at the back of the restaurant.

'I do feel a bit more relaxed - although I'm sure it's just a temporary lull in hostilities. All the nastiness will probably begin all over again soon. I just don't understand why he has suddenly stopped.'

Richard poured me a large glass of wine and one for himself.' Cheers!', he said, smiling.

'Cheers!' I replied, clinking our glasses together.

Richard swallowed a large slug of wine. 'I think I know why it's stopped, Rachel.'

I stared at Richard. 'What do you mean?'

'I called him on Monday.'

I tipped my glass too far to the left and wine spilled onto the tablecloth. I grabbed my napkin.

'You called him? You called Tim?' I asked, absently mopping up the wine, my heart pounding under my shirt.

'Yes. I knew his address because you had it written in your book in your room.'

I ignored the fact that Richard had been through my address book without my permission and continued to listen.

'So, I called him up.'

'And what happened?' I drank what was left of the wine on my glass in one large slug.

'Let's just say that you can be sure that he won't be contacting you again.' Richard finished his glass and topped us up. He stared at me with a smug grin etched across his face.

'How? I mean, what did you say exactly? Tim isn't going to give up that easily, surely? Not after all the effort he's been making.'

'I simply explained what would happen to him if he kept this up - and he seemed to come to his senses. Quite quickly, actually.' Richard buttered a piece of ciabatta slowly, smiling smugly.

'And what exactly did you say would happen?' I asked, my mouth gaping open like a small child waiting for the punchline at the end of a bedtime story.

'I merely pointed out to him that he would never have a career as a solicitor if you filed a police report, which you were now intending to do. No legal firm in a small provincial town, let alone at a Magic Circle company in London, would come near him once you'd done that. It's quite difficult, if not nigh on impossible, to hold down one of those important legal jobs when you have a criminal record and a restraining order against you.'

I gawped at Richard. 'But what did he say?' I had finished my wine without even realising it and Richard filled me up again. Signalling over to the waiter, he ordered another bottle.

'Very little actually. I spoke, he listened. I guess he must have mulled it over fairly rapidly with that supersized brain of his and concluded that he must, as always, put himself first. That is his forte, isn't it?' Richard grinned his beautiful grin.

I stared at Richard in stunned silence. I could not believe that he had found a solution or that it would actually work. And he had done all this for me, and I loved him for it. I thought I might explode with pride, happiness, and red wine right there in the middle of The Spaghetti House.

I leaned across the table, grabbed Richard's shirt, and planted a huge kiss on his lips. 'I don't know what to say. I love you. Just saying thank you doesn't seem anywhere near enough somehow. I, well, I…what can I say or do?'

Richard stretched his hand across the table and grasped mine.

'Oh, I bet we can think of something,' he smiled. 'More wine?'

Chapter 20

Christmas loomed large on the horizon and both Richard and I managed to wangle the period between Christmas and New Year off work. As it happened, Richard also hailed from just outside Manchester, so we drove home together. The traffic was horrific and three hours in, we had not yet negotiated Spaghetti Junction. Almost six hours later, we crawled up to the front door of Richard's house.

'Thanks for the lift, Rachel. I'll see you in a couple of hours at the pub, I hope.'

I saluted in the manner of all good chauffeurs and chugged off home.

My mother was pleased to see me for approximately thirty seconds, before regaling me on the dreadful state of my dress, my messy, dirty hair, and poor, disinterested general demeanour. She then set about providing me with a long list of chores, which had to be completed within the following hour if we were ever going to be ready for Christmas Day. We may have been Jewish, but that did not prevent my mother from cooking a full-on Christmas dinner, even if it did begin with smoked salmon and bagels.

'But Mum, the table is set, the food is prepared, the presents are under the tree – or at least mine will be shortly – so where's the fire? Anyway, I'm going out in an hour, so I need to shower and change.'

'Well, you'd better not be late back. I've got to get up at three in the morning to put the turkey in the oven.'

'How big is this sodding turkey?' I laughed.

'It's the size of a baby elephant,' my father commented from behind his newspaper. 'Perfect for four.'

'Really, if any of you had any idea how much work it takes to make Christmas dinner, you wouldn't be so bloody glib about it.' My mother stomped out of the room.

'It's going to be another relaxed Christmas Day, I see,' I sighed.

My father said nothing, but merely jiggled his newspaper slightly.

At that moment, Catherine burst through the living room door. Despite it being December – and it was a chilly one at that – she almost wore only an off-the-shoulder Bardot style top and tracksuit bottoms, which were so low you could see her knickers if she turned in any direction. Almost eighteen, she had just blitzed her A Level mocks, having already secured a place to study medicine at Cambridge. She was going to live my parents' dream.

'Oh, you're back already,' she commented, flinging herself onto the sofa with a thud. 'Well, at least you can drive me about, now you're home. Fancy taking me to the pub tonight?'

'Not really. I'm meeting some friends there - and anyway, you're underage.'

'I'm eighteen in three weeks, for Christ sakes! Let me come with you. Pleeze. I'll be really well-behaved, I promise.' She stared at me with her big doe eyes.

'Rachel, the least you can do is take your sister out with you. It will be good for you two to spend some time together anyway. You haven't seen each other for ages.' my mother snapped, entering the room again with a handful of crackers. 'And I've got a splitting headache and having you two out and not bickering here for a few hours will do me good.'

I rolled my eyes at my mother and huffed, 'Alright, Catherine, but don't be embarrassing. Any crap from you for one minute and you can piss off home again.'

'I'll be angelic, as always,' she smiled, fluttering her mascaraed lashes at me.

'Save it for someone who cares, Catherine. And I suggest you put some more clothes on before we go, or you'll freeze your tits off,' I snorted, leaving the room to change my clothes.

'Rachel! Since when did you use such coarse language? Is that what you learn at that bloody university of yours? Just make sure you look after Catherine in the pub, that's all,' my mother shouted in my wake. As if Catherine needed any looking after.

An hour later, I was in the pub with Mary. my old friend from school. We chatted about everything and nothing while I waited for Richard to appear. Catherine sat quietly, sipping a gin and tonic, listening to our chatter, and glancing around like a meerkat in season, hoping to meet a mate.

'It's the one night of the year that my father insists I turn up on time,' Mary prattled to me. 'I'm driving to stop myself from overdoing it before I get back. Last year, I got a just little too tiddly and ended up singing *Four and twenty virgins went down to Inverness,* instead of *We Three Kings* in the middle of Daddy's midnight mass. One of the parishioners has still not recovered.' Mary's father was the local vicar and Mary was a typical vicar's daughter – very lively and practised in the art of concealing the less Christian of her antics.

She tootled off after two lemonades. There were quite a few old friends from school in the pub, so we bedded a few beers, before deciding that we all needed something to eat to soak up the alcohol. I was reluctant to leave, however, as Richard had still not appeared, and I had no way of contacting him to tell him we had moved on.

'Who are you waiting for, Rach?' asked Catherine, poking me in the ribs with her elbow.

'Cut it out. No one,' I answered quickly. 'No one at all.' I stuck my nose into my wine glass and drank.

'So why do you keep staring at the door. Expecting Santa Claus, are you?' Catherine chortled.

'Very amusing, Catherine. You should go on tour,' I sniped. I scratched the inside of my arm.

Just then, a blast of icy air entered the pub as the door swung open and Richard appeared. Flushed from the cold outside, he rushed straight over and pecked me on the cheek. 'I'm so sorry I'm late, Rachel. I couldn't get away from my blasted mother. She had made enough food to stun a large buffalo,' he gasped.

'That's OK,' I replied, 'I'm only glad that you made it, as we were just about to go to get something to eat. I can introduce you to everyone at the restaurant. Are you still hungry after you've had such a big meal?'

'I can always eat, you know that,' Richard laughed.

'Come on then.,' I cooed, taking his arm.

'Aren't you at least going to introduce me now?' squeaked a small voice behind me.

I glanced over my shoulder at Catherine. For a brief moment, I had forgotten that she was there. Sighing, I turned back towards Catherine. 'Richard, this is my little sister, Catherine.'

'Hi, Catherine, it's great to meet you,' replied Richard, reaching over, and shaking Catherine's hand.

Catherine grabbed Richard's other arm and gave him a swift peck on the cheek. 'Good to meet you, Richard. So...are you two an item then, or what?' she giggled.

Richard and I glanced at each other, but neither of us answered. Richard turned and headed for the door, and I followed him, Catherine scurrying behind in our wake.

'Well, you kept him incredibly quiet, didn't you?' whispered Catherine behind me. 'He's bleeding gorgeous. How the hell did you manage that, ratbag? I'm utterly flabbergasted. He's so much hunkier than that dreadful gorilla you went out with a Durham.'

I let go of the pub door and allowed it to swing back into Catherine's face.

Our family Christmas dinner was relatively uneventful and inevitably, the only person who became tired and emotional was my mother. We shuffled her off to bed early with a couple of sleeping pills, and then settled down to a thrilling night of *The Two Ronnies* and *The Sound of Music*. We really knew how to enjoy Christmas in our house.

Boxing Day morning miraculously saw me up at nine, fiddling with my hair and having an anxiety attack over what to wear. Richard was coming over for Boxing Day lunch. I never usually bothered too much about what I wore, but somehow, today, at home, I felt like I needed to make more of an effort. My mother was a stickler for dressing properly when the relatives came over, although no-one knew why, as they were hardly the height of sartorial elegance themselves...I had brought my only two dresses up with me from London, but this fact did not prevent me from trying each one on several times. I asked my mother for her preference, but she simply told me that I looked appalling in both and that the best thing I could do was to lose a bit of weight. I replied that it was unlikely that I would be able to achieve that before lunch, and sulked back to despair once more in front of the mirror in my bedroom.

In the end, I plumped for my royal blue dress, with a sweetheart neck and a slightly flared skirt. Frankly, I hated it, but it seemed the more suitable for the occasion. I fiddled with my mascara one last time, sticking the wand into my eye in my haste so that it turned red and bloodshot. A black streak ran down my left cheek.

The doorbell rang and I raced to answer it. Richard stood there, stunningly handsome in a plain white shirt, navy chinos, and a baby blue crewneck sweater. He was holding a bottle of wine in his hand. He kissed me on the lips surreptitiously on the doorstep before I led him through to the living room. My mother had been hard at work from early morning – how she managed to wake up after sleeping pills and anti-depressants was a medical mystery - and the room now appeared to have been temporarily transformed into a full-blown Christmas grotto. Every surface was covered with rolls of cotton wool and myriad gaudy baubles hung from the light fittings, mantelpiece, Welsh dresser, side, and dining tables. I was surprised that my mother did not have a compulsory glittery adornment hanging from her own person. Fairy lights blinked on and off with terrifying regularity. An enormous, illuminated Father Christmas waved slowly from the corner of the room. This house was an epileptic nightmare.

'My mother goes a bit nuts for Boxing Day,' I explained to Richard, as I stood there wishing that this was not my home.

'You don't say. Where are the bloody elves?' he stage-whispered.

'Elvis? Did someone say Elvis? I'm not sure we've got any of his records,' called my father, entering the room wearing a bright red jumper with a reindeer on the front. The reindeer sported a pair of googly eyes, which moved as he walked. I wanted to curl up and die on the spot with embarrassment.

'Dad, this is Richard,' I announced.

My father held out his hand and shook Richard's with vigour. The googly eyes on his jumper danced in alarm.

'Of course. Richard, it's lovely to meet you,' said my father, while looking at me as if to ask who this person was and if he had been expected.

I smiled and pulled at a thread on the sleeve of my dress.

'Can I offer you a drink? Gin and tonic? Wine?'

Before Richard could reply, my mother sailed into the room, resplendent in a shimmering, loose, gold kaftan and matching shoes, both of which were very much in keeping with the festive decorations yet clashed rather with the yellow floral pinny she was wearing.

'Martin, don't stand there like a great lemon. Go and open the wine and sort out the nibbles. Everyone will be here in a minute.' She glanced over at me, reappraising my dress once again, and sniffed. 'Go on, Martin, move. We don't have all day.'

My father slunk away.

'Hello, I'm Richard. Happy Christmas. It's a pleasure to meet you,' Richard ventured, holding out his hand.

'And you, Richard dear,' my mother replied, blushing slightly. 'Do you think you could untie the back of my apron, please.' Richard removed said apron and folded it carefully, handing it to my mother, who giggled like a schoolgirl.

Catherine bowled through the door and wiggled her way over to us. She was wearing a simple T-shirt dress, which was so tight that it left nothing to the imagination.

'Hi, Richard, Happy Christmas. Good to see you again,' she said, brushing me out of the way and planting a hefty kiss on Richard's cheek. Her lips left an imprint in deep red.

'Hi, Catherine. Happy Christmas, I hope you got everything you wanted in your stocking yesterday,' Richard replied.

'Not quite everything,' Catherine retorted, smiling at Richard, and fiddling with the pendant on her necklace.

'Catherine, I think Mum needs some help in the kitchen,' I whispered.

'Well, why don't you go and help her then, Rach? You know I can't boil an egg. It's not my thing, you know. But I can pour drinks. Can I top you up, Richard?'

With that, she wheeled Richard away to the table where the drinks were lined up like soldiers waiting to enter battle.

The doorbell rang. 'Catherine, get the door, will you?' called my father, forcing her to relinquish Richard's arm. Catherine, in a rare moment of obedience, left the room and I grabbed Richard's hand.

'It's the relatives, I'm afraid. I hope you can cope.'

'I'll be fine,' Richard replied and gave my hand a little squeeze. 'They can't be any worse than mine.'

My aunt and uncle were led into the room by my mother. 'Jenny, Reg, do come and meet Richard, Rachel's new young man,' cooed my mother with pride.

'Hello,' barked Aunt Jenny, inspecting Richard over her pince-nez. 'Rachel, when's lunch? It's been a long journey.'

'Shortly, I think,' I muttered. 'And Richard, this is Uncle Reg.'

''Hello, Richard,' spat Uncle Reg. He wiped his mouth with a large spotted handkerchief, which he had retrieved from his pocket. 'Good to meet you,' he continued, his wet spittle flying in all directions.

'And this is my cousin, William,' I persevered. William had been lurking behind his parents and did not even glance up at me. He kept his bottle-top glasses fixed firmly on his shoes and said absolutely nothing.

117

Aunt Jenny, Uncle Reg and Cousin William looked as though they had just emerged from a 1940s re-enactment. They were all tweed, tank tops and sensible shoes. Aunt Jenny even wore a small hat, which she did not remove at any stage during her visit. I always half-expected them to bring a tin of Spam with them as a gift.

Eventually, we sat down to lunch. My mother ensured that Richard and I were positioned at polar opposites at the table, so that I was placed opposite Uncle Reg, with Cousin William on my left and Aunt Jenny – on my right. Richard was sandwiched between my mother and Catherine.

'Now, everyone, it's the traditional Boxing Day fare. There's beef, new potatoes, and plenty of vegetables, so tuck in. Don't be shy. Did you know that William also studied at Oxford, Richard,' boomed my mother, as she attempted to entice William into conversation.

'Ah, that's interesting. Which college did you go to?' Richard enquired, turning to face him.

William regarded him with wild panic, before finally stuttering the word, 'Worcester.'

'Ah, good college. So, you must have picked up your MA by now, William. I'll be able to collect mine in a couple of years,' boasted Richard.

'It's totally outrageous that you receive an MA for essentially doing nothing, when you actually have to study for one everywhere else,' I quipped.

Richard laughed, and even William managed a tiny titter.

'But Rachel,' my mother countered, 'a degree from Oxford or Cambridge is worth at least twice more than a degree from Durham, obviously, because only the crème de la crème is chosen to go there. So, of course, they should get their MA without any further effort, when they have worked so much harder in the first place. One mustn't be bitter about these things, just because one didn't achieve them.'

'I couldn't agree more,' said Catherine, giving me the finger behind her back.

I blushed hard and stabbed at my mushy vegetables, which had clearly been on the boil since November at the very least, rendering any form of cutlery redundant. 'I fail to see how you can justify the fact that Oxbridge degrees are worth more than those from other leading universities,' I mumbled.

'I see what you mean,' piped up Aunt Jenny, addressing my mother. 'She really can be a tricky little bitch, can't she?'

I felt as though someone had slapped me across the face. I glanced over at Richard, who was only partially visible next to my mother's bulky frame. His face had drained of all colour. 'Rachel, shall we help to clear the table?' Richard muttered through clenched teeth.

I nodded and was about to stand when Uncle Eric coughed violently. As he did so, his false teeth shot out of his mouth, sailing through the air towards me. Before I could react, he had stretched out his arm and recaptured his dentures in mid-air.

'Howzat!' he called out in triumph, before replacing them back into his mouth. 'I haven't lost my touch, you know. I used to be a decent fielder, back in the day,' he drooled, wiping his mouth with his serviette.

'Pudding, anyone?' enquired my mother.

Having met my family in Christmas mode, it only seemed fair to introduce Richard to our Jewish side. Two days later, we swopped tinsel and baubles for suits and yarmulke, when my extended family held a function to celebrate the birth of my cousin's baby. I invited Richard to join us. It seemed like a decent excuse to drag him away from his mother and for me to see him again. Richard seemed keen to accept. He drove over

119

to our house and then manoeuvred himself into the backseat of our car for the journey over to North Manchester. Catherine took full advantage of my mother's request for me to go back into the house to fetch the present she had left on the table to shove Richard into the middle, hooking her arm around his, because it was, as she commented, all a bit of a tight squeeze, 'Huddle up, Richard, so Rachel can get her big bottom in,' she cackled, as I returned with the gift.

The noise level in the car grew, as we chatted all the way, and in reply, my father turned the radio up louder and louder to drown us all out. Unperturbed, my mother attempted polite conversation with Richard from the front seat, blushing and giggling whenever Richard addressed her. All the while, he resembled a terrified animal caught in a painful trap. The concept of having to shout to be heard over many voices was totally alien to him, having been reared as an only child in a holy shrine of peaceful contemplation, where his parents hung on his every word. By the time we reached our destination, Richard had shellshock.

But if he was expecting things to be calmer on arrival, he was going to be disappointed. This was a big family gathering. Hundreds upon thousands of aunts, uncles, cousins, and friends had congregated for the celebration.

'There are an awful lot of people here just to wet the baby's head,' exclaimed Richard, who knew nothing about the true purpose of the get-together, except for the fact that he was required to wear a suit.

'It's a bris, Richard,' my mother informed him. 'Everyone always comes'

'A bris?'

'A ritual circumcision, Richard,' chirruped Catherine, banging him playfully on the arm. 'You know, where they slice off the end of the baby's chopper. They don't use anaesthetic or anything – they just rub on a bit of alcohol and the foreskin is cut off by a rabbi, not a doctor. It's a truly barbaric act when you think about it.'

Richard swayed slightly and cupped his hands involuntarily in front of his genitals.

'Don't worry, it's not your knob they are shortening – well, not yet, anyway,' Catherine laughed, threading her arm through Richard's to steady him.

'Alright, Catherine, enough,' I barked.

Undeterred, Catherine continued. 'It doesn't matter what the occasion is - wedding, bar mitzvah, bris, or funeral – we all get together, eat too much and drink too much. Then someone has a blazing argument with someone else and we all go home. This seemed as good a time as any to introduce you to the extended family, so you can see it in action for yourself .'

'As good a time as any? Are you serious?' Richard's face had drained of all colour.

I dragged Richard from Catherine's grasp and led him towards the house. 'Don't let her wind you up, Richard. She is just so immature,' I muttered, taking a deliberate step backward to stamp on Catherine's toe.

People were milling about in all directions.

'Rachel, what is this? A munchkins' convention? I am taller than everyone here by at least a foot. I'm struggling not to trample them.'

Richard did indeed tower over everyone. My father was usually the tallest at family functions – all five foot eight inches of him – so Richard, at six foot two, was like Gulliver in Lilliput. He told me later that his back ached for hours afterward from all the bending down he had to do in order to hear everyone as I introduced him.

A heavily overweight man, my Uncle Charlie – not a birth uncle, but a friend uncle – introduced himself. 'Well, Richard, you'd better come with me and let's make it fast. There is one rule and one rule only about attending a bris. You race into the room as quickly as you can, and you stand as far away from the action as possible. Go in too late and you can't avoid seeing the whole thing – and that really puts you off your chopped liver, I can tell you.'

'You'll need this,' I called after them, producing a yarmulke from my handbag and stuffing it in Richard's sweaty palm.

'Pop it on the back of your head, pronto, there's a good man, and let's go,' instructed Uncle Charlie.

Richard was whisked away, and I sought out the rest of the women, who were mercifully spared the sight and sound of a small child having his privates mutilated in public.

Chapter 21

'So, your family liked Richard from the sounds of things?' Dr Blake commented, flicking a spec of white lint off her blouse. 'That must have pleased you.'

'You'd think so, wouldn't you, Doctor?'

Chapter 22

It was amazing to me how quickly I got used to living in London, with its frenetic pace of life, at work and at play. The whole country was being privatised–the gas, the electricity, the water, the telephones, even the planes. Everyone was being offered a share of something. The economy was booming, and London was on a high.

My flat in Child's Hill was also only fifteen minutes away from Richard's flat, which meant that he tended to spend quite a few days during the week at my place, leaving Peter the run of his. My parents were oblivious to this partial co-habitation, on the grounds that they would disapprove vehemently – even if they were secretly relieved that a man as handsome as Richard had shown an interest in me. Neither Richard nor I ever picked up the receiver without letting the call move to the answering machine first. That way, Richard could be absolutely sure when it was safe to reveal his presence.

Work was intense. I was in by eight and rarely home before ten. I was often in over the weekends. We were pitching for new business, and we were winning. Every Friday evening around six, a trolley loaded with champagne and crisps was wheeled into the office to celebrate the achievements of the last seven days. The weekend started then and there. My copywriting manager, who I reported to, was a garrulous Dutchman called Marco. He had a wonderful way of schmoozing the clients. He was also rather too fond of the drink, but this never stopped him appearing in the office bang on time every morning. He swept in, his leggy secretary scooting in his wake with an enormous flask of coffee, struggling to keep pace. He would drink two large, strong cups without speaking, before leaning back in his chair and squirting drops into his blood-shot eyes.

'Rachel, these blue drops are the real secret. Pop them into your eyes and no one will know that you had no sleep last night. Talking of which, you'll never believe what happened to me yesterday.' He blinked and blue tears teemed down his cheeks.

As I steadied myself for his latest shaggy dog story, Marco leaned so far back in his chair that I was sure he was going to topple right over and hit his head against the cupboards behind his desk. Somehow, he remained upright.

'So, I went to Madame JoJo's last night – you know, the groovy club – and I met this gorgeous girl. She was all over me, you know, like a tickly rash, and after a few drinks, I think to myself, I'll take her home. I mean, why not. Kristen is away, and she will never know.'

I nodded, like I was an expert at picking up strangers in bars and having illicit extra-marital affairs.

'So, we go home together, we have a few more drinks, and one thing leads to another and then – well, you will simply not believe what happens then. Can you guess?'

I shook my head. I should have guessed, given Madame JoJo's reputation, but I was far too closeted.

'So, suddenly, she takes off her tiny panties and there it is. She has got a huge dick just like me. Bigger, in fact. I tell you - it was a real shock.' Marco threw his head back and guffawed so loudly that people outside his glass office stopped work to watch.

'But, Marco, didn't you suspect that she might be a man?'

'No, not at all. There all these real girls in the club, dancing, *nacked* with a smoke machine behind them, so I thought they were all, you know, women.'

'Nacked?'

'You know, nacked – with no clothes on.'

'Ah, naked.' Marco's English was ninety-nine percent perfect, but the odd word still caught him out.

Jenny, Marco's secretary, raced in. 'Marco, the client from Heinz is waiting in the meeting room. You need to go now.'

'OK, OK, I go.' He paused. 'You OK, Rachel? You look a little green. Have you also been burning your candle at both its ends?'

'No, I'm just a little tired, that's all,' I mumbled, still recovering from Marco's story.

But the truth was that I did feel a little nauseous and, as the day wore on, I began to feel worse. I decided to leave the office early, around six, and staggered onto to the Tube. I just about made it home before I was violently sick. I put myself to bed and was asleep before Richard arrived home.

I spent a very restless night, which frustrated Richard, as he had an early flight to catch the following morning. When he got up at five in the morning having been disturbed by me all night, he showered and changed, but he appeared reluctant to leave me in such a state.

'I'll be fine,' I groaned. 'I'll call the doctor at eight if I don't feel any better.'

'Alright, as long as you're sure,' whispered Richard, stroking my hair. 'I've left the phone by your side of the bed, and I'll be back as soon as I can tonight.'

I threw up again, narrowly missing his shoes.

I called the doctor's surgery as soon as it opened. The receptionist assured me that the doctor would come over within the hour. Three hours later, the doctor called to ask if I could attend the surgery instead.

'I can't stand up,' I moaned.

'So, you can't come here then?' the doctor retorted, sounding rather miffed.

'No, I can't move. I definitely can't walk.'

''Oh, well that's extremely disappointing,' replied the doctor. 'I'm rather busy this morning. Leave it with me.'

I tried to replace the receiver but missed, and I was in too much pain to reach down to retrieve it. A while later – I had no idea how long - I heard a key turning in the door and Richard came rushing in.

'Oh my God, Rachel, you look terrible. You're burning hot. I tried to call you, but there was no answer. Didn't you call the doctor?' Richard knelt beside me, feeling my forehead.'

'I called, but he said he was too busy to make a house call and he asked me to go there.' I paused. 'Aren't you supposed to be on a plane?' I mumbled.

'Yes, but I missed it - and then the next one would have got in too late for me to make my meeting, so I thought I'd come back to see how you were. I was worried about you.'

I smiled wanly. 'Thank you.'

'Right, we need to get you to A&E. Come on, Rachel, let's get you up.'

With difficulty and with a great deal of moaning and groaning on my part, Richard stood me up, helped me on with my dressing gown and crammed my slippers onto my feet, before manoeuvring me downstairs very slowly – inevitably, I lived on the top floor and there was no lift. He shovelled me into his Ford Escort. In retrospect, an ambulance might have been a better call, but he was in charge now. Richard wound the seat back as far as it would go, so that I could lie flatter, and we drove to The Royal Free. Every speed bump was utter agony.

A&E was a zoo and the mere fact that I could not unfold myself into an upright position seemed of no consequence to the triage nurse. After what seemed like weeks, I was finally taken into a cubicle and a doctor sidled in beside me. Richard remained in the waiting room.

'So, who have we here today?' the doctor asked. He seemed rather worn out, with ingrained dark circles under his eyes. His tie was loose and halfway around the side of his neck. He looked like he needed to lie down more than I did.

'Rachel,' I groaned.

'And Rachel, what seems to be the problem?'

'Well, I've got terrible stomach pain, I keep being sick and I can't walk.'

'Right. So, tell me, does it hurt when I press here?'

The doctor jabbed his finger into the lower right-hand side of my stomach, and I howled.

'Well, that settles it. It'll have to come out.' The doctor began to scribble on his clipboard.

'What will?'

'Your appendix – and the sooner the better, by the look of you. Let's get you sorted out.'

So, I was admitted and then left on a trolley in the corridor for the next four and a half hours. Richard never left my side.

'You know, Richard, I think I feel much better now,' I confided, wincing. 'Maybe we should just forget this whole thing and go home.'

'Rachel, you can't go home, just because you don't want the operation.'

'Seriously, I think I'm alright now. Why don't we just...' But I never finished the sentence, because I vomited all over Richard's shirt before I got to the end of it.

Once Richard had found some paper towels and attempted to clean his chest, he said,' I think should call your parents to let them know, don't you, Rachel?'

'Don't leave me, Richard, please,' I whined.

'There's a payphone right here on the wall next to us.' Richard pointed behind my head. 'Remind me of their number.'

I dutifully spelled out the numbers and Richard dialled. The phone rang out for several minutes.

'Hello, it's Richard here.' There was a pause. 'Richard Anderson.' Another pause. 'Richard? I've been going out with your daughter Rachel for a while now...we met at Christmas...Yes, that Richard. Yes, hello. I'm fine, thank you. You? That's good. Look, the reason that I'm calling is that Rachel has got appendicitis and we are at the hospital. They are going to operate shortly, and I wanted to let you know...yes, I'll hold.'

'What's going on?' I called.

'He's gone to find your mother. He had no idea who I was, you know.'

'That doesn't surprise me,' I giggled. 'Ow, I mustn't do that.'

'Hi, yes, hello, it's Richard. Yes, that's right. Yes, I'm well thank you. How are you? Yes, it appears to be appendicitis. Shortly, yes...The Royal Free. No, it's NHS... No, I haven't asked about a private room... You're coming down now? OK. Right. I'll let her know. Bye.'

Richard's face had turned ashen.

'Your mother says they are coming down tonight.'

'You mean tonight? Oh shit'

'Exactly. I'll have to go back to your flat and remove all traces of myself before they get here.'

'Yes, absolutely. Bugger. Why didn't you suggest she waited until tomorrow?'

'I wasn't given the opportunity,' he sulked. 'Your mother was on transmit.'

At that moment, a nurse arrived to remove me from the corridor and transfer me to the ward prior to my operation.

'Rachel, I'm going to go now, because it will take me a while to clear the detritus, and they could be here in three hours if they leave straight away. I'll come back later, I promise. Good luck.' He kissed me on the cheek and scuttled off down the corridor.

As it happened, my parents thought better of a late-night dash down the M1 and did not arrive until the following day, appearing by my bedside around late morning.

'Rachel, how are you? We came straight from the station,' soothed my mother.

'OK,' I mumbled.

'You don't look wonderfully comfortable, Rachel. Let me sort out your covers.'

'I'm fine, honestly, Mum. Please don't fuss'

But my mother had already pulled back the sheets. 'Good grief, Rachel, is that the best you can do?'

I looked at her puzzled, my eyelids still sleepy.

'You've come into hospital to have an operation wearing that grotty old T-shirt. Didn't you have any good nighties to bring?'

I bent my head to my chin to remind myself of my outfit. I was wearing a faded brown t-shirt with an orange printed on the front saying, 'Squeeze Me'. 'My attire wasn't really my top priority yesterday, Mum, if I'm being strictly honest. It was a bit of an emergency.'

My mother harrumphed, 'And to be frank, my dear, I have to say that the state of your flat wasn't up to much either.'

My stomach lurched. What incriminating evidence had Richard left behind?

'The wardrobes, Rachel. The bloody wardrobes. They are a disgrace. Do you know how much dust there is on the top of them?'

'Funnily enough, Mother, when I was doubled over in agony yesterday, my first thought was that I must check the tops of the wardrobes, but unfortunately, I couldn't quite reach them.' I was already beginning to wonder when they might go home.

'Well, I was shocked, really. Weren't you, Martin?'

But my father had already settled himself by my bed and started in on the large box of All Gold chocolates which they had brought from Manchester for me. He slowly disappeared behind that day's newspaper. 'Yes, darling,' he muttered.

Sadly, my parents kept a vigil by my bedside all day long. Richard arrived at eight in the evening, I suspect hoping to have missed them, but he was out of luck. He wandered onto the ward, squinting in a haphazard manner at the occupant of each bed before finally recognising me. I waved weakly and Richard smiled.

'Richard, hello,' called my mother, rising from the hard chair by my bed. She leaned forward and flapped her arms, clearly unsure whether to kiss Richard, or to shake his hand. In the end, she did neither, blushing scarlet. My father remained seated, but he did at least fold his newspaper down and nod in Richard's general direction.

'Richard, thank you so much for bringing Rachel in yesterday, and for staying with her. I hope it wasn't too inconvenient,' gushed my mother. 'We must find a way to thank you. Perhaps we can take you to dinner while we are here?'

'No, no, that's not at all necessary,' Richard answered too quickly. 'Anyway, I have to go up North tomorrow on an errand.'

I glanced over at Richard, somewhat surprised, as he had not mentioned a trip to me.

'I was extremely worried about Rachel,' Richard continued, 'but hopefully, she will start to feel better now. I know that when my appendix decided to blow, I certainly felt the benefit of surgery very quickly. Mind you, it was in Bangor hospital, where no one spoke any English on the ward. It was all slightly disorientating.'

'Goodness me! Your appendix going bang in Bangor. Imagine,' gasped my mother, intending no pun whatsoever. My father rolled his eyes.

'Well, we'll be getting back to the flat now. It needs a really good clean, Richard, I can tell you. If only you could have seen the state of the top of the wardrobes...'

'Mention the bloody wardrobes one more time, Mum, and I will ensure you're in the bed next to me,' I muttered.

My mother huffed and gathered up her things. 'Well, there's no need for that, Rachel. You're clearly feeling slightly stronger. See you in the morning.'

'Don't rush,' I hissed under my breath.

My father gave me a peck on the cheek. 'Sleep well.' He turned to Richard. 'Bye, er...,' he looked somewhat confused, 'bye. Thank you.'

They waddled off towards the exit at the end of the corridor and Richard slumped down onto the chair beside me.

'You look more tired than I do,' I laughed. 'Ow. Oh, I must remember not to do that. It hurts.'

'How are you feeling?' enquired Richard, tearing open the paper bag he was holding and taking a large bite out of a club sandwich. 'Sorry, I'm starving. Do you want some?'

'No, thanks. I haven't been able to keep anything down yet.'

'Poor you. Maybe you'll feel a bit better tomorrow when you've got the anaesthetic out of your system. Anyway, the thing is, Rachel, now that you're alright, I'm going to go back to Manchester tomorrow. There's a car I really want to buy, and I've arranged to test drive it tomorrow afternoon,' Richard informed me between munches.

'A car? Now? When I'm still in hospital? Can't it wait?'

'Well, it's alright, isn't it? You are stuck in here anyway - and your parents are down looking after you. There's not much more I can actually do, is there?'

'Except be here for me,' I whined. 'Surely you'd like to be around to see how I'm getting on and so that you can visit me every day?' I felt on the verge of tears.

Richard stuffed the remains of his sandwich into his mouth and chewed. 'Look, Rachel, it's all arranged now. I'll see you when I get back. I really don't want to miss out on this car. I've been looking for this model for ages and it's a great price. Please don't be difficult about it, please. It's not very fair, is it?'

'Well, at least you've got your priorities straight,' I huffed.

''You're being really silly about this, Rachel, you really are.'

'Am I?' Tears pricked at the corners of my eyes and my throat hurt as I tried to hold them back.

'Come on now,' soothed Richard, stroking my hand. 'It's only for a couple of days. I'll be back before you know it.'

He bought the wretched car – it was a flame red Sierra Cosworth, with a nasty racing fin stuck on the back of it. I hated that car on principle for the rest of the time that he owned it.

Chapter 23

Richard had been acting extremely oddly ever since he returned to London with his new, treasured, flashy car. He began to stay longer and longer in the office and spent less and less time with me at my flat. I rarely bumped into him at work, and he suddenly seemed always to be too busy for lunch. I kept asking him if anything was wrong, but he assured me that everything was OK. He told me that he was just extremely tired and overworked. But something was nagging at the back of my mind. I just could not work out what it was.

Richard's birthday was looming and so, as a special treat to cheer him up and to inject some new excitement and romance into our stagnating relationship, I arranged for us to spend two nights away at a bed and breakfast in Ely. I chose Ely because it was not too far out of London to travel after work on a Friday night – and because neither of us had ever visited it previously.

I presented Richard with a handcrafted invitation, scribbled on the back of a postcard:

Rachel cordially invites Richard to spend two nights away at a secret location to celebrate his birthday

R.S.V.P

I popped the invitation into an envelope and left it on his desk at work. I assumed that he would call me during the day to reply, as he often used to do during the working day, or that he might wander up to the creative department to see me, but he did not. I reasoned that he must still be extremely busy and that we would discuss it in the evening, but when I returned home, Richard was not there. He had obviously decided to stay at his place again and had forgotten to tell me.

The following day, I sought him out at the agency and tackled him on it. He was hurrying down the corridor to a meeting as I headed towards his desk, and I had to run to catch up with him.

'Did you get my invitation?' I puffed, struggling to keep up with Richard, who never broke his long-legged stride.

'What invitation?' Richard spluttered.

I raised my eyebrow at him.

'Ah, yes, that one. Yes, I did.'

No thanks, no smile.

'Well, are you coming then?' I pressed.

Richard continued to stare straight ahead at the swing doors, as if they were an insurmountable obstacle in his path.

'Have you already paid for the room?' he asked, banging through the doors, and almost knocking me over in the process.

'Yes. I had to pay for it in advance to get the best deal,' as we slammed down the next corridor. I paused. 'Don't you want to go?'

Richard stopped and faced me. 'It's not that I don't want to go as such, Rachel. It's just that it's my birthday… and I usually spend it with all my friends.'

'I just thought it would be a nice surprise, you know, for the two of us to go away to celebrate together. You can see everyone else when we get back, can't you?' My chest felt heavy, as if I had a large weight pushing down against my ribs.

'I suppose so,' Richard replied, 'but I really wish you'd asked me first. I hate surprises. You ought to know that by now, Rachel. Really.' He glanced at his watch. 'Shit, I'm late,' he yelled, bolting away from me.

The following Friday, we left London straight from work around eight in the evening and crawled out on the

A1 towards Ely. Richard was silent most of the way, fiddling with the channels on the radio and staring out of the window, even though it was pitch black outside and there was nothing to see. When we arrived at the bed and breakfast place, it was already quite late. We knocked on the door and an older gentleman answered. He was rather stooped and spoke extremely slowly, which only increased the level of Richard's irritation. I could sense Richard's annoyance by the way he was breathing.

The man showed us to our room, which was in a granny annexe at the back of the house. The accommodation was rather small, rather shabby, and more than a little disappointing. It smelt strongly of damp. The man handed us our key and wished us a pleasant stay. I knew already that it was not going to be.

'Let's see if we can catch last orders at the pub,' I suggested to Richard, who had thrown our overnight bag onto the bed and was surveying the room with obvious distaste, seemingly unwilling to even sit down.

We went back out and wandered down the high street, which I had expected it to be rather quaint and picturesque, but which was, in fact, somewhat dilapidated, with a variety of rundown shops and a couple of fish and chip and kebab take-out places. Groups of drunken youths roamed the pavements, having just fallen out of the pubs.

'Let's just go back, Rachel,' whispered Richard quietly, grabbing my arm rather too forcefully, and steering me back the way we had come. 'This is no fun.'

Back in the room, we undressed quickly, as the room was freezing cold, and dived under the covers. I snuggled up to Richard to try to get warm, but he turned his back on me and was soon snoring loudly. I lay awake all night under the thin blanket, shivering and fretting about my poor choice. I prayed that Richard would wake in a cheerier state of mind.

The following morning dawned sunny and cold. Richard awoke cold and not even vaguely sunny. I suggested that we walk over to the cathedral after a short breakfast of toast and weak, grey tea. The cathedral dominated the town in the early sunshine. It was hard not to be over-awed by its architectural beauty, yet Richard was so unutterably miserable and seemed determined not to derive any pleasure from it whatsoever.

''It's gorgeous, isn't, Richard?' I commented as we walked around the perimeter of the cathedral.

'Hmm, yes, I suppose so,' Richard murmured, clearly less than impressed – or at least, doing his level best not to be. He walked on ahead of me, his hands in his pockets, head down.

I scurried to catch up with him. 'Shall we have a drive out to Cambridge after this? I've never been, and I hear it's lovely.'

'Well, I've already been there several times before, but we can if we must,' Richard replied, his frown unbroken.

So, buoyed by Richard's overwhelming enthusiasm, we drove to Cambridge. I scratched at a cut on my hand as I drove along.

'I hate this part of the world,' Richard moaned as we tootled along behind a tractor piled high with straw. ' It's as flat as a pancake. There's literally nothing of interest to look at.'

'You can always look at me,' I joked.

My joke fell as flat as the Fens.

We dragged round Cambridge, Richard studiously not admiring the mighty Kings, nor wishing to take afternoon tea, nor to punt romantically on the Cam. 'Rachel, it's bloody freezing. You've got to be joking about going out on the river. If you want to come to places like this, let's at least do it in the Spring when the weather is a bit warmer,' Richard moaned.

By the time we returned to the car park to return to Ely, I had reached the end of my patience. 'Richard, what the hell is the matter with you? I booked this trip as a special treat for you and you're behaving as though I've given you bubonic plague. You're being a totally ungrateful git.'

'I told you I didn't want to come, Rachel, but as usual, you didn't want to listen,' Richard sulked.

'Well, thanks a bunch. I'm so pleased I've spent my hard-earned money on taking you away.' I felt tears forming and swallowed hard to stop them. 'It was supposed to be a treat for you.'

Richard did not reply, but merely opened the passenger door and got in. I opened the driver's door and slammed it behind me so hard that the little car shuddered in pain, before I started the engine, revving it with force.

'So, shall we just go home then? I can't see the point of spending tonight here if you're just going to be so sodding miserable.'

Richard stared out of the car window. 'Yes, I think that's probably for the best.'

Richard may as well have slapped me across the face.

'I won't be able to get the money back, you know that!' I shouted.

'Sorry,' Richard answered in a monotone.

We returned to the bed and breakfast place, where I made up an excuse to the owner about us needing to return to London for work, but I was struggling not to cry while I was having the conversation with him, so I suspect he just thought that Richard and I had had an enormous row, which was effectively true. I stuffed all my sexy lingerie – which was basically anything I owned that was not greying - back into my holdall and we travelled back to London in silence.

'Can you drop me at my flat, Rachel?' Richard requested.

I jumped, as they were the first words that Richard had said to me for the past two hours.

'Yes, sir,' I snapped, saluting with my free hand.

I pulled up outside his flat and put on the handbrake. Clearly Richard had no intention of inviting me in, getting out of the car and retrieving his luggage from the boot as fast as he could. I jumped out of the car, slamming the poor door with an almighty thud once again, and followed him in any way. I felt such gigantic, rising panic within me that, as much as I was totally furious with him, I just wanted him to wrap me in his arms and tell me that he was sorry and that he loved me regardless. I wanted to grab at his shirt and beg him to stop pulling away from me. Instead, the moment he unlocked his front door, Richard disappeared into his bedroom, closing the door behind him.

Peter was still in his pyjamas watching television and eating cornflakes at five in the afternoon. I collapsed onto the sofa next to him.

'Hey, I thought you guys weren't back until tomorrow?' he commented, spilling milk down his top. 'Did you have a good time?'

I dropped my head into my hands and burst into tears.

Peter patted my knee, spraying my leg with a couple of corn flakes and a little more of the milk. 'Hey, come on, Rach, what's the matter?'

'I don't know,' I sobbed. 'I thought Richard would really like to go away, but he clearly didn't want to spend his birthday with me. He wanted to be with you and all his other friends.'

'The boy is insane,' soothed Peter. 'I don't know what his problem is, but if I was invited away for a dirty weekend with a gorgeous girl like you, I'd jump at the chance.'

I tried to smile, but my mouth would not co-operate.

'Come on,' said Peter, jumping up. 'I'll throw some proper clothes on, and we'll go out for tea. I've lived on cornflakes for the past two days as it is, and as the well-known saying goes, man cannot live on cereal alone.'

Peter and I walked to the local café down the road, where we stuffed ourselves with cake for an hour or so. Peter did his best to cheer me up – and the sugar binge helped a bit as well. As we walked back, Peter reassured me that he would speak to Richard 'He's just being a silly ass. There was no one around this weekend except me anyway, and I can't compete with you. I think he just gets scared of commitment, that's all - despite the fact he's clearly crazy about you. If it is any consolation at all, I think he's behaved really badly.'

I kissed Peter on the cheek, and he blushed vermillion, after which I drove home and spent the evening intermittently crying while eating more of the cake, which we had taken home in a doggy bag. Before bed, I sliced a little at my left arm.

I did not hear from Richard at all for the next three days and instead, I focused ridiculously hard on not seeking him out, which took all of my willpower and more. When he did finally call, he did not say much, except to ask if he could come over to my flat after work. I said fine in the most disinterested voice I could muster, but under my shirt, my heart was pounding so loud that I was sure my colleague at the next desk could hear it.

I arrived home as early as I could to check my face and arrange it as stonily as possible for Richard's arrival, but as soon as he came through the door and took me in his arms, muttering into my neck how sorry he was and how he just had a stupid fear of missing out on what his friends were doing, I had forgiven him. Ten seconds later, we were in bed. We had no need of sexy lingerie.

The following morning, I rolled over, squinting at my alarm clock. It was blinking zeros at me, so I fumbled for my watch and screamed.

"Jesus! Richard, wake up. It's ten o'clock.'

'What? It can't be. I've got an early meeting. I'll be in so much shit.'

'There must have been a power cut.' I jumped out of bed and flicked on the lights. Nothing. 'Bloody hell, we've got no electricity. How am I going to shower and dry my hair?'

I pulled on my dressing gown and marched into the lounge to find *The Yellow Pages*. I located the emergency number for the electricity board and dialled. It rang for an eternity, but eventually, someone answered.

'Hello. I wonder if you can help me. We appear to have had a power cut and have no electricity at the moment.'

'You and the rest of southern England, love,' the man at the end of the line snorted.

'Excuse me?'

'Look, darling, I don't know if you're deaf or something, but we had an almighty storm last night, which has taken out the power in half of the country.'

I muttered my thanks and, replacing the receiver, threw back the curtains. A magnificent oak tree lay horizontally across the main road. Another had landed on two parked cars, their roofs caved in. Dustbins were upended and litter was strewn everywhere. Detritus was suspended in the air in the still gusting wind. We had slept through Armageddon.

Richard later insisted that it was the power of good sex, so we decided to test the theory again, before eventually getting up and slowly driving into town. We had no choice, as the tubes were out of action and there were no buses running. We reached the agency around lunchtime to find that very few people had bothered to do the same. We both felt most happy and virtuous.

Chapter 24

'So all was well again? It was just a bit of a blip, was it?' asked Dr Blake, doe-eyed.

'A blip? A blip of happiness, a moment of reprieve. But as you know, it didn't last all that long.' I ripped at a scab on my wrist.

'Why not?'

'Why not? Now, that's a particularly interesting question, Dr Blake, isn't it?'

Chapter 25

'It's a total nightmare,' I sobbed into my Chardonnay. 'Richard has changed completely.'

'Oh, Rachel, come on. It can't be that bad,' soothed Sarah, topping up my wine glass to the brim, so that I had to slurp it without lifting it from the tabletop. 'I thought things had got better again. What the hell is going on?'

We were ensconced in a corner of *The Crusting Pipe* wine bar in the bowels of Covent Garden, perched on wooden stools which were still slightly sticky from wine spilled previously during past boozy lunches and evenings. In front of us were three empty plates, littered with cream cracker crumbs, which we had eaten because we were not really hungry enough to buy real food. Sarah waved to the waiter and asked for another plate.

'Well, ever since he came back with that foul car, he's been offhand with me. Essentially, he's been absent.'

'Maybe he's just super stressed with work as he told you. Isn't your boss a bit of a bastard to him?' Sarah lit a new cigarette off the one she was just finishing and handed it to me. I accepted it, even though I never smoked. I had tried it once at a school disco when I was fourteen and it had made me sick on the dancefloor. My date at the time had been less than impressed. I watched the fag's orange tip winking at me, before returning it to Sarah, who stubbed out her old one and started in on the new.

'He's always been busy with work, but that has never seemed to stop him from staying at my place every night in the past. We have been practically living together for the last eighteen months. But now he says he must stay at his flat because he needs more space. It's simply a pathetic excuse. I know something is up, but I don't know what.'

Sarah nodded in agreement. 'I wish he'd move in with you, because then I could rent his place. I desperately need new digs and his flatmate has moved out, hasn't he?'

'Yes, he's got his own place now. Hang on. I thought you were living with Rupert?'

'Oh, Christ no. That's fallen through. He was a decent shag but had the most dreadful personal habits. He cut his toenails in bed and farted like a geriatric hound. There's only so much I can put up with.' Sarah took another drag of her cigarette, thoughtfully blowing the smoke onto the next table rather than at me. 'Shame though. He had such a lovely pad in Chelsea.'

'I would suggest it to Richard, but he's barely communicating with me. He never answers when I call him at work, and when I do see him, we just seem to argue,' I sighed, leaning forward to take another huge slurp of wine.

'Argue about what?' Sarah asked as the crackers arrived. Sarah stuffed a whole one into her mouth, crumbs sticking to her lipstick.

'About everything and nothing. Mostly everything. Apparently, I'm too possessive and he wants to see more of his friends. I also love him too much, as if that's even a thing. How can you love someone too much?' I drained my glass and Sarah dutifully poured the end of the bottle into it.

'I'll get another one in a minute,' she promised, sensing that I might dissolve into a puddle without the continuous prop of alcohol. 'He's just being an utter prat. Ignore him. Play hard to get and he'll come running. Usually works for me.'

I stared, somewhat blurrily, at Sarah, and blinked. Sarah was many things, but hard to get was not one of them. She was more of a Paul Young sort of girl…wherever she lay her hat.

'I can't. I've tried, but I just feel this horrible sense of panic all the time. I really want everything to go back to being like it was before.' A tear slipped unbidden from the corner of my eye and dropped into my wine.

Sarah dragged her chair to the other side of the table, so that she was sitting next to me, and draped her arm around my shoulders. 'He'll come round, Rachel, you'll see. He is just behaving like an immature idiot. You know full well that he's crazy about you. It's just that he doesn't want to admit it to himself. He's just being a bloke.'

I could not reply, because if I opened my mouth at that moment, I was just going to howl.

'Come on, I'm starving, and you need something to soak up the booze if you're going to make it into work tomorrow. Let's go and stuff our faces with lasagne,' Sarah suggested, smiling.

The following evening, Richard made a surprise guest appearance at my flat after work. 'Hi, gorgeous,' he cooed, wrapping me in his arms and holding me against his warm body. We were naked in seconds.

A while later, I lay with my head on Richard's chest, listening to the rhythmic sound of his heart beating against my ear. Running my fingers through his dark chest hair, I murmured, 'I'm ravenous. Shall we eat here, or in the lounge?'

Richard rolled away to the side of the bed and stood up, pulling on his underpants. 'I'm not staying, Rachel. I need to get back home.'

'Seriously?' I stared at the dark mole in the centre of his back.

'Yes, I've got an extremely busy day tomorrow.' Richard buttoned up his shirt quickly, before searching for his trousers, which lay crumpled in a heap by the window. 'I've got a meeting with a new client.'

'So, you just came over here for sex, did you?' I screeched, my voice too high.

'No, of course not, Rachel. It was great to see you, but...' Richard's voice trailed off into nothing.

'But what, Richard?' I sat up, covering myself with the duvet. 'You keep doing this. Popping in, shagging me, then pissing off again. I'm not here just to service you, you know.'

'I know that Rachel. It's not like that, really it's not.' Richard stuffed his tie into his trouser pocket.

'So, exactly what is it like, Richard? Because it's not what it was, is it? What's changed exactly? Talk me through it.' My chest was heaving with anger.

Richard flumped heavily onto my dressing table stool, which rocked in violent protest. 'I don't know, Rachel. I think that maybe we just need a bit of time apart. I'm feeling rather hemmed in.'

I pitched forwards and buried my head into the duvet cover. 'Not this again,' I sighed.

'Perhaps we should stop seeing each other for a couple of weeks. You know, not speak, or meet up at all during that time. I just need to get my head straight.'

I re-emerged from the duvet with a jolt. 'Straight about what exactly? I feel the same about you as I always have, but you've just been weird ever since you went up to Manchester to buy that disgusting boy racer car.' I reached onto the floor for my dressing gown and pulled it on, before sliding out of the bed. I moved towards Richard and held out my hand, but he did not take it.

'I just feel under a lot of pressure right now, that's all,' Richard muttered.

'Who's pressurising you? Not me.' I sat down on the floor in front of him and gazed at him. 'Don't you love me anymore? Is that it?' I could feel the tears searing the back of my eyelids, as I tried to force them back. I felt so utterly weary.

'Look, Rachel, let's agree to two weeks with no communication – nothing at all. We will avoid each other at work. Then we can arrange a date to meet up and sort everything out. OK? I just need that time. Please try to understand.' Richard kissed the top of my head, jumped up and fled, his socks and shoes in his hand. The front door banged shut.

We met up again at my flat just over a fortnight later. It was a bitter November day, and I was looking far from my most alluring. My legs were chapped from waiting at the bus stop every morning - my thin tights offering no protection against the biting wind. My nose was red raw due to a heavy cold - and from too much crying in the early hours in bed. I had bags for life under my eyes and a livid network of new scars.

I bunked off work early to prepare for our reunion. I did not know what to expect or know how long Richard might stay – if he arrived at all - so I kept things simple, purchasing some wine and a few packets of crisps from Tesco. Back at the flat, I jumped in the shower and shaved my legs - just in case. Wiping a patch of condensation off the mirror, I screamed at the image which stared back at me. Slapping Sudocrem onto my nose and wiping the remainder onto my sore legs, I dried my hair hurriedly and set to work on my face. Twenty minutes later, I had a little more colour, but my nose still looked as though it was auditioning as a lighthouse. I knew the only solution was to stop looking in the mirror. I did not. Instead, I continued to apply further layers of concealer to my nose, so that now it resembled an enormous, rather nasty, brown scab. 'Shit, I look terrible,' I shouted at my reflection, which nodded back at me in agreement.

I was about to scrub it all off and start again when the doorbell sounded.

'Who the hell is that?' I asked out loud. I assumed it was not Richard, because he had a key, and I hoped it was not my neighbour with a parcel, as I would not be able to get rid of her for hours. She would witter on about the latest scandals in the block. Number 12 had blocked the drive again, Number 17 had jammed the rubbish chute - and I had to hope that she did not start on the goings-on at Number 4, or I might need to take some Valium. I pulled my bathrobe cord tightly around my waist, so as not to flash her, and opened the door.

'Oh, it's you,' I muttered.

'Weren't you expecting me?' Richard hesitated on the threshold, breathtakingly handsome in his long black overcoat, absently swinging the bottle of wine he was holding in his left hand.

'Yes, I, well yes, but I thought you would have used your key.'

'I thought under the circumstances that I should probably ring the bell.' Richard stood hopping from one foot to the other.

'Right, sure. Well, come in – it's cold out there.' I stood aside to allow Richard to enter. 'Look, I'll just throw some clothes on. Why don't you open the wine? I'll be with you in a second.'

I bolted into the bedroom and pulled on a pair of jeans and an old shirt, which was one I knew Richard really liked. I reasoned that it might distract him from my face. I found Richard in the living room, staring out of the window at the relentless, unmoving traffic on the main road.

'It's bloody freezing out there,' Richard remarked, turning around, and handing me a glass from the table. 'It's getting quite foggy too.'

'Yes, the forecast said it might get misty overnight.'

Christ. We were reduced to talking about the weather. I sat down at one end of the sofa and Richard sat at the other.

'So...' we both said together and laughed.

'What have you been up to?' Richard enquired, pulling the cork out of the bottle he had brought with him and pouring red wine into my glass.

'Oh, nothing exciting. Just working. We are really busy, actually. I'm working on that new pitch for tampons.'

'Right, yes, I heard about that.'

'Yes, it's a great conversation starter at dinner parties too,' I laughed, my heart sinking. 'I bet you're sorry you're not working on it too. And you? What have you been doing?'

'The same as you. Working hard. Thinking hard.' Richard stood up and moved to the table to refill his own wine, which he had downed at warp speed. He returned to the sofa and sidled closer, holding out his hand. I took it. 'Rachel, I've been a mess these past two weeks. I haven't been able to concentrate on anything at all. I love you and I miss you and...'

I genuinely cannot vaguely remember what he said next. All I can tell you was that, several hours later, we were giggling, while finishing off the crisps and more wine in bed. In the morning, we made love again and ate toast under the covers to keep warm.

Around noon, Richard went to take a shower and I lay luxuriating in bed. I felt exhilarated and utterly content. I knew now that Richard loved me, and I had always adored him – I had felt that way from the very first time we met, even if I had not fully realised it at the time. This last fortnight had been utter hell for both of us, but now we knew we were destined to be together.

Richard returned from the bathroom, drops of water glistening on his chest hair, and perched on the edge of the bed in his towel.

'Rachel,' he said. 'There's something I need to tell you.'

Chapter 26

It had grown dusky in the room and Dr Blake appeared to be slightly fuzzy and out of focus. I rubbed my eyes, but it did not seem to help to restore my vision. I felt utterly exhausted, as I flopped across my chair.

'So, what did Richard have to say?' whispered Dr Blake.

I shot straight out of my seat and leaned across the table. I was so close that I could almost feel her breath on my face. Dr Blake flattened herself against the back of her chair, clutching her notepad so tightly that I could see her knuckles whiten.

'How can you ask me that question? You know the bloody answer already.' My whole body trembled - and then I collapsed backward, narrowly missing the base of my own armchair. I fell at the foot of the seat and began to sob. Dr Blake said nothing but slid a box of tissues across the coffee table. I ignored it and wiped my nose on my sleeve, smearing it with a glob of yellow snot.

'I know it's not easy to talk about,' murmured Dr Blake. Her voice sounded distant, like a faint echo. 'It's exceedingly difficult to relive traumatic past events, but it's especially important to talk about them. It's cathartic.'

I raised my bloodshot eyes upwards. 'I don't need catharsis, Doctor. I need exorcism.' I cackled. 'Can you exorcise me, Doctor? After everything I've done?'

Dr Blake made no reply, but I thought I saw her wipe a tear away from her eye - or it might just have been a trick of the dimming light.

'Let me remind you then, my dear witch doctor, of what happened. I must admit I'm more than slightly surprised that you want to relive it with me all over again, but I guess we must both continue to suffer it.'

Chapter 27

I shivered, suddenly feeling icy cold, and hoisted the duvet up over my shoulders so that just my head poked over the top. Underneath the covers, my heart was pulverising my ribs, as if it were trying to run away and escape. I struggled to catch my breath.

'Rachel, the thing is,' Richard hesitated. 'Well, there's no easy way to put this, but I've been seeing someone else.'

I stared at Richard, unblinking, saying nothing. My heart was about to explode.

'I thought it was just a one-night stand – nothing more than that initially – but I find that I can't get her out of my head. I need to progress things with her - see what develops - or I will never know whether it's important, or whether or not I can forget her. And as I say this, I know what I'm throwing away with you is so precious - and how much I'm hurting you, especially when you find out...'

Richard faltered, his face scarlet. A small trickle of sweat escaped from his hairline and ran over his right eye. He wiped it away.

'When I find out what, Richard?' I gulped.

Richard made no reply.

'When I find out what?' I repeated. I was shouting now.

Richard looked down at his hands. 'When you find out who it is,' he stammered.

'It's someone I know?' I felt suddenly overwhelmed by nausea.

Richard nodded.

'Christ, is it someone at work? I don't think I could bear the humiliation,' I whispered, trying to hold back the lump of terror which threatened to force its way out of my throat and onto the bed. 'Is it that blonde tart from finance, who is always sniffing around your desk, supposedly querying your billing?'

Richard shook his head.

'You're not going to tell me that you've shagged Sarah, are you? What a total cow. I can't believe she'd do that to me. I know she's loose, but she's supposed to be my best friend. Is it Sarah?' I was shouting louder now, crying.

'No, no, it's not Sarah, Rachel. She wouldn't do that to you. You know that and I wouldn't, well, you know, I just wouldn't...' Richard's left hand was shaking. He lunged at it with his right to make it stop.

'So who is it then, Richard. Who the fuck have you been fucking?'

Richard was silent, wringing his hands.

'Answer me, you bastard,' I screeched, dropping the duvet, and grabbing at his towel.

Richard raised his eyes and looked straight at me. 'Well, you know I went back to Manchester when you were in the hospital, and I bought my new car?'

I nodded. I hated that car. I knew it would bring bad karma.

'So, the night before I went to the dealership, I met a few friends in the pub... and Catherine was there.'

'Catherine who?' I searched my mind for people I knew with that name. There was no one, except, oh, Christ no, except...'Catherine – as in my little sister, Catherine?'

'Yes. She just wandered over to me and said hello. I had not seen her sitting there, but she said she had spotted me as soon as I arrived. Well, we got chatting and I told her about going to see the car. Anyway, to cut a long story short, she asked if she could come to view it with me. She said she was at a loose end, as your parents were in London looking after you when you had your operation.'

'And, let me guess, she was lonely,' I snarled.

'I suppose so,' muttered Richard. 'Anyway, she came with me to buy the car and then I dropped her home.'

'You dropped her home. Was that it?'

'Well, no, not exactly. Catherine offered to make me some lunch and I hadn't eaten since breakfast, so I said OK and then…'

'And then she dished up her perfectly nubile self for dessert, did she? She just spread her legs and said come on in, and you said, OK, I haven't eaten much today, so I don't mind if I do…' I spat, tears coursing down my face.

'It wasn't like that, Rachel.'

'So, what exactly was it like, Richard. Go on, paint me a picture.'

'It just kind of happened. I can't explain it.'

'And then you did what? Fucked her a few more times? Came back to London and kept on fucking me for comparison? Lucky you. Two sisters for the price of one. But clearly, I'm nowhere near as good as my darling sister Catherine in the sack if you're dumping me for her.'

'It's not a competition, Rachel,' Richard muttered.

'It's always been a competition with Catherine, Richard, 'I shouted at him. 'You know that. How many times have I told you about her and her fucked up, controlling ways? And I always keep losing out. I just can't ever measure up to my dazzling sister and she always has to best me. How could you let her manipulate you like this? Can't you see what she's doing? It's deliberate. She's just using you to get at me again.'

Richard made no reply, so I slapped him hard across the face, my palm leaving a flaming imprint on his cheek.

Richard stood up and grabbed his clothes from the chair where he had thrown them last night - before he made love to me.

'You're totally wrong. It wasn't like that, Rachel. I can't explain it, but it just happened. It felt right. I'm not proud of myself. It was an unforgiveable thing to do, but she, I – well, we couldn't help ourselves.'

'Sound to me like you helped yourselves absolutely fine.' I suddenly felt quite calm. Richard hovered next to me, an alien, a repulsive, brainless animal rather than the man I thought I loved, and who I thought had loved me. And Catherine, who had always taken what was mine had now grabbed the one person who was the most precious to me. I couldn't blame Richard, because he was just a pathetic pawn in her strategic game of ultimate superiority. Catherine believed that she had outplayed both of us and had achieved checkmate. Or so she assumed.

'Get out, Richard. Get out and go and see how happy you'll be with that stinking whore of a sister of mine. I give it a month - tops. And don't even think about crawling back to me when it all goes tits up, because I won't be vaguely interested. I honestly hope I never see you or her ever again. Now fuck off!'

I picked up my hand mirror from my dressing table and hurled it at Richard. He ducked and it hit the wardrobe door behind him, shattering into a million shards. Seven years of bad luck for me– minimum.

Chapter 28

'What do you mean, you got fired?' my mother replied down the phone when I called her to say that I was no longer working at the agency. 'That was a great job with a good firm. You seemed to be really going places. What happened?'

'Why don't you ask Catherine what happened?' I mumbled.

'Rachel, what the hell has any of this got to do with your sister? She is in Cambridge studying to be a doctor- and you're in London. What is it with you that you always have to blame your younger sister for everything which you fail to achieve? You know, jealously is a terrible thing, Rachel. It will destroy you in the end.' She paused for breath. 'Rachel, are you still there?'

'Yes, mother. I'm still here,' I sighed.

'Look, whatever has happened has happened. It might not be too late to reapply for accountancy. I can help you with the applications if you like, and...'

'I'd rather slit my own throat than become a bloody bean counter,' I snarled, twisting the phone cord round and round my hand like a tourniquet until my fingers blanched.

'So, what exactly do you intend to do, Rachel? Your father and I can't support you if you won't make the effort yourself, as you well know.'

'I don't need your support and I haven't asked for it, have I? I'll manage absolutely fine as I am, no thanks to any of you,' I muttered, slamming the payphone receiver back onto its moorings. It missed, swinging in the air limply, the monotonous dialling tone drilling through my ears.

Roja had fired me because I had become so unreliable – apparently. Admittedly, I was often slightly late getting in to work and sometimes, I did forget the deadlines. My output was slightly lame at times. So, I missed the odd thing here and there, and I did not always churn out top-class ideas. Personally, I did not think that it was such a major issue.

The truth was that I could not bear dealing too much with the reality of my life, so I tried to take the edge of it a little. After Richard left, I was in a mess. I was cutting myself every day. I was wide awake all night and exhausted during the day. I went to see my doctor, who had prescribed some sleeping pills for me, as I was struggling with insomnia. After a while, they did not work so well, but I found that if I slugged them down with a glass of brandy before bed, they seemed to do the trick. The problem then was that I was quite drowsy in the morning. After a while, I solved that issue with a Bloody Mary breakfast, which seemed to kick-start me enough to get me onto the Tube, even if it was a much later one than I really needed to be on. However, I tended to find that, by the time I reached the office, I was knackered again, and I seemed to need a quick power nap at my desk around eleven. Roja informed me that people had started to notice - to complain even. I said that no one ever seemed to care too much about his various peccadillos when it came to his own working hours. He told me to pack up my desk and get the hell out of there immediately. I asked if he would give me a reference - and he told me to fuck off and never to darken his door again.

So, that was that and there I was. No job, a mortgage to pay, no references, no real skills to speak of. So, I was forced to downsize my life choices. I decided to opt for something less demanding anyway. I touted myself around various West End pubs looking for bar work. I figured it was the only way I could kill two birds with one stone – get paid and get sufficiently drunk to manage day-to-day. In actuality it proved more difficult than I thought. In the mid-1980s, trendy bars were springing up everywhere, frequented by yuppies, who wore smart suits and flashed their fat wads of cash. The bar owners wanted hot girls with lengthy legs, who could squeeze their nubile, lusty bodies into tiny, short dresses, thus encouraging their clientele to part with their cash on bottles of champagne and overpriced food. A girl who had allowed herself to get a little out of shape with tangled hair, spots and a network of strange scars and scabs on her arms was not really the image they were seeking to portray.

Eventually, however, I got lucky − or rather ultimately, I got unlucky − depending on your point of view. I stumbled across a tiny pub in one of the seedier streets in Soho, rather ironically named *The Maiden*. In the main bar, there were half a dozen rickety wooden tables and to the side was a small snug, which reeked of smoke and urine. The owner and head barman, Dave, was as wide as he was tall. Essentially, he sported the figure of a top darts player. Each day, he wore the same stained, baggy grey trousers and a matching crumpled, checked shirt, over which strained a maroon waistcoat, working overtime as a corset to contain his gigantic girth. His lower lip was fat and swollen and he dribbled over the top of it when he spoke. He wore holed carpet slippers on his feet, as he lived upstairs above the pub and as far as I was aware, never stepped outside into natural light. As a result, his skin was grey and ashen, as if he were already slightly decomposing.

The clientele frequenting *The Maiden* was hardly more attractive. The regular punters were normally summoning up Dutch courage to visit a sex show or a brothel around the corner or had just enjoyed either or both of the aforementioned local attractions. They were not a chatty bunch on the whole, which suited me fine to be honest. I had little to say for myself these days. I turned up at lunchtime − roughly - and worked slowly until closing time. I watered the regulars, washed up, swept up and kept myself topped up with any dregs the customers left behind, or any ends of bottes which I could justifiably finish off. Dave did not seem to mind. He had a drink with every one of his regulars and by mid-afternoon, he was usually snoozing in the snug, his slippered feet resting on a low stool as he snored gently. I would leave him there when I left in the evening, locking up the front door and catching the last tube home.

Home was increasingly becoming a struggle to maintain. I could no longer make my mortgage payments and I kept ignoring the plethora of red letters which crashed through my letterbox on a daily basis. Eventually, the flat was repossessed. I was forced to scour the pages of Loot until I could find a suitable room, which turned out to be a highly unsuitable bedsit above a launderette on the Caledonian Road, just opposite Pentonville Prison. The room was tiny, consisting of a rock-hard single bed, one small armchair missing its stuffing, a countertop with a small electric ring for cooking and a miniscule shower compartment, which resembled a plastic cupboard, which leaked all over the nylon carpet whenever I used it. The flat vibrated constantly from the ever-rotating washing machines on the floor below. When they were all in use together, I swore I could actually levitate off my bed. I used to spend a great deal of my spare time staring out of my window at the incarcerated inmates opposite me, whose shadows I could glimpse occasionally, hidden behind the bars. It was difficult to decide which of us was more isolated. At least they had their cellmates and activities. I envied them.

Yet, I had little choice. I had no one to call. I had stopped communicating with my parents shortly after leaving the advertising agency, sparing them the excruciating embarrassment and obvious disappointment which I so clearly wrought on them. I had not spoken to or heard from Catherine since Richard had told me about their affair. I had even rebuffed every call from my best friend Sarah for the last few months. I knew she meant well, but our lives were now so different. She was earning stacks of money and shagging ever richer guys, one of whom would eventually nab her. She was attractive and vivacious. I felt ugly, depressive, and drunken in her wake. She did not need a total loser like me dragging her down.

Richard had left the agency almost as soon as he had dumped me. He had clearly already been interviewing elsewhere, and soon, in addition to a new girlfriend, he had also secured a new job – a promotion, in fact – in another top agency across town. Frankly, leaving the agency was the least he could do. While I had still clung to my job, I had not had to worry about bumping into him in the corridors at work, or worse, having to work on one of his briefs. Yet, bizarrely, I still longed to see him. I was tortured by the fact that I had not proved to be enough for him and that he had chosen Catherine over me. I thought many times about making an impromptu visit to his flat, to confront him and to ask him to explain. I wanted to beg him to take me back. I needed to explain to him why he had made the wrong decision. But in reality, what would I have actually said or done if I had seen him? What could he have said to me which could possibly justify his behaviour and allow me to trust him again? What could he have said to make me feel any better? And worse, what if Catherine had been there when I turned up? It was all so completely unbearable.

Yet I could not stop thinking about Richard - sometimes, often, always - whenever I was too sober to forget him. His face would zoom back into focus, his smile melting me with its warmth, his manly body wrapping itself around mine. In my dreams, he would rescue me from Tim all over again and we would swear our undying love to each other. And then I would wake up and remember the horror of his leaving and relive all those dreadful things he told me. I would reimagine him naked with Catherine in my parents' house. And every single time I did, it was as if it was for the first time. It was as if Richard and Catherine could stab me through the heart repeatedly - and yet still, I could not die.

Chapter 29

'It must have been extremely difficult, having the rug completely swept from under you like that. How did it make you feel?' asked Dr Blake, dim in the twilight of the room.

I shifted on my uncomfortable chair. 'I felt alone. I felt betrayed. I felt overwhelming anger – and it was no longer enough just to hurt myself.'

Chapter 30

I had absolutely no idea if Catherine was still seeing Richard, or whether - having lured him away from me. She had achieved her objective and had now moved on to new fodder. She may have already broken Richard's heart as he had broken mine. She would not have cared.

When Richard had first told me about Catherine, I had tried to call her a thousand times at her college in Cambridge to rant and rave and scream abuse at her, but the payphone on her corridor was the only phone available - and Catherine never answered it. Many of her fellow students did pick up the receiver and they faithfully promised to leave a message on her door to ask her to call me, but she never did. She almost certainly wiped them away as easily as she wiped out everything else in her path. So I resorted to writing to her. I penned long letters, short notes, even postcards. Not one of them was ever answered. So, in the end, there appeared to be only one solution. I jumped on a train, and I went to find her.

Weaving my way through Cambridge, I began to reminisce woozily about my own time at university, a time when I had had some hope of a reasonable future for myself, even though it had been mired by poor choices and unhappiness. Durham had been undoubtedly beautiful, yet Cambridge seemed to surpass it in every way. Of course, it did. This was the place that had chosen Catherine. The crisp spring sunshine illuminated the walls of Kings, the magnificent college at the centre of this academic beacon, with its famous chapel, and stunning grounds bleeding onto The Backs, where lovers and tourists punted lethargically together along the River Cam. This was the place where I had brought Richard for his birthday, when he had refused to engage with either the city or with me.

The cobbles bothered the soles of my feet as I walked along, my shoes being worn through and totally ill-equipped for such uneven ground. Even though this was a student town, I felt shabby in comparison to the smiling youths who cycled past on their bicycles, their pristine woollen college scarves flying in the wind. As I wandered past the expensive shops and restaurants which I could ill afford to enter, my throat and mind felt parched, so I dipped into the supermarket and emerged with half a bottle of vodka. I sipped it from inside its carrier bag as I walked along, the strong, clear, camouflaged liquid soothing my gullet and settling my thoughts.

At the end of the high street, I turned left into St Johns College and entered through Great Gate, stuffing the remains of the vodka bottle into my duffle bag. I stopped for a moment and gaped at the lengthy path which stretched far ahead of me through the first courtyard, then into the second, followed by the third. I walked slowly, breathing heavily in the hallowed air, overwhelmed by the sheer size of the college, which could easily have encompassed the whole of Durham within it. I reached the Bridge of Sighs – named ostentatiously for its famous cousin in Venice - and passed over the Cam into New Court. This is where I believed that I could locate Catherine. I lurched around the quad slowly, checking the bottom of each staircase for names, many of which I could never have even attempted to pronounce, and some of which were so long that they spilled over the edge of their nameplates. On the third staircase, I found Catherine's name. She was living on the top floor. I began to climb the stairs, holding onto the banister for support, my shoes clacking on the concrete as I climbed. When I reached her door, I waited there for quite a considerable length of time, my heart banging against my ribs. I felt unable to move any further, unable to raise my hand to knock.

With a sudden jolt, the door flew open, and Catherine emerged, colliding straight into me, and knocking me backward. I clutched the banister harder to steady myself.

'Christ, Catherine, you nearly pushed me down the fucking stairs,' I yelled. My voice bounced off the walls and echoed around the quiet quad.

Catherine blinked, then wrinkled up her nose as if she smelt something extremely malodorous. 'Rachel? Is that you? What the hell have you come as? Mum would have a complete fit if she saw you in that state.' Catherine threw her head back and laughed.

I grimaced and pushed past her into her room. I plonked myself down clumsily onto her bed, muttering to myself, 'Hello, Rachel. How are you doing Rachel? I'm fine, thank you, Catherine. How are you? Still shagging my ex?'

'What do you want, Rachel. I'm busy,' asked Catherine, re-entering the room, and closing the door behind her.

'What do I want? Why do I need an excuse to visit my darling little sister? I was at a loose end, it was a lovely morning when I got up, so I thought to myself, Rachel, why not jump on a train and go to visit Catherine. I'm sure she'll be delighted to see you.'

Catherine stood by the door, arms crossed over her ample chest. 'Rachel, you stink.'

'Sorry if I offend your delicate sensibilities, Catherine. I am so sorry, your majesty. I should have dressed for the occasion.'

'You should have washed at the very least,' she retorted, wafting her hand in the air.

I paused 'Are you really living as a student? This place is pathetically tidy,' I remarked, standing, and lifting up a random medical textbook before slamming it

167

back down onto the desk in the wrong place. I examined her pristine room. Her desk was immaculate, with papers and books stacked just so. There were no clothes strewn across the bed or on the floor. Her mugs were washed and arranged neatly by the small sink. Arty posters were blutaked to the walls without any of the edges crinkling up. Her bed was made as well as any army cadet could have achieved.

'What do you actually want from me, Rachel?' Catherine hissed, turning her head towards me.

'Oh, I don't know, Catherine, I just felt like popping in, I suppose. Chew the fat, you know. It's been a while, hasn't it? I don't think we've seen each other since, well, when was it exactly? Since…ah, I remember, that's it. Since before you pinched my boyfriend and slept with him. We haven't seen each other since you fucked Richard.'

Catherine sighed theatrically. 'I didn't pinch anything from you, Rachel. Richard was just like any other bloke I have ever met – weak as piss and with his brain in his cock. He didn't need much persuasion either, I can tell you. I only offered to make him a sandwich, and the next thing I knew, he was munching me for lunch.' She moved over to the bed and sat down next to me. 'He wasn't any good at it either.'

I turned to face her. 'You're a foul, twisted, little whore, you know that? No, you're far worse than that. You're a treacherous, adulterous vixen.'

'Ah, it's pleasing to see that your English degree has furnished you with such a wonderful breadth of vocabulary. Bravo.'

I ignored her. 'You thought absolutely nothing of stealing the only good thing that has ever happened to me. And you still don't give a shit, do you?' I suddenly felt utterly exhausted, wondering why I had ever bothered to come here.

'If he's the best thing that ever happened to you, then I pity you, Rachel. Look, you're not the most attractive thing I've ever clapped eyes on, that's true, but if you made some effort and didn't wander around looking like – and more sadly, smelling like – an intoxicated tramp who drinks Special Brew under a bridge, you might be able to hook yourself a decent catch. But just look at you.'

I glanced down– and she was right. I was overweight and my once baggy tracksuit bottoms now strained across my flabby thighs. The bottoms were badly stained and even though I could not smell myself, I would not have been surprised if they stank. Deodorant was expensive and, on my budget, it rated as a luxury item.

'What are you up to these days anyway, Rachel?' Catherine enquired, getting up and moving over to the window. She threw it open and took a deliberate deep breath.

'Nothing much. Working in a grotty pub in Soho,' I muttered.

'Enjoying it?'

'No, not at all.'

Catherine did not seem to hear me, or she chose not to do so. 'You should get in touch with Mum and Dad, you know. They worry about you,' she smiled.

'Very amusing. I'm sure they don't, Catherine.'

'No, really they do. They are not thrilled with your life choices so far, but you are their elder daughter, and they do care about you. They are upset that you have become effectively incommunicado.' Catherine paused and turned to face me. 'You know they've spent their lives worrying about you and whether or not you'll ever have the ability to manage, given your issues.'

'My issues?' I felt cold suddenly, freezing, despite the stuffiness in the room.

'Oh, come off it, Rachel. I've heard Mum and Dad discussing your bizarre behaviour a thousand times over the years. Sometimes, it seemed to be all they ever talked about. I got so sick and tired of hearing about it at one point, that I told them to stop bloody talking about how odd you were and to bloody well do something about it for a change. But as usual, they chose to do absolutely fuck all.'

My brain struggled to locate anything to say in reply. I flumped backward onto Catherine's pillow, suddenly exhausted.

Catherine turned her head and regarded herself in the vanity mirror, which was perched on the side of her sink.

'Yes, you're still gorgeous, Catherine. Christ, you're so bloody vain, and so full of yourself.'

Seeing Catherine admiring herself, I remembered why I had come to see her in the first place. Forcing back the tears which had sprung up in the corner of my eyes, I whispered, 'So, are you still with him?'

'Still with who, Rachel?'

'With Richard.'

'Are we still harping on about him? God, no, I'm not still with him. Christ, he became so bloody boring after a while. He was way too keen and kept wanting to visit me here all the time. It rather cramped my style - if you know what I mean. I was done with him ages ago. You can have him back now if you're really that desperate.'

My head suddenly grew extremely hot, and I jumped up from the bed and lunged at Catherine, knocking her off balance. I tore at her cotton shirt, which ripped easily in my hands, and then I spat in her face, a pure bullseye, right onto her perfect lips – those adulterous lips - which had sucked everything away from me. I loosened my grip on her collar, momentarily satisfied. Catherine sank down and lay panting on the floor, breathing hard.

Catherine eyed me from the carpet, unmoving. I began to roam around her room once more, shifting this, examining that, poking into something else. I found Catherine's lack of movement vaguely disconcerting, so I turned to look at her, just to check that she had not really hurt her head as she fell. As I did so, she grabbed my ankle and I lost my footing, toppling over and landing on the floor beside her. I rolled towards her and thumped her in the chest. She responded by biting my shoulder, drawing blood.

'You're a total bitch, you know that don't you?' I hissed, slapping her across the face. Catherine grabbed my hair and pulled out a fistful, waving it in her hand. Her lip was split and bleeding. We scrapped like two wild alley cats until exhausted, we ended up lying together side by side on the floor, panting like a pair of geriatric dogs.

After a few minutes of complete silence, Catherine jumped up, unbuttoning what was left of her shirt and reaching into her wardrobe for a replacement. Her clothes were hung in a colour coded row running light to dark. Her fingers moved to the end of the rack, where she picked out a black shirt. She pulled it on and lobbed the torn one in the bin. 'I'd offer it to you, Rach, but I don't think it would fit,' she snorted. She grabbed a tissue from the box on her desk, spat on it and began dabbing at her split lip.

'Are you ever going to apologise to me, Catherine? I mean, will you ever say sorry properly?' I murmured, propping myself up onto my elbows.

'Say sorry for what?' Catherine faced me, her eyes hard, defiant.

'For totally ruining my life,' I answered, tears seeping out of the corners of my eyes.

'Oh, don't be so bloody melodramatic, Rachel. For fucks sake, I have not totally ruined your life. If anyone has done that, you have. You lost your man, who wasn't worth keeping anyway, and then you inexplicably went to pieces. Who gets dumped, then gets fired, and then chooses a dead-end job as a way of moving on? It's utterly ridiculous. If you just stopped playing the victim all the time and actually attempted to get on with your life, you'd be fine - but you always have to blame everyone else for your own personal catastrophes. It's genuinely pathetic. Why don't you just grow a pair?'

'What do you know about my life?' I faltered, sitting up.

'Well, for one thing, I know that you let that hairy ape knock you about in Durham.'

I felt as if Catherine had winded me. 'How do you know that? Did Richard tell you?'

Catherine laughed. 'Jesus, Rach, it didn't take a fucking detective to work out that the bruises I saw when I came up for the ball were not caused by you simply falling over by accident – and anyway, you could just tell from the way Tim acted around you. It was a clear case of coercive control.'

'What do you know about it, Catherine? You're not a bloody psychiatrist. You're not even a doctor.'

'Not yet, but I will be soon. And as ever, you're totally missing the sodding point. Stop allowing your life to be dominated by useless men and quit caring so much about what other people think of you. That's always been your issue. – or one of them anyway. You always need constant reassurance and attention. Just go out there and grab whatever it is you want – or whatever it is that you think you want - if you've any bloody idea what that is.'

'Just like you do, you mean?'

'Yes, just like I do.' Catherine grabbed her hairbrush and started to smooth out her ponytail.

'But I don't want to be like you, Catherine. I don't want to be someone who is only ever out for themselves and never thinks about the effect they can have on other people.'

'Look, Rach, you've only got one life and it's up to you how you live it. Just don't expect me, or anyone else for that matter, to live it for you. You need to sober up, toughen up, and for Christ sake, stop hacking at yourself. All those things would be a good start. Or, alternatively, you can just carry on as you are, feeling sorry for yourself and continuing to spiral downhill. It's a simple life choice. And frankly, I don't really give a shit which direction you decide to go in. Just don't come crawling back here to bother me with it, because I really can't be arsed.' Catherine sighed heavily. 'If only Mum and Dad had got you some help when you were younger.'

'Help with what? With my so-called issues?' I spat.

'Look, Rach, I don't know all the gory details. All I know is that when you were at primary school, Mum and Dad took you to see someone. I was far too young at the time to be told much else, but nothing came of it at any rate. They fobbed me off with something about polar bears at the time. I've no idea what they meant. Anyway, it's a great shame. Perhaps if they had persevered, you might not be in the state you're in now.'

I opened my mouth to speak, but no words emerged.

Catherine grabbed her coat from behind the door and pulled it on. 'Look, I'm extremely late for a lab session, so you'll have to piss off now, Rach. Good to see you and all that, sis. Don't be a stranger, and all that bollocks.'

And with that, she yanked me by the arm with surprising strength, so that I was hoisted off her floor and found myself outside her room before I realised what was happening. Catherine locked the door behind us and skipped off down the stairs and into the rest of her charmed life, while I simply stood there, fossilised.

Chapter 31

'I didn't think I would ever see her again after that. I mean, what was the point? I hated her and she despised me. She would never apologise – she clearly had no moral compass - and I would never forgive her. There was no way back.'

'And did you ever see her again?' asked Dr Blake.

'You know the answer to that, so why are you asking me such a redundant question? Seriously, what's the matter with you?'

'It's not really about me, Rachel, is it? It's about you.'

'Is it?'

'Yes, I'm here to help you.'

'Ah that's just terrific. So now you want to help me.'

Chapter 32

I slunk back to my life at *The Maiden*, pulling pints, mopping up spilled beer and wiping away misdirected urine. Dave paid me a pittance to work there, and there was never any hope of any tips from the regulars, none of whom appeared any more affluent than I was. My life contracted a little more day by day, as I shuffled between bedsit and pub, pub to bedsit. Fortunately, I realised I could effectively live without food, as long as I had regular access to alcohol. Sometimes, I nicked the odd bottle from the pub. Dave had put me in charge of the inventory, so it was easy to squirrel away one here and there if I was clever about it. Vodka one week, whisky the next. I supplemented it with a little from the optics during the day to keep myself sharp.

One empty afternoon, I was half-heartedly polishing the top of the bar when a guy walked in. He was younger than the usual clientele - scruffy, but in a trendy way. He sauntered through the door with his faded denim jacket slung over his right shoulder, whilst taking a drag of his cigarette with the other. He was as thin as a needle, his jeans sagging around the crotch. His dirty hair was long to his shoulders and clearly untouched by a brush for many months.

'Scotch on the rocks – make it a double please, darlin'' he drawled, leaning against the bar, and scratching at his stubble. I nodded and aimed a glass at the optic – once, twice.

'Pour one for yourself, love. It's on me.' He stubbed his cigarette out with force into the full ashtray on the bar top and reached into his top pocket for his pack. He flipped the top open with practiced alacrity and held it out to me. I took one and nodded thanks. I smoked on and off these days. He flicked his lighter and leaned over to light mine before igniting his own. I took a short drag and coughed.

'Not much of a smoker, then?'

'No, not really,' I gasped. I grabbed my whisky and downed a large slug.

He laughed. 'What's your name?'

'Rachel,' I murmured, concentrating on draining my glass.

He nodded appreciatively. 'Well, Rachel, you certainly know how to drink whisky. Can I get you another?'

I glanced behind me. There was no need. Dave was fast asleep in the snug and a nuclear explosion would not have woken him. 'Yes, thanks. That would be nice. Can I get you one?'

'Go on then. Why not. After all, it's Tuesday.'

I giggled and filled up our glasses.

'I'm Doug, by the way,' he said, holding out his hand to shake mine. His louche hand fell limply into mine. The contact made me shiver. It was the first time anyone had touched me in quite a while.

'Hey, Rach, come and sit with me.'

'Well, I'm working, so I really shouldn't.' I peeked over at the snug again.

'What's in there?' enquired Doug.

'My boss. He's napping.'

'That giant walrus in there? Well, you know what they say...while the master's away, and all that. Come on, Rachel, darlin', take a load off.'

I shrugged and sidled out from behind the bar, joining Doug at one of the tables near the back. I picked up a bar mat and started to peel the top from it.

'So how come a good-looking girl like you is working in a dump like this?' Doug leered.

Despite myself, I felt my cheeks redden. 'I don't know. It's just a job, I suppose,' I muttered.

'Worked here long?' Doug lit another cigarette off the back of his current one and then stubbed the old one out on the table.

'A year or so,' I murmured.

Doug dragged his chair closer to mine. It scraped the floor, but there was no obvious movement from the snug. 'Here, have one of these. My treat.' He held out a small pink pill in the palm of his hand.

'What is it?' I queried.

'I call them my happy pills, and you look like you could do with a bit of cheering up, my love. Go on, try one. I guarantee it will do the trick.'

I took the tiny pill from his palm and rolled it back and forth between my fingers. Glancing up, Doug smiled at me and then he reached up, parting my lips with his fingers.

'Go on. You know you're curious,' he coaxed.

I placed the pill on my tongue and washed it down with the last of my whisky.

'Good girl,' Dave cooed. 'How do you feel now?'

'No different,' I admitted.

'Give it a minute,' he smiled.

We sat there in companionable silence. Doug started to edge closer to me. He took my arm and traced the lines of new and old wounds without speaking. Then he shifted his hand, so that it was stroking my thigh, but oddly, it did not feel like my own thigh. He moved his fingers higher until he reached the waistband of my sweatpants. I could not be sure, but I think his hand was now inside my pants, moving. My breath quickened.

'You like my happy pills, eh, Rach? I knew you would,' Doug panted. 'Come on, baby, come on.'

He took his hand away and used it to take mine, guiding me away from the table. I followed him, watching myself walk with him from somewhere on the ceiling. He walked me into the Ladies' loo, where he shoved me down onto my knees onto the filthy, broken tiles and unzipped himself.

'My turn for happiness now, my dear. Off you go.'

Chapter 33

After our first intimate introduction, Doug began to pop into the pub on a regular basis. He always made certain to arrive in the afternoon, when he could be sure that we could watch Dave's enormous stomach moving rhythmically through the window in the snug, and thus, remain undisturbed.

'I wish I could sleep like that,' Doug commented. 'Mind you, he must wake up with one hell of a bad back, the poor bastard.'

Doug and I helped ourselves to drinks from behind the bar with nonchalance. Doug no longer paid, as officially he was never there. He was like a more unsavoury version of Macavity the Mystery Cat. We would toss down a couple of doubles with a pill each, and then I would watch myself in wonder as somewhere else, Doug performed more and more perverted acts on my body amongst the dirt and squalor of the pub toilets.

It was only much later, as I sat alone in the dark and damp of my bedsit, scissors poised, that I felt the guilt and shame crawling over me like lice. I cut myself repeatedly. The knife, as it entered my flesh, was the only thing I could actually feel, numbed as I was to everything else in my life. My scabs and scars were my only genuine proof that I was still alive.

I hated myself, yet, on the days Doug did not appear, I was frantic with worry. I doubled my stolen alcohol consumption, but it did not help. I really needed those pills.

'Doug, can you leave me a couple of extra tabs, just in case you don't show up tomorrow,' I begged him one afternoon, as I retrieved my misshapen tracksuit bottoms from the stinking floor of the men's toilet.

'No, darlin', I can't. If I left you more pills, you might not look forward to me coming to see you - and where would be the fun in that?'

'Please, Doug. Just one then,' I simpered.

'Rach, these pills don't come for free. You have to pay your Uncle Douggie in kind, don't you? You know that.' He tugged on my matted hair a little too hard. Turning on the tap at the rusty sink, he splashed some of the brown water which spattered from it onto his face, and then ran his damp hands through his hair. Drying his face on his shirt sleeve, he said, 'Of course, if you'd like to get some more of these terrific little uppers, you could come to a little get-together I'm hosting on Saturday. You could pop along after your shift and meet some of my mates. They are a great group of guys, and they are dying to meet you. Would you like that?'

I nodded.

'Well then, my darlin', it's a date,' Doug announced and stomped out of the loo.

After I finished my shift on Saturday, I downed a couple of vodka shots for Dutch courage. In the Ladies' loo, I stared at my image in the cracked mirror. My hair was unkempt, and my skin had the deathly pallor of a just killed corpse. I slapped my cheeks a couple of times to try to coax some colour into them, but it faded as quickly as the pain. 'You look totally crap,' I told myself. I tugged hard at the mirror until it came loose, and I hurled it to the floor. Stamping on it for good measure, I knew that I had already run out of luck. Smashed mirrors held no fear for me anymore.

Doug lived in Kentish Town on a relatively urbane side street close to the tube. He had given me vague directions, but I still managed to get lost and had to ask several people for help finding the address. They eyed me suspiciously, as they might behave towards someone who was acting oddly on a night bus, but eventually, someone pointed me down the right street. Doug rented the basement flat of a dilapidated converted terraced house. As I descended the stairs, something scuttled beneath a large pile of rubbish by the door, and I jumped in fright. I hated rats, even though they had the run of the pub.

I pressed the doorbell and waited. No one came, but I could hear voices from inside the building. I peered through the ragged net curtain, which hung loosely inside the window, but I could only see outlines of bodies. I rang again, leaning harder on the buzzer. This time, Doug came to the door.

'Hold your horses, Rach,' Doug slurred, slouching in the doorway. Patting me on the shoulder, he ushered me inside. The air was thick with weed, tobacco, and body odour. My stomach gave a sudden lurch.

'Don't just stand there, Rach. Take your jacket off and come and meet the gang.'

I kept my jacket on and followed behind Doug as he sashayed into the front room. There were half a dozen guys – some sitting, some standing – all staring - as I entered. There were no other women there. The coffee table was strewn with used cigarette butts, Rizla papers, tobacco, and a couple of syringes, as well as several dirty glasses and a few bottles of spirits.

'So, Rachel, say hello to the gang. Hey, gang, say hello to Rachel,' Doug instructed.

'Hi,' I muttered, raising my hand into a half-wave. They nodded, but no one spoke to me. One guy standing by the fireplace whispered something I could not catch in his mate's ear and his friend laughed, before beginning to cough so badly that he had to sit down on the floor. Doug grabbed a dirty glass from the table and filled it halfway to the top with whisky. Rummaging in his trouser pocket, he produced a couple of pills – one of the usual pinks and in addition, a white one.

'As you've come all this way, Rachel, you get two specials for the price of one tonight. Get those down you my girl - and let's party.'

I jiggled the pills in one palm and my drink in the other. Glancing around the room, the gang did not exactly look like party animals, but maybe I just needed to loosen up. I had been working all week and I was shattered. I had very much been looking forward to the pills. Without further hesitation, I downed them both with the whisky. Doug topped up my glass and wandered away.

I stood alone by the bookcase, which housed no books whatsoever. The shelves were completely bare, except for a smattering of car magazines, intermingled with some girlie ones. I began to feel a little unsteady. Suddenly I began to overheat, sweat forming in pools under my armpits and around my waist. Swaying slightly, I made a move towards the door.

'Hey, where are you going, darlin'?' Doug asked me, appearing at that moment by my side.

'I don't feel very well. I just need some air, I think,' I slurred.

'You're OK, Rach. You're just a little overtired. You need to relax, baby. Come over to sit on the sofa with me.'

He guided me over to the settee and I stumbled into the seat. Doug knelt in front of me and began to remove my boots. He slipped off my socks and rubbed my feet.

'Does that feel good, baby?' he crooned.

'Mmm,' I groaned.

He leaned forward and began to remove my jacket. I felt him pulling my sweat top up over my head. My head got stuck and Doug tugged at it a little too hard.

'That's better, isn't it,' he crooned.

My eyes were closing. I had no control over the weight of my eyelids. Somewhere in the distance, I could feel Doug fumbling with the buttons of my shirt and then reaching round me to unclasp my bra.

'No, Doug. Not here. The others are watching,' I mumbled.

'Don't worry about them, Rach. We are all here to enjoy ourselves, aren't we? We are all very much looking forward to it.'

My eyes fluttered open, and I could see the outline of the gang, crowding around me, leering, joking. Doug tugged at the waistband of my jeans - and then the world fell away from me.

I was woken by a sharp shaft of light, which speared my eyes through a gap in the thin curtains. I was lying on my side on a mattress in a room I did not recognise. On the floor next to me was a pool of vomit. Smelling it, I vomited on top of it. The pain shooting through my head was unbearable, as if thousands of boots were stamping on it with every tiny movement I made. I rolled gingerly onto my back, away from the mess on the floor. I touched something - someone - and screamed. A naked man lay beside me, unconscious. I recognised him vaguely as one of the nameless gang from the previous night. Pushing myself up slowly onto my elbows, I realised that I was also naked. There were small burns all over my stomach, which looked as though I had been used as a human ashtray. Bolts of pain shot through my entire body as I tried to sit up. My thighs were swollen and black like overripe fruit, and I was lying in a pool of dried blood.

I slid off the bed very slowly, in agony, and hunkered on the floor on all fours, shaking like a wounded animal. I stayed static for a few moments in that position, listening, but there was no sound, except for the laboured breathing of the body on the bed. I began to crawl. Every move speared pain through my body. I wiggled through the door and emerged onto a narrow hallway. Still on my hands and knees, I inched my way towards the bathroom door, which was open. I hoisted myself up using the doorknob for support, hobbled inside and shot the bolt on the door.

The bathroom smelt even fouler than the toilet at *The Maiden*. I staggered over to the toilet and vomited bile. Slowly, I moved over to the basin, and ran some water. It was ice cold, but it felt good against my face. There was a scrofulous towel by the sink. I ran it under the water and then dabbed at my body, wincing with every touch. I washed between my legs. Dried blood and mucus stained the towel.

Behind the door hung an old blue dressing gown. I pulled it on and slid the bolt on the bathroom door again. With every creak, a flash of cold fear shot through me. I inched the door open millimetre by millimetre. Silence. Slowly, I wobbled my way down the stairs. At the foot of the staircase, I glanced to my left. Doug was asleep, his head resting on the kitchen table, wearing only his underpants. There was no sign of anyone else. Carefully, I lifted the latch and it opened easily. Pushing the door open as narrowly as I could, I slipped outside. The cold air slapped me in the face, and I vomited again on the pile of rubbish. More fodder for the rats. Dragging myself up the steps, I emerged onto the road and began to hobble towards the main road, holding the dressing gown around my body, as it had no tie. Every step I took required immense concentration, as if I had never walked before. I watched my own bare feet as they worked to remove me pace by painful pace from this place, but eventually, even they gave way on me. I dissolved onto the pavement and began to weep.

Chapter 34

Neon lights blinked intermittently over my head, as if they were about to peter out and die. My eyes were closed, but I could hear bustling and bleeping all around me. Occasionally, someone banged the end of my bed as they passed by, jolting me. But I was not yet ready to open my eyes.

'She was brought in this morning, Doctor,' I heard a female voice declare. 'They found her collapsed in the street. Her bloods show extremely high levels of toxicity, although we have not had the results back from the lab to identify the substances as yet. There is serious bruising to her thighs and some internal damage.'

A man asked, 'What's her name?' A light was brought closer to my face, illuminating my eyelids.

'We haven't been able to identify her. She was only wearing a dressing gown and had no ID on her. The police are working on it,' the woman replied.

'Right. Let me know when she wakes up - and see if you can find out what happened. It could be just drug use that got out of hand, or she might be a victim of domestic abuse. Or maybe she has a history of mental illness. When do we expect the toxicology report back?'

'In the next hour or so, I hope.'

'OK. Well, hopefully we will know more soon. In the meantime, keep her on an IV fluid drip, but let's not administer any opiates until we know what she's taken.'

Footsteps receded. The overhead light flickered.

Sometime later – minutes, hours, days, I could not tell you – my eyes fluttered open. My mouth felt desiccated, and I struggled to swallow. Turning my head to the left, I could see waves of green running across a monitor. The machine beeped intermittently. I attempted to lift my left arm, but it was too heavy. A tube trailed from the inside of my elbow and clear liquid ran through it from the drip overhead. I rolled my head back and stared at the light. On and off, off and on.

'Ah, good, my dear. I see you are awake finally,' announced a woman in a blue apron, arriving as if from nowhere by the side of my bed. 'How are you feeling now?'

I tried to move my mouth to answer her, but my tongue would not cooperate.

'You must be very thirsty. Here, let me give you a sip of water.'

The nurse placed her hand behind my head and with her other hand, she tilted a plastic cup of water towards my mouth. I dribbled most of the contents down my hospital gown, but a small amount went into my mouth. I swallowed it gratefully.

The nurse replaced my head back onto the pillow. 'Now, mystery lady, tell me your name,' she smiled.

'Rachel,' I mumbled.

'Hello, Rachel. My name is Alice. Do you know where you are?'

'I'm not sure. Hospital?' I ventured.

'Yes, that's right. You are in The Royal Free in Hampstead. You were brought in this morning wearing just a dressing gown. Can you tell me what happened?'

'Water,' I muttered.

'Here you go.' Alice brought the cup to my lips again and I sipped.

'Now, let's try again. What happened?'

'I don't know.' I closed my eyes again.

'Rachel, try to remember. It will help us to make you better if you can tell us what was going on.'

I opened my eyes again and tried to concentrate on Alice's face. She had a chubby face and her nurse's hat was perched askew on the top of a heap of unruly curly red hair. I wondered how it managed to stay on. She was probably around the same age as me, give or take, but I looked much older.

'You had a fair amount of drugs in your system, Rachel. Do you know what they were?'

'One pink and one white,' I whispered.

'OK. Good. Do you know what they actually were?'

'No. Just the colours.'

'OK, that's fine. And where did you get these pink and white pills?' Alice smiled and reached out to hold my hand. I shuddered. I could not remember the last time someone touched me like that - gently.

'I went to a party.'

'OK. And where was this party, Rachel?'

'I don't know.' I turned my head away from her, towards the waving lines on the machine.

'That's OK. Do you know who you went with?'

'No. I didn't go with anyone. I didn't know anyone there, except...' I turned my face away from her.

'Except who?'

Alice moved around to the other side of the bed to face me again.

'Except no one. I didn't know anyone.' I closed my eyes. I wanted to go back to sleep.

'Right, so what happened at the party? It's OK, Rachel, you can tell me. I promise that I'll keep it to myself.'

'I don't remember. I had a drink - and that's honestly all I remember.'

'Did anybody hurt you?' Alice patted me on the arm and leaned closer to me.

'No. No, nothing happened. I took the pills, I had a drink, I woke up in here. I don't know why I'm here. Can I go home now?' I wanted Alice to leave me alone. She had no right to ask me all these questions. I had not done anything wrong.

'I don't think you're in any fit state to go home just yet, Rachel. Don't you worry. Get some rest and we will chat again later.'

Alice offered me another sip of water, checked my bleeping machine, made a couple of notes, and scooted away.

I closed my eyes. The overhead light kept blinking away.

Later – I don't know precisely when – a doctor was standing beside me and, behind him, there was a gaggle of other people wearing white coats with stethoscopes snaked around their necks.

'Now - Rachel, is it? Good morning. I am Doctor Donaldson. I work in the psychiatric department here at The Royal Free. We haven't had the chance to talk for the last couple of days, as you have been going in and out of consciousness.'

Two days?

'Now, how are you feeling, Rachel? Do you feel any pain anywhere at all?'

'I'm fine,' I winced, trying not to move.

'OK,' the doctor replied, glancing over the top of his glasses at me. 'Well, Rachel, you had an interesting concoction of drugs in your system. Enough to stun a large rhinoceros, never mind a girl of your size. Do you take drugs regularly?'

'No, never,' I stuttered. My skin felt hot and clammy. I pushed the sheet down from my neck.

'OK. Well, if you say so.' The doctor frowned and turned to address the cloud of doctors dressed in their white coats. All of them immediately stood to attention like soldiers on the parade ground when he spoke to them.

'So, can anyone tell me the preferred course of action in a case like this?'

No one replied.

'Come on, how the hell are any of you going to become psychologists if you can't even open your mouths?' He sighed heavily, removing his glasses, and rubbing his hand over his face. He replaced his spectacles.

A hand shot up at the back of the group.

'Yes, Catherine. Ideas, please?'

'I think that, once she has been stabilised medically, we should assess her mental state to ascertain whether or not she is suffering from depression or another form of mental illness. If we rule out any form of mental disturbance, we should ask one of the specialist nurses to assess her needs and decide whether she requires further help in terms of rehabilitation.'

'Good. Anything else? Anyone?' the doctor enquired of the listless group.

I recognised that voice. I would recognise it anywhere. 'Catherine,' I whispered, attempting to prop myself up on my elbows. I groaned with the effort and collapsed back down again.

'Rachel, that was a lady called Catherine speaking. She is one of my students. Do you know someone called Catherine? It might help us to identify you and to find your family,' asked the doctor.

'Family. Yes, I know this Catherine,' I whispered. 'She's my sister.'

'Are you sure? You may still be feeling a little confused after your ordeal,' the doctor suggested.

'It's her. I know it's her,' I muttered.

'Catherine, is this your sister?' asked the doctor, turning towards Catherine. 'Come closer so that Rachel can talk to you.' The doctor beckoned to her.

Catherine walked from the back of the group so that she was right beside my bed. She looked exactly the same as when I last saw her, except somewhat more professional in her white coat. She bent down towards me, peering at me closely, her cold stethoscope brushing my hand. For a moment, I thought that she was about to plant a kiss on my cheek, and I waited for her touch. But suddenly, she straightened up again and, addressing the doctor directly, she pronounced, 'I am afraid I have never seen this woman before in my life, Doctor Donaldson. She must be delusional. I suppose it is possible that she has mistaken me for her sister, who might also be called Catherine. It could be a mere coincidence. But regardless, it's not me. I don't even have a sister.' And she stepped back into the shadows.

'You are a lying bitch!' I only managed an inaudible croak. When my voice did sound, it was as a whisper, hoarse and out of practice. 'You are a filthy, lying whore,' I tried to shout. I do not believe anyone heard me.

I attempted to sit up, but Doctor Donaldson placed his arm across my chest to hold me back.

'Call the nurses. We might need a sedative, as the patient is clearly distressed.'

In my head, I was screaming, 'I don't need a sedative. What I need is justice. It is all her fault I am here in the first place. She has stolen my life. She has stolen everything I ever had. She's a liar and a cheat. She really is my sister. She's my sister.' Tears were cascading down my cheeks –tears of anger and frustration and sheer humiliation.

Two nurses arrived. One grabbed my arm and injected something into my catheter. Within seconds, I was yelling in my dreams.

Chapter 35

I was released back into the wild just a few days later. I had been interrogated by the psychiatric unit and by the sexual health clinic at the hospital, but I managed to convince both of them that this had just been a one-off event. They all seemed rather relieved that I did not want to consider further treatment, and that they did not have to do very much more. They were busy enough dealing with actual sick people.

The police were trickier. They repeatedly questioned me about where the party had taken place, who had I been with, whether or not I could supply names, addresses, or identify faces, what the drugs were that I had taken. I kept firmly to the line that I simply could not remember anything about it. I spun what I considered to be a rather convincing story about meeting some guy in the toilet roll aisle of Sainsburys, who had chatted me up and had invited me to a party. I had been rather lonely and at a loose end, so I had thought, why not. I got lost on my way there, hence I could not tell them where I had ended up, nor could I recollect the house number, street, or the name of the random man who had invited me.

They asked me again which specific drugs I had taken, and I told them I did not think that I had taken anything of any note. I had mentioned that I had a headache to one of the people at the party and they had given me what I thought at the time were painkillers. It was as much of a shock to them as it was to me that they might have turned out to be other kinds of drugs.

They quizzed me further. Had I had sex at the party, willingly or unwillingly? I said I could not remember, as my memory was hazy after taking the so-called painkillers, and I also recollected that I had had a drink or two. So, they persisted, how could I account for the bruising and my other injuries. Did I believe that I could have been raped? I said I did not think so. Surely, I would have remembered something as horrific as that. Did I want to file a complaint again any specific person or persons. I told them no, I did not. I gave them nothing to go on - and eventually, they gave up on me.

I was completely terrified on so many levels. Obviously, I feared being prosecuted for illegal drug use, or worse, being sent to prison. I had absolutely no intention of ever mentioning Doug just in case he shopped me to the police for regular drug use. In truth, I was completely petrified of what had actually occurred at the flat, as I genuinely could not remember. Whatever it was, I knew that it had been horrific and that I had now sunk into a slough of despond so deep and so cataclysmic that even I could not believe that I had fallen so far. Essentially, I was desperately frightened of myself and of what I had allowed myself to become.

Even worse, when I was at my lowest ebb, drowning face down in the quicksand of what had now become my life, Catherine – my own sister, my only sister, fashioned from the same blood and sharer of some of my DNA - had refused to recognise me as family. Even when she saw me in my moment of greatest need, she stamped me down even further into the mire, rather than holding out her hand to pull me back up and out. Our blood was clearly thinner than water.

Back in the squalor of my bedsit, I hibernated inside my dirty, unmade bed for many weeks, alternatively crying, screaming, writhing, bleeding and sometimes, sleeping. Terrifying monsters flew down at me from the ceiling, screeching, and clawing at my face. The walls palpitated in and out, out and in. I was nauseous most of the time, I vomited often. My body emptied out as my mind fought my demons by night and by day.

Then, one day, I awoke. The sun streamed through the filthy window, illuminating the disgusting state of my surroundings, and of myself. I arose and walked over to the cracked mirror above the sink, both thick with grime.

I ran the cold tap and splashed icy water over my face and into my mouth. Then, I made a series of solemn promises to my own hideous reflection. Never again would I play the victim. No one would ever ignore me again. I would arise from my heap of ashes. I would make a new life for myself. If I were ever betrayed again, I would be avenged.

Chapter 36

'And you know what happened next, don't you?' I whispered, my words dispersing into the fetid air of the consulting room.

Dr Blake remained silent, a shadowy outline against a darkened wall.

Part II

Ten years later

Chapter 37

I dropped my bags with relief onto the floor, my arms wilting from carrying them all the way from the supermarket and up two flights of stairs to my flat. I wrenched my handbag off my shoulder and began to ferret inside for my keys. I resolved - by no means for the first time - to buy a bag with proper compartments, so that I could find things straight away, rather than searching for the one thing I needed, which had always inevitably journeyed to the bottom.

As I rummaged, the front door flew open and Rob draped himself across the door frame, his tie loosened around his neck.

'Hey, gorgeous, I thought I heard you mooching about behind the door.' He leaned forward and planted a gentle kiss on my lips. 'Here, let me grab those bags for you.'

Picking up the shopping as if it were weightless, Rob headed into the kitchen. It was a small galley, long and thin, with precious little passing space for two people. I loitered at the entrance and removed my coat.

'Have you been in long?' I asked, slinging my coat onto the stand in the hall. It missed and stayed where it fell in a forlorn heap.

'No. I only arrived five minutes ago - if that. I must have just missed you struggling up the road. You should have called me.'

I shrugged, manoeuvring my shoulders round and round to alleviate the lactic acid which had accumulated from carrying the bags.

Rob unfastened his tie and threw it towards me. I failed to catch it and kicked it towards the coat stand.

'Sit down, Rachel, and I'll bring you a glass of wine. You look like you could do with one,' Rob smiled. He wrenched the kitchen drawer open, but it stuck halfway. 'I've got to fix this bloody drawer,' he commented, snaking his hand inside to retrieve the corkscrew.

'So you keep saying,' I laughed.

Rob ran his hand through his mane of blonde hair. I never thought I would end up with a blonde. They had never been my type in my previous life. Mind you, for quite a while, I had been convinced that I would never end up with anyone ever again. In the small moments – sitting on the tube observing others or walking down the street – I would often ponder how lucky I was to have found a way back. *I am the new me,* I would tell myself, pulling my sleeves down firmly over my wrists.

I wandered into the living room and opened the curtains. We were both hopeless at remembering to open them before we went to work. The sun was setting behind the terraced houses opposite, rendering the rooftops orange. Our flat was the top half of an identical house, arranged on two floors, with the kitchen and lounge at the top of the stairs and the bathroom and bedroom up another short flight. Before we got married just over five years ago, we had cobbled together everything we had to get our deposit. This was the perfect space for us as a couple, although clearly, we would have to think again if we were ever to have children.

I catapulted myself onto the sofa and exhaled heavily. Kicking off my shoes, I curled my legs underneath my bottom and stretched my head back onto the cushion. Something in my neck clicked pleasingly

'Tired?' asked Rob, handing me my wine.

'Yes, I am. Friday tired.' I slurped my wine, and a trickle ran down my chin.

'I see your old drinking problem has returned, Madam,' Rob quipped.

I stuck my tongue out and licked around my lips to catch the drip.

Rob settled down heavily beside me, causing me to spill more wine.

'Careful,' I laughed. 'Watch the sofa!'

'Why, what's it going to do?'

I pulled a face at him. 'Ah, the old jokes are always the best,' I replied, placing my glass on the table beside me. 'Was there any post?'

'Yes, it's in the kitchen. Shall I grab it?'

'No, I'll go,' I replied, heaving myself back off the sofa with all the elegance of a baby hippo. I tried to smooth my skirt, which was crumpled after my day at the office. 'I think we will have to call in at the dry cleaners tomorrow, Rob. I need to get this skirt cleaned and few other bits and bobs,' I called from the kitchen. I grabbed the pile of letters and returned to the sofa.

'I can't believe how much crap we receive on a daily basis,' I commented, hurling various leaflets and flyers onto the floor as I sifted for any actual mail. I came to a letter stamped NHS and held it in my hand for a moment, turning it over and over. Reaching for my wine, I took another sip, before I ripped into it.

'They've finally sent us an appointment, Rob,' I said, facing him.

Rob's face reddened. 'Really. When for?'

'A week on Tuesday. Two o'clock at The Royal Free. I'll have to ask for the afternoon off – and so will you.'

Rob gazed deeply into his wine glass as if it were a crystal ball. 'I'm not sure I can do that day. I've got a meeting with the team coming down from Edinburgh and it will be difficult to move it.'

'Rob, we have been waiting for months for this appointment and we are both going. That's the end of the discussion.' I could feel chilly beads of panic pricking at my chest.

'Can't we just keep practising?' Rob giggled, sidling over, and running his hand over my knee.

'I'm sure we can, but it's not working, is it, so we need to find out why.'

'I'm sure it's nothing, Rach. We just need to give it a little more time.'

'Rob, we've been trying forever. We are going to that hospital appointment – no arguments. Please, Rob. We have been over and over this - and we need to get everything checked out. Alright?' I grabbed Rob's hand and squeezed it a little too hard.

'Alright, boss, if you say so,' Rob replied, leaning in to kiss me. 'Do you think there will be a hot nurse there to help me with the, well, with the, you know?'

'You are an awfully bad boy, Rob.'

'I know. Let me show you just how bad…'

Chapter 38

The truth was that I was as terrified as Rob was about getting my fertility tests done– if not more so. There was so much that I had not told Rob about my past life or sex life - and I was certain that past events had affected my ability to conceive. Even if I could get the physical side of things to operate, and I did not have any permanent damage in that department, something somewhere in the back of my mind whispered darkly that I could never be a good mother anyway. How could I be, when I had proved incapable of sustaining a relationship with anyone within my own family? I had not communicated with my parents - or with my sister, Catherine - for many years now. We had disowned each other.

On the other hand, my hormones shrieked far louder. They had remained completely silent until I turned thirty, at which point, they had leaped out of their Pandora's box in my brain, screaming and shouting at me about how I must have a child - and how I must have one right now. No matter how hard I tried to think about something else – quite literally, anything else - they just kept clamouring for my complete attention. In the end, I simply could not ignore them.

I conducted extensive research about the fertility process, as I knew that I would be quizzed by the doctor about my sexual and reproductive history. Equally, I knew I would have to lie about all of it. As far as Rob was concerned, I had only ever had one sexual partner – that being Tim back at university. I had never told him about Richard, because then I would have had to explain how and why that relationship ended, which would have inevitably spiralled into a confession about Doug and then, possibly, about Doug's party and 'the gang'. It was all far too raw, shocking, and frankly, too complicated to explain. When I had first met Rob, I was convinced that if I had told the truth and nothing but the truth, Rob would have run for the hills.

So, as far as Rob was concerned, I was a completely different Rachel with a totally alternate past. I was a relatively innocent woman, who – having had a traumatic experience with a domineering guy at university – had lost all confidence in men and had therefore shied away from any form of intimacy for over a decade. I had effectively been a practising nun – without the religious bit, obviously. This was the story I wove for Rob, and one in which, if I was being honest, I now believed myself - at least half of the time. Rob was also under the impression that I was an orphan and an only child – my family having perished in a car accident when I was a baby. I told him that I had been raised by an aged aunt, who had sadly died just after I left university. My labyrinth of scars on my arms and legs were a by-product of my inability to cope with my own childhood trauma. Once I had a newly invented past, I simply could not unravel it.

It was not that I enjoyed bending the truth as such, but much more that it was quite simply easier. Why complicate my current relationship with irritating details about people I cared nothing for, and who clearly cared nothing for me? If I had come clean, then Rob would have wanted to know why we did not speak to my family and worse, possibly wanted to meet them – which I had no intention of arranging. That had not tended to work out so well in the past. And frankly, what was the point? What good would it do either Rob or me?

I first met Rob when we both worked at a merchant bank in the city. He was working as an investment banker, and I was the personal assistant to his boss. I had moved up from my initial lowly secretarial job at the stationary supplier once I had regained a little confidence, and been lucky enough to land a new job, which paid better and was certainly more intellectually taxing. I was positioned at my desk at one end of the gargantuan banking floor, strategically placed outside Mr Willow's door to enable me to screen all visitors. Rob's desk was way over on the other side of the office, which was almost the length of a football pitch. Despite this, he began to make a staggering number of trips over to the coffee machine on our side of the floor, always smiling as he passed. I enjoyed watching his pert little bottom as he added his milk and stirred sugar into his regular latte. He eventually plucked up the courage to nod hello, followed a week later by a brief chat about the weather. It was miserably cold and rainy given that it was May, wasn't it? We probably would not have a good summer, would we, having had a better one the year before and good summers only happen every seven years in England.

Thankfully, conversations progressed beyond whether we might need an umbrella to nip out together for a sandwich at lunchtime until eventually – when it was impossible for Rob to invent any further excuses to be on the wrong side of the banking floor for most of the day – he asked me out to dinner. We subsequently had more and more dinners and took a couple of short holidays together. I moved jobs to the bank across the street, so as not to break the rules prohibiting office romance. Eventually we got hitched. For the first time in my life, I felt contented, settled, and safe. Rob was the one relationship that I was determined would be a success.

Now, I was convinced that my wretched hormones were out to ruin it all for me – and I had to sort it out.

When we lay together in bed, Rob would often trace with his fingertips the crisscrossing scars which laced across my arms and spread over my thighs.

'Did it hurt when you did this to yourself?' he would ask, gently kissing each and every line better, as if they were still livid and sore.

'I can't remember, Rob. I was incredibly young at the time. I probably didn't even know what I was doing.' I raised his head and kissed him, hoping to distract him.

'But how did you get hold of a knife? Wasn't your aunt careful about that sort of thing?' Rob questioned, examining my left wrist.

'Yes, of course she was, but I mostly did it with the nail scissors. My aunt kept them in the bathroom for cutting my toenails and they were easy for me to access. She never knew what I was doing.' I turned onto my side away from him.

'Didn't she ever notice?' He stroked my hair, trailing his fingers along the curve of my naked spine.

'No, Rob, she didn't. She was pretty old, and her eyesight was awful. It wasn't a big deal, really. I've survived it, haven't I?'

Rob cocooned me in his arms and rocked me slowly to sleep, as I stared wide-eyed at the pale cream wall, waiting for morning.

Chapter 39

It had been an excruciatingly slow crawl back to life as I now knew it. After I was discharged from hospital following Doug's party, time melded into one lazy lump, and I was wedged underneath it for weeks, horrors leaking slowly from my body and my mind. It took every ounce of my energy simply to crawl to the toilet and back again. I did not change my bed sheets for weeks, nor did I bathe or clean my teeth.

Most nights, I dreamt of Lucy, forever sixteen. I shared her pain and her shame. I could see her so clearly, calling to me, begging me to join her. I could, she urged me, forget the terrors of life on earth and the constant censure and judgment of everyone around me and meet her in a place where no one cared a jot about such things. It would be easy. I was used to cutting myself. All it would take would be a little more courage, a slightly deeper slice of flesh, and voila, we could be together again, as we had been so many years before. We could laugh and joke around, with our whole lives stretching ahead of us for infinity. I was so tempted to go with her. It would have been such an easy path to follow.

Yet, when I awoke each day, contemplating my foul body lying in my stinking bed, I knew that I could not go through with it. I did not possess either the strength or the willpower. I was stuck on this unforgiving earth and if I could not transcend it, I had to find a way to live in it again. I think Lucy must have sensed this, as she stopped entering my dreams quite so often. One night, she failed to appear at all. She had decided to wait.

The following morning, I woke up with nauseating, needle-sharp stomach cramps. I guess this must have been some nine or ten weeks after I was discharged from the hospital. I felt unpleasant stickiness between my legs and, when I reached down, my fingers emerged from under my sheets covered in blood. I had been vaguely fretting about why my period was so late, but then again, I had always been irregular, so I had not been overly stressed about it. My mind and body had been scrambled for so long. At least now my period had arrived – and with a vengeance it appeared. I tried to sit up, but the cramps overwhelmed me. When they subsided, I tried again, inching slowly over to the toilet in the corner of the room. As I squatted, lumpy clots of blood fell away from me as my abdomen contracted fiercely. When I had cleaned myself up, I looked down into the toilet bowl. It was a bloody mess of tissue.

The next three days were agony, as more contractions ebbed and flowed - and as I writhed and screamed. I vomited several times, and I passed more blood and then more. I was not entirely sure what was happening to me. I had no desire to return to the hospital, so I soldiered on alone. When the horror stopped, I lay wasted, my old life aborted.

I orchestrated my comeback slowly, working on the basics, step by step. One morning, I told myself that, on the count of ten, I would get out of bed. On the next count of ten, I would shower. Once out of the shower, I would pull on clean sweats. I achieved it all, counting. Then I found an old comb and dragged it through my tangled hair. My hair was so knotted that the comb snapped, so I carried on brushing using my fingernails, which had grown hideously long. I slapped some Nivea from an old pot I had lying by my bed onto my parched, dehydrated skin.

Sitting cross-legged on the floor, eating dry Rice Krispies from the packet with my hands, I grabbed an old envelope that was lying on the floor near the bin. I started to draft my blueprint for my new life plan on the back of it.

Things to obliterate

Mum and Dad

Catherine

Tim

Richard

Doug

Men in general

Drugs

Cigarettes

Advertising

Cutting myself

Me

Things I am able to do

Read

Write

Things I could do better

Lose weight

Wear better clothes

Get a proper job

Live somewhere decent

I had the beginnings of a plan. Baby steps.

I created a disciplined daily routine for myself, such that I was awake by eight and showered by nine. At ten, I ventured out as far as the corner shops and bought my food for each day. I had to be extremely frugal. I had saved a little from my days at the pub, but not very much. Every day, I made sure to buy a newspaper. At first, I merely read it, re-familiarising myself with the outside world. It was cathartic to immerse myself in wars, famine, political intrigue, sex scandals, heatwaves, and storms – a macrocosm of my own past life. I spoke to no one, except to nod hello to the tiny, wizened man behind the till at the newsagent, who smiled at me beatifically every day as he handed me my change. I wondered if he would even notice if I ever failed to show up and whether he might sound an alarm. Most probably he would not.

Eventually, I ventured on to the jobs pages and circled the ones which might be feasible for someone like me. The advertisements were for a mix of retail assistants, supermarket work or secretarial. I soon decided to avoid fashion retail, as I could not envisage myself being a jolly and positive sales assistant to customers who almost certainly would wish to be encouraged to buy garments for which they were unsuited. Working in a supermarket stacking shelves or pressing the electronic labelled buttons on the till's keyboard would inevitably allow my brain too much freedom to roam – and I knew what dangers lay in boredom. What I really needed was a certain amount of intellectual stimulus without too much stress. There were various administrative and secretarial options on offer, which I had initially dismissed, as I possessed no shorthand skills and my typing was two-fingered, if relatively speedy given that impediment. However, I would be capable of organising an office, making tea, and arranging meetings, so I reasoned that this might be the most feasible career option to pursue.

The next day, when I visited the newsagent, I bought a pad of Basildon Bond notepaper and some matching envelopes, as well as a biro which did not leak and a book of second-class stamps. Returning home, I cleared some space on the counter in the kitchenette and wiped it down to avoid the paper getting wet. I spent the whole day honing a one-page letter to a supplier of office products in central London, wasting most of my precious notepaper as I drafted and redrafted. I embellished my past employment – lead copywriter at a major advertising agency, manager of an entertainment establishment etc. In the end, it read reasonably well. I sealed it and skipped down to the post box to catch the last collection, hoping that the company would not require a reference.

I had no phone in the bedsit, so I could only supply a return address. I did, however, have the foresight to include a stamped addressed envelope, hoping that this might magnify the level of my enthusiasm. I resolved to write no more applications until I had heard back from this first one, which effectively meant that I had nothing to do except wait around for the post to arrive. Three weeks later, I had still heard nothing and resolved to begin a new application the following Monday, even though I was already fairly certain that there was no real point.

Suddenly, there was a knock on my door. I lay on my bed, transfixed. No one ever knocked on my door. The knock came again, except stronger and more insistent, so I moved warily towards it and undid the lock, keeping the chain rigidly fixed.

'Hello?' I whispered.

'I fink this is for you, love,' rasped a voice, shoving a tattered envelope through the crack in the door. 'I found it wedged behind the front door downstairs.'

'Thanks,' I stuttered, my vocal cords rusty through lack of use, but the disembodied voice had already gone.

I closed the door, my heart banging against my ribs, and stared at the envelope. The front of it was muddied by a large footprint and was slightly damp, but it was definitely addressed to me. In fact, it was written in my handwriting, which confused me for a moment, until I realised that it was my own stamped addressed envelope. I carried it back to bed with me and placed it on my pillow as if it were a precious object, which might be easily shattered. My brain was pounding with fear. I lifted the envelope up to the light to see if I could read it without opening it, but it was completely opaque. I placed it back down again and went to make a cup of tea. When I returned to the bed, the letter was still there, winking at me.

'Oh, for Christ sakes, stop being so pathetic, Rachel,' I shouted at myself, and tore open the letter.

Dear Rachel,

Thank you for your application for the post of administrative assistant at Wilkes Office Supplies.

We would be delighted if you could attend an interview at our offices on Thursday, March 26 at 09.30 a.m.

We assume we will meet you then unless we hear otherwise.

Yours sincerely,

Maxwell Ford

Thursday. That was in two days' time. I had neither clothes, nor shoes, nor hair to wear. Obviously, I could not go.

'Oh, for fuck's sake, Rachel, pull yourself together,' I admonished myself. 'What the hell are you going to do with the rest of your life if you don't at least try? Live in this shit hole like a recluse forever?' If I did not drag myself out of my current predicament, I would soon be like the ragged lady who stood every day on the corner of my street, muttering to herself, and occasionally shouting obscenities at other passers-by.

I bent down and reached under the bed for my ancient, battered shortbread tin, which served as a trusty safe for my most treasured possessions. It contained a faded photograph of myself and Catherine as small children. I had no idea why I still kept it, but every time I tried to throw it away, it seemed to stick to my fingers like a magnet, and I replaced it back into the tin. There was a large black button that had fallen off Richard's overcoat once. I found it after he had left me and for many months, I carried it around in my handbag, hoping it might lure him back to me like the Sirens singing to the sailors from their rock, before I gave up and condemned it to the sanctity of my tin. My graduation certificate was also in there. I also kept my cash in there. I tipped it all out onto the bed and counted it twice. My total worldly wealth was £37.02. Clearly, a high street shopping spree was out of the question, but I had to do something. Dragging my sweat top over my head, I grabbed my house keys, shoved the money into my sweat bottoms – checking first that the pocket did not have a hole - and headed out with purpose into the world.

Two streets away from my flat - at the dead-end of high street next to the pound shop - was a rather rundown charity shop. I dawdled outside it for a few minutes, pretending to admire the haphazard display of bric-a-brac which filled the shop window. Eventually, I took an extremely deep breath and plunged through the door. A pathetic, little bell tinkled over my head, announcing my presence. Pulling my hood further down over my face, I headed towards the back of the shop. It was a miniscule place, but seemed even more so, because there was stuff piled everywhere – on the floor, on shelves, on rails. The clothing racks were stuffed so full, that it was nigh on impossible to see what was hanging from them. It was more of a warehouse than a retail establishment. I began to flick through the clothes as best as I could. I dismissed any dresses or skirts, reasoning that my legs had not been exposed to the light for many years and a job interview was not the time to reveal them and their scars to the unsuspecting world. Then there was the obvious fact that I would have to buy a depilatory, for which I possessed neither the cash, nor the inclination.

I was losing the will to live, irritably rifling through the clothes, when I spotted a black trouser suit. I manhandled the hanger off rack and held the jacket against my front. It looked to be vaguely the right size.

'Would you like to try that on?' asked a disembodied voice. I jumped and glanced around, but I could see no one. I felt an imperceptible tap on the back of my arm and spun around in panic. In front of me was the tiniest woman I had ever seen, wizened like an overly dry raisin.

She smiled at me and the gap where her missing front tooth should have been blinked at me. 'Is it for something special?' she asked, her voice a faint whisper.

'I, well, no, well, yes, I suppose so. I've got a job interview and I've got nothing to wear.'

The little goblin clapped her minute hands together in glee. 'Oh, how thrilling, my lovely. I do love it when I have a customer who is on a mission.' She took a hop closer. 'I think that suit would look gorgeous on you.' She looked me up and down. 'Yes, you're a definite size ten. I have a lovely green blouse to go with that suit, which will set your eyes off perfectly. Let me go and find it for you.'

A size ten? This woman must be mental, I laughed to myself. And then, I stared at myself in the mirror in the corner of the shop, which was cracked and partially obscured by a faded hobby horse and a pair of wellington boots. I was shocked to realise that I did look quite thin. I had always been a bigger girl, but I seemed to have shrunk to half the person I once was – both mentally and physically. I gasped, unsure whether to be pleased or disappointed.

'Come on, my lovely. I have a small room in the back where you can try everything on,' called the tiny woman, beckoning me to follow her.

She led me into the overly cluttered storeroom, which made the shop itself appear tidy and ordered. Weaving her way through myriad cardboard boxes and black bin liners, the woman found a clear square of flooring.

'Change here while I go to see if I can find you some shoes,' she instructed, before disappearing behind the piles of junk.

I glanced around to check that no one else was looking, and then quickly donned the new clothes. The green rayon blouse was so soft against my skin that I could hardly feel that I was wearing it, and the trouser suit fitted as though it had been tailormade made especially for me.

The old woman appeared again by my side as if by magic. 'Well, just look at you. A proper businesswoman,' she crowed. 'Now, slip these on.' She handed me a pair of black court shoes with a low heel. They were a precise fit.

'How did you know my size?' I asked, my mouth agape.

'Oh, I'm just a good guesser,' the woman laughed, revealing further missing teeth. 'Now, we need to sort out your hair.'

'My hair?' I lifted my fingers to the rat's nest above my face.

'Well, I don't know when you last had it cut, my lovely, but it does resemble a badly tied bale of straw.' The old lady giggled and blushed slightly pink, 'if you don't mind me saying so.'

She motioned me towards a sealed cardboard box. 'Change into the clothes you arrived in and sit down.' Mutely, I did as I was told.

Out of nowhere, the woman produced a pair of scissors and an exceptionally large towel. She threw the towel across the front of my body and tied it like an expert hairdresser around my neck. Then she proceeded to snip, snip, snip away. I perched in silence as great lumps of hair fell around my feet. I felt unable to speak and the lady was also silent as she concentrated on the task in hand.

'Voila, my lovely. Have a look at yourself in the mirror. You look gorgeous. You are an absolutely beautiful, young woman.'

She swivelled me around on the box. There was a mirror on the back wall. I stared at this alien woman, who looked almost attractive - and who was crying silent tears.

'I don't know what to say,' I gulped.

'There is nothing you need to say, my lovely.' The woman replied, handing me a clean tissue. 'I'm simply extremely glad to be of help to you. Now, let me bag up your new clothes and send you on your way. I'll pop in some moisturiser and a little bit of mascara for you too.'

'How much will all that be?' I asked in panic, fingering the meagre roll of notes and the smattering of coins in my pocket.

'Oh, don't you worry, my lovely. These are all a gift from me. When you get back on your feet and are prospering again, pop back in to see me and make a small donation to the shop. I'll look forward to hearing all about your progress.'

When we were very young, in rare moments of contented togetherness, Catherine and I used to love watching a television programme called *Mr Ben*. Mr Ben would visit his favourite dressing up shop, and each time he visited, he tried on a different outfit, thus causing him to embark on a new adventure. Just like Mr Ben, this lady had enabled me to begin again as someone else. I never told anyone about my visit to the charity shop and the kindness of the woman in there, who helped me to make a new start - but I was forever grateful. When I was successful at landing the job at the stationers and had been able to move out of my grotty bedsit and found somewhere decent to live, I returned to the shop to give a donation as promised and to thank the old lady - but it was all boarded up. Every so often as my career progressed, I had still wandered past, in the vain hope that it may have been reopened - but it never did.

Chapter 40

Rob and I waited within the white walls of the clinic. I sat there flicking through a leaflet on infertility, detailing its various causes and the options to remedy it using a variety of line drawings. The pages jiggled about in front of my eyes, goading me to make any sense of them. Rob just sat staring at the blank wall, his left leg shaking up and down.

'Rob, can you stop that, please?' I hissed, tapping his leg.

He stopped – only to begin again a few seconds later.

'Rob, please. You look like you've got St Vitus' dance.'

'Like I've got Saint what what's?'

'It's a phrase my aunt used to use. It's a problem to do with uncontrollable movement, or something like that. Whatever it is - just quit, please, will you? It's so bloody irritating.' I placed my hand on his leg to steady it.

'I'm nervous, that's all, Rachel. It's really embarrassing for me, having to come here and do my thing. It's alright for you.' His leg started up again.

'Really, Rob? You think so? You'd rather be all legs akimbo while someone has a rummage around inside you with a cold, metal stick, would you? All you've got to do is jiggle your togger around for a while – which is something you seem to enjoy doing in general.'

'Yes, but I never do that in public, do I?' Rob whispered.

'I don't think you'll be doing it in public today, either, as you might get arrested,' I giggled.

Well, no, but - oh, never mind. You just don't get it.' Rob sighed.

'They're ready for you now, Rachel,' the nurse at the desk called.

Rob kissed me lightly on the cheek and I rose to follow the nurse. 'See you soon,' I said. 'Good luck.'

Rob nodded, his leg beginning to vibrate yet again. 'You too.'

We rendezvoused back in reception an hour or so later. Tests completed, we said nothing to each other as we exited the building. We merely held hands as we walked down the street towards the tube station in silence, neither of us wanting to know how the other had got on.

A fortnight later, we met with the doctor back at the clinic. He was fifty-ish, with greying stubble and telescopic glasses which magnified his eyes, so that you could not quite tell if he was looking at you, or at an object much further in the distance.

'Come in, come in,' he boomed, ushering us towards the two chairs in front of his desk. 'Have a seat, do. It's Rachel and Rob, isn't it? Terrific. Right. Excellent.'

There was a prolonged period of quiet, apart from the sound of the doctor shuffling a mound of papers and occasionally humming to himself as he read. He must have spent a good five minutes going over all the notes, flicking backward and forwards through the reports. As he did so, he fiddled constantly with his glasses, moving them up and down his nose. Eventually, with a flourish, he removed his spectacles and placed them on top of the papers.

'Right, Rachel. Ladies first, so let me start with you. You will be pleased to hear that it is all good news. You're ovulating as you should be, your tubes are all clear, and generally you appear to be as fit as a fiddle.'

I exhaled heavily - not realising that I had been holding my breath. My back was wet with perspiration as

I relaxed into the seat of my chair. So no damage. I was amazed.

'Now you, Rob. Your sperm count is normal, so you have no problem with either the quantity or the strength of your swimmers.'

Rob grinned and slapped his leg, his virility confirmed. 'See, Rachel, I told you we just needed to keep practising.' He grinned, his dimples bursting from his flushed cheeks.

'However,' interrupted the doctor, 'there does appear to be a small lump on your right testicle, which we would like to investigate further. Have you noticed it at all?'

Rob's smile had faded. 'No, never. Is it anything to worry about?' Rob fidgeted on his chair and crossed his hands involuntarily over his groin.

'Hopefully not, no, but I'd like to refer you for an ultrasound, if that's alright with you?'

'What will that do?' asked Rob, his leg shaking up and down once again.

'It will check for - and confirm - the presence of any lumps or bumps, and we will also run some blood tests. It is all standard procedure, but we need to err on the side of caution, obviously. I'll send a request to the relevant department, and they will be in touch with a date for an appointment soon.' The doctor replaced his glasses onto his nose, signalling that our time was up.

Rob's cheeks had drained of all colour. I reached over and squeezed his hand. 'I'm sure it will be fine, Rob. Honestly.'

Rob squeezed my hand in return but made no reply.

'Do you think it could be anything serious?' Rob asked the doctor, his voice wavering.

'I really can't say until we've run the tests, Rob, but glass half full and all that. Let us just wait and see,' the doctor replied, rising from his chair, before opening the surgery door for us to leave.

The next two weeks were the longest that either of us had ever spent together. Rob shrunk into himself, drowning in a heady mixture of mind-numbing television programmes and daily bottles of red wine. Every morning and every evening, he would present his right testicle to me for inspection.

'I can definitely feel the lump, Rachel. I think it's bigger today. What do you think?' he asked, ball in hand.

'It barely noticeable, Rob – and no, I don't think it's any bigger. I think it just seems like it is to you, because you know it's there and you're worried. I get that, but I'm sure once you've had the tests, it'll be nothing.' I stroked his balls gently, hoping to distract him, but there was no reaction. I could definitely feel a lump.

'Rachel, there's no point in saying everything will be fine all the time, because you've got no bloody idea whether it will be or not,' Rob snapped.

And the obvious truth was that I did not have a clue, but I desperately hoped that it would be alright and that we could just go back to normal. If only I had not pushed for the fertility tests, Rob might never have known about the lump, and everything would have just carried on as normal. Somehow, I had managed to create a crisis instead of a life.

A couple of weeks later, Rob returned to the hospital for his ultrasound and his blood tests. He would not allow me to accompany him.

'They are just routine tests, Rachel, as you keep reminding me. There's nothing you can do to help.'

'I can be there for moral support,' I argued, scratching the inside of my arm.

'There's no point in both of us taking time off work. I'll be in and out in no time.'

'No change there then,' I quipped – and, in a rare moment of levity, he threw a cushion at my head.

But the results were not routine or fine. The ultrasound confirmed the presence of a lump and the bloods highlighted raised markers for cancer. Even though we had both half-expected bad news, the confirmation was utterly devastating. Rob cried like a small child. I had never seen him cry before.

When I was not with Rob and trying to be brave for his sake, I wept intermittently for days -in the shower, at work, whenever Rob could not see me. At night, we clung to each other as though we were shipwrecked, hoping desperately for rescue. I loved him so much that the worry hurt me physically, like a sharp pain stabbing at my chest. I simply could not bear the thought of Rob suffering, or worse, of not surviving. I had no idea how I would manage to go on alone, without this wonderful man, with whom I had hoped to spend the rest of our long lives. I prayed constantly to a god I did not really believe in that Rob would be alright. I touched wood, threw salt over my left shoulder, read our horoscopes religiously, and crossed my fingers until they ached as much as my heart. I would do whatever I had to do to keep Rob safe.

Rob was duly booked in for an orchidectomy – 'It sounds like I should be in the Chelsea Flower Show,' Rob joked to the oncologist, who failed to understand the joke. They had to remove his lumpy testicle.

'I'm just like Hitler now,' smiled Rob from his hospital bed, his eyelids opening and closing over his bloodshot eyes in his post-operative haze.

'I don't think having one testicle removed automatically turns you into a fascist dictator and mass murderer,' I commented, holding a glass of water to

Rob's lips for him to sip, 'but I shall be on the lookout for the obvious signs - and if I spot any, I'll suggest they remove the other one as well.'

Rob winced. 'That's what I love about you - your unfailing sympathy.'

'I know. I have the best bedside manner, don't' I? Perhaps I missed my vocation, and I should have trained to be a nurse,' I laughed, climbing gingerly onto the bed on the good testicle side, and kissing him lightly on the forehead. We lay there together for a long while until a genuine nurse appeared to turf me out for the night.

I staggered home that evening, barely able to lift one foot in front of the other to walk. I felt as if I had been operated on instead of Rob and worse – I felt utterly drained already as I looked ahead to the battle he and I had to face from here.

Chapter 41

Rob had radiation treatment post-surgery and then had to undergo two cycles of chemotherapy, each of which lasted around three weeks. Rob attended the appointments alone, but I liked to collect him in a taxi, as he tended to feel quite nauseous and generally tired after the sessions. The oncologist appeared reasonably optimistic regarding Rob's prognosis and assured us that one testicle could do the work of two when it came to conception. I was not convinced, given that two had not done the job before, but frankly, that was the least of my concerns. I just wanted Rob to get better – and to feel less afraid.

It was an odd thing – caring for someone who had cancer. I worried incessantly about Rob – obviously - and desperately prayed to any deity who would listen that he would recover permanently. Friends telephoned and popped round regularly to see how he was. Everyone was fantastic. Yet no one ever asked me how I was doing. Now, there is no particular reason why they should have done so. After all, there was nothing wrong with me - and I felt very selfish feeling sorry for myself. But Rob's illness had changed everything. While he was in recovery, he needed to be looked after. We could not go out as we had before – nor could we stay in to make love like we had before. I had to do pretty much everything around the flat myself – and I really hated doing the cleaning. I was bored, yet shattered; worried, yet annoyed. Some hours of the day, I felt like I was a saint and at other times, I was sure I was the devil.

Towards the end of Rob's first cycle of chemo, I was loitering outside The Royal Free Hospital waiting for him to appear, while keeping an eye out for the taxi I had booked. I was perched on a low wall, stuffing my face with a tuna mayonnaise Subway sandwich, purchased on my way there from the tube. The incessant worry was making me hungry, and I seemed to be constantly stuffing my face with something. The spring sunshine caressed my face, and oddly, I felt a wave of optimism wash over me. I was suddenly sure that Rob and I would survive all of this.

I took another healthy bite and wiped away a trickle of mayonnaise stuck to the corner of my mouth with the back of my hand. I glanced up at the entrance to the hospital and saw Rob dawdling in the entrance, chatting to a female doctor, her white coat shining in the sunshine. My grip on the remainder of my sandwich dissolved and it fell from my hand, landing on top of my new, black suede boots. I stared, my mouth agape in disbelief. Rob was laughing and joking. The doctor was smiling and fiddling with her stethoscope. She placed her hand on Rob's shoulder - and left it there far too long. Her sleek, blonde ponytail swayed as she giggled and increasingly invaded his personal space.

Eventually, Rob waved his goodbyes to her and began to stroll towards me. The doctor remained in the entrance, shielding her face from the sun while watching him walk away.

'Hi, gorgeous,' Rob smiled, pecking me on the cheek. 'Hey, Rachel, did you know you've got a sandwich on your shoe?'

'Who was that?' I snarled.

'Who was who?' Rob replied, looking behind him.

'That doctor. Who was she?'

'Oh, her? She works in the psychiatric department She has been assigned to me to help me through the psychological issues that can affect people dealing with cancer. She is newly qualified, and she has been immensely helpful, actually. She seems extremely sweet, and I think she likes me.' Rob laughed. 'What's the matter, Rachel? You look like you've just seen the angel of death.' Rob slumped next to me on the wall and draped his arm across my shoulders. I batted his hand away.

'What's her name?' I asked, staring straight at Rob.

'Catherine. Why?'

'And she's your doctor, is she?' I persisted.

'Well, one of them, yes. Not my main oncologist, but I will see her occasionally. What is this, the bloody Spanish Inquisition? What the hell is the matter with you?' Rob stood up, pale and slightly unsteady on his feet. 'Come on, Let's go. I'm tired and I'm starting to feel sick.'

I remained where I was, stuck on the wall immobile, staring at the hospital entrance, where Catherine had disappeared into her labyrinth.

'Come on, let's move, Rachel. I think this must be our taxi.' Rob turned and began to walk towards a minicab that had stopped a few yards away. 'Are you coming or what?' Rob snapped.

I remained rooted to the spot, unsure whether I could even stand up. Catherine. How was it possible that she had come back to haunt me – and what the hell was she doing with Rob?

Chapter 42

A few days later, I returned home from work before Rob. The day had been particularly warm for April and the flat was extremely stuffy, so I threw open the windows in the lounge as soon as I got in. Stale air and the thud of traffic from the main road outside flooded through them. I removed my jacket and flung it onto the armchair. I would hang it up later. My habit of leaving my clothes everywhere rather than hanging them up was one of many which really annoyed Rob, who believed that every garment with sleeves should be placed on a hanger as soon as it was removed. I could not have cared less.

The phone trilled and I moved over to the side table by the television to answer it.

'Hello?'

'Hello, could I speak to Rob, please?' asked a man. I strained to hear him, as the noise of beeps and other people talking in the background overwhelmed his rather quiet voice, as did the traffic outside my own window.

'He's not here at the moment. Can I take a message?' I asked.

'Could you ask him to call the psychiatric department at The Royal Free when he has a moment regarding his next appointment, please,' the man requested.

'Is there a problem?' I questioned, pushing the receiver into my ear to block out the noise at my end.

'Yes, we need to rearrange it, as his doctor would like to ensure that she can see him when he comes in to review his treatment plan – and currently, she is not due to be in on the day that Rob had his appointment.'

'I see,' I replied, my palm sweating against the phone.

'Great. Well, if you could just pass on the message, that would be brilliant. Thank you so much.'

He rang off and I stood there like a stone, holding the phone in mid-air as if I had forgotten what to do with it

Rob came crashing through the front door and into the lounge.

'Hi, Rach. Are you OK?' he smiled, large sweat patches visible under his arms. 'It's bloody baking on the tube. Gross!'

'Yes, I'm fine,' I replied, remembering suddenly how to replace the receiver.

'Who was on the phone, Rachel?' Rob asked. He scooped my jacket up from the chair. 'I'll hang this for you, shall I? So, who was it?' he repeated.

'Oh, it was no one,' I blustered. 'Wrong number. We seem to get them a lot at the moment, have you noticed?' I felt my face run hot.

'Not particularly. Maybe you're just lucky!' Rob laughed. 'Is there anything in the fridge, or shall we pop out for pizza? I'm in that week of my cycle where I'm ravenous. Jesus, I sound like a pre-menstrual woman.'

I made no reply, my mind racing away in an alternative direction.

'Rach, did you hear what I said?' Rob asked.

'You're a pre-menstrual woman?'

'No. I asked whether we are intending to eat here, or do you want to go out? I really don't mind either way.'

'Oh, I don't mind either. I'm not very hungry. It's far too hot. You choose.' I picked my handbag up off the floor and pushed past him into the bedroom.

'Let's go out for an hour then,' Rob shouted after me. ' Saves cooking here, doesn't it? I'm going to take a shower and then we can leave.'

We wandered up the Finchley Road to our favourite Italian restaurant, L'Artista. It was easy to locate, as you could smell the heady garlic long before the restaurant itself came into view. It was a place of utter chaos, with waiters in stripey T-shirts yelling in Italian at top volume whilst balancing at least six plates of food on each arm. The passing spaces in the eatery were extremely narrow, and it was a miracle that the food ever arrived at the tables intact, rather than crashing to the floor.

'Buona sera, bella signora,' warbled the greeter at the door.

'Buona sera,' I muttered in reply.

'Do you have a table for two' Rob enquired, in his best English.

'Un tavolo per due. Fammi dare un'occhiata per te,' the greeter replied, beetling off into the depths of the restaurant.

Rob and I waited, sidestepping every so often to avoid being poleaxed by the gigantic pizzas as they sped past from all sides.

'Sì. Vieni da questa parte, per favore,' screeched the returning waiter, waving his arms wildly, as if he were trying to park a petulant jumbo jet.

We followed him to the back of the restaurant, where he seated us before lobbing two enormous, laminated menus at us. We stared at each other, exhausted before we began.

'I love this place. It's crazy, isn't it?' giggled Rob. He waved at one of the careering waiters and ordered a carafe of red wine and some tap water.

'Rachel, what's up with you? You seem a bit distant tonight. In fact, you've seemed a bit off for a few days now,' Rob asked, reaching across the table to stroke my hand. 'Is everything OK at work?'

'I'm fine, Rob, really, but I have been thinking.' I fanned myself with the menu. The lazy overhead fan was useless.

'Oh no, that sounds ominous,' laughed Rob, taking a swig of the Barolo, which had already been delivered to the table.

'Very amusing, darling,' I replied without smiling. 'But seriously, do you think that you are getting the best treatment at The Royal Free, or do you think you should go private for this last bit? Just to be sure.' I downed a glass of wine and refilled it.

'Why would I do that now? Firstly, everyone says that the best place for cancer treatment is on the NHS and secondly, the doctors at the Royal Free have been bloody brilliant - and I have every confidence in them. They are really pleased with my progress, and I don't see why I would even consider changing at this point.' Rob picked up his menu. 'Right, now that's out of the way, what do you want to eat?' He began to scour the menu, even though he knew it off by heart.

'But, Rob, honestly, before we go totally off topic, don't you think a second opinion would be a good idea. Especially if we want to still have kids.?' I fiddled with my napkin, tearing off small pieces and rolling them into smaller balls.

'No, Rachel, I don't. It's my body and it's my problem - and I'm happy exactly where I am. Let me at least get through chemo and sort my own head out before you go banging on again about having kids. That's not the priority right now, is it?' Rob waved the menu at me. 'Now, what do you want to eat?'

'I'm not hungry,' I answered, lowering my menu to the table.

229

'So why the hell did you say you wanted to come out?' Rob banged his menu down, knocking his wine glass over in the process. Red wine gushed across the plastic chequered tablecloth. Rob jumped up just in time before the red flow hit his trousers. 'Shit, now look what you made me do,' he barked.

'I didn't make you do anything,' I retorted, as a stripey body arrived at speed to replace the tablecloth and napkins. 'You were the one who wanted to come out - not me.'

'I asked you what you wanted to do,' Rob snapped, sitting back down at the table, and refilling his wine glass.

'And I said it was up to you,' I sulked.

'Yes, but why didn't you just say you didn't want to come if you wanted to stay in?' Rob leaned back on his chair and folded his arms.

'Because said that you wanted go out and I didn't want to upset you.' I finished my wine. 'I didn't want to be selfish. But if I'd known you were going to a total arse, I wouldn't have bothered,' I glowered.

We sat across from each other and glared; two potential prize-fighters squaring up across a red and white tablecloth.

'I think we should just pay and go,' Rob muttered.

'OK, if that's what you want to do,' I sulked.

Rob signalled for the bill. The waiter was most perturbed that we were leaving without eating, his arms entering full windmill mode, but we assured him that it was fine. One of us was not feeling too well, that was all. We did not elaborate on which of us that might be. The waiter disappeared into the kitchen and returned moments later with our food wrapped in tin foil cartons. Rob threw some cash on the table, downed the rest of his wine and we wandered home in silence, which was not companionable.

'I'm going to bed,' I announced, as Rob fumbled with the key in the front door.

'Fine by me,' he replied.

I undressed, dumping my clothes on the floor where I stood, and threw on my pyjamas. I cleaned my teeth in the bathroom and grabbed a glass of water from the kitchen before getting into bed. I lay there, staring at the black mark on the ceiling, which I had made a mental note to paint over on many occasions. My blood was racing around my body too quickly and my heart was performing perfect somersaults every so often, as my adrenalin revved itself up. The image which had been seared on my brain for days lit up like the beginning of a West End show. Catherine - full of joie de vivre and venom – bounced in front of me, all boobs and bravado, taunting me. I closed my eyes, but that merely illuminated her further.

But if Catherine really thought I would let her outshine me again, she could not have been more misguided. If she wanted to come for Rob, let her try. This time, I would be waiting.

Chapter 43

'Did you take a message from the hospital about changing my psychiatric appointment the other day and forget to tell me?' Rob shouted, slamming through the front door.

'And good evening to you too, Rob,' I replied, lowering my book. I had returned home around thirty minutes earlier with only the last few pages to finish off my novel, which I had been reading on the tube.

'Well, did you?' Rob repeated, standing there, his hands locked onto his hips.

'I have absolutely no idea what you're talking about, Rob – and I'm certainly not going to discuss anything with you if you come home and start yelling at me.' I picked my book up again.

Rob slumped onto the sofa next to me.

'Sorry, Rach, but when I got to the hospital today, they didn't have my appointment in the diary. They said they had called and left a message for me to rearrange it. They said they spoke to a woman.'

'Well, they must have rung the wrong number and spoken to some other woman then, because I didn't take that call - and there was no message left on the answering machine,' I replied, pretending to continue to concentrate my novel.

'That's weird. Anyway, I was pissed off, because I had to race out of work in order to get there on time - and now I've got to go again next week. Their inefficiency really hacks me off. It's as if my time doesn't matter at all.'

'Well, there's no need to take it out on me,' I sighed, lowering my book to my lap. 'Did you manage to rearrange it?' I queried.

'Yes, I'm going on Tuesday at 4 o'clock,' Rob sighed.

'Who's it with?' concentrating on my book.

'I don't know. The usual doctor, I suppose. Right, I'm going to get changed out of this suit.' Rob rose and removed his jacket.

'Which doctor is that then?' I asked, avoiding his eye.

Rob wheeled round. 'I don't bloody know, Rachel, do I? I rarely see the same one twice. What's it to you who I see at the hospital anyway?'

'What's it to me?' I shouted. 'I am concerned about you, obviously. I've been through this whole process with you, holding your hand, and you've got the gall to ask what's it to me? Go fuck yourself, Rob.'

Rob turned and slammed out of the room.

We seemed to have spent most of the last two weeks bickering with each other. I lobbed my book onto the cushion next to me and brushed away an angry tear from my eye. I rose and went to find Rob into the bedroom. He was removing his shirt.

'Sorry, Rob. Let's stop arguing, shall we? We are so close to the end of all this, and I know you're tired. So am I. When the chemo is over, let's book a holiday away somewhere. We could both try to get a bit of additional time off and make it an extended break?' I wrapped my arms around Rob's waist and leaned my head against his broad, naked chest. His chest hair tickled my nose.

'I'd love to, Rach, but I won't be able to take any holiday for ages. I've had so much time off sick already- and it's really slowed me down.' Rob gently unpeeled me from his torso.

'But they'll understand, Rob. They know how sick you have been,' I wheedled.

'Yes, but I don't want to appear to be a slouch - and there is a possible promotion looming. I don't want that dick Henderson getting it when he's useless and I'm not.'

233

Rob sat down on the bed and began to unlace his shoes. He had dark circles under his eyes and his cheeks were hollow.

'But surely…' I persisted.

'Rach, leave it alone, will you? I don't know why you've become such a bloody nag recently. It's so sodding boring.' He rose slowly. 'I'm going to have a shower.'

My thoughts raced after him. I wondered why he was taking a shower straight after work. He never usually did that. I scooped up his dirty shirt from where Rob had dropped it – unusually - in the middle of the bedroom carpet and sniffed it like one of those tracker dogs you see working at the airport looking for drugs. I had made the mistake once of bending down to pat one as I disembarked at Heathrow, only to be pulled swiftly away by Rob, who told me that stroking the dogs was what traffickers did to distract attention from themselves. If they had searched me, they would have found that I was carrying only an excess of menthol in the form of both Vicks and Olbas Oil. The shirt smelt purely of Rob. I examined the collar and the cuff and the buttons, but I could see nothing, except for a faint line of grime from the filth of the tube. I sank onto the bed and threw Rob's shirt over my face to hibernate from my own thoughts.

Chapter 44

'I'll pick you up from the hospital later,' I offered when the day arrived for Rob's next appointment.

'I'm fine, Rach. It is a slightly earlier appointment than usual, and there's no need for you to take time off. I'll grab a taxi and see you back at home when I'm done.' Rob finished tying his tie, glancing at himself in the mirror as he straightened it. 'I've got to go, or I'll be late for the early morning meeting,' he announced, pecking me on the cheek.

'It's no bother, really, Rob,' I called after him, as the front door slammed shut.

I spent the day at work running through mundane tasks by rote and ignoring any of the more urgent and complex ones. I had decided to meet Rob after his hospital appointment anyway, just to make sure he was alright after his session. My boss was always accommodating about this stuff, and I had promised to come in early the next day to begin planning the quarterly conference, which by rights I should have already begun to arrange.

I jumped onto the tube and alighted at Belsize Park. The sun warmed the back of my head as I hurried along the street towards The Royal Free Hospital, past the regulars supping their pints in The George on the corner. I never felt hugely comfortable around a pub these days, and I quickened my pace as I marched past it. Normally, I waited for Rob outside the entrance, but today I thought I would surprise him by meeting him up on the ward. My footsteps echoed on the hard linoleum as I scurried through the hospital to locate the lifts. The department of psychiatry was on the seventh floor, so that the patients could admire the panoramic view of London while discussing their innermost fears and alleviating their stress. The lift seemed to take forever to come, and we stopped at every floor on the way up. I was worried that Rob might have left by the time I arrived.

As I emerged from the lift, I moved to turn right towards the nurses' station, but stopped short, causing the orderly walking behind me to bang into my back.

'Sorry,' I murmured, as the woman tutted at me and moved on.

Catherine bounced along the corridor, ponytail swinging in tandem with her stethoscope. It was nestled between her perfectly pert breasts, which seemed able to make themselves known even under her lab coat. I hung back, frozen.

'Hi, Catherine,' called a chubby, red-faced nurse sitting behind the desk. 'How are you doing?'

'Hi, Jenny, I'm fine. How are you today?' Catherine replied, reaching into her top pocket for a pen and scribbling something onto the clipboard she was carrying.

'Not too bad, all things considered,' Jenny replied. 'What can I help you with?'

'Have you got the notes for the gorgeous chap in Room 4? I need to go and give him the once over.'

They giggled like two infantile co-conspirators.

'The blonde guy? I know, he is rather dishy, isn't he?' Jenny warbled, her red face beetrooting even further. 'I always try to linger over his papers for a while when he comes in. He's so cute.'

'Oh, Jenny, you are a very naughty girl! Anyway, I hate to tell you this, but I think he's taken, unfortunately,' Catherine informed her, 'but then again, it's always worth a punt, don't you think?'

They tittered together like thirteen-year-old schoolgirls.

Jenny handed Catherine a manila file. 'Well, Catherine, if anyone can turn his head, I'm sure you can,' laughed Jenny.

'Well, I'll always give it a go, you know me! Wish me luck,' Catherine replied, tossing her hair as she wiggled her bottom back down the corridor.

Jenny turned to her fellow nurse, who was perched on a stool further behind the desk. 'Christ, that girl thinks she's something special,' bitched Jenny. 'That poor bugger doesn't stand a chance!'

I burped loudly and bile lurched up into my mouth. I turned and dived into the toilet. I spat my venom into the sink and ran the tap to wash out my mouth. Looking at my face in the mirror, I appeared extremely drawn and haggard. Dark rings lined my under-eyes and a network of wrinkles had stencilled themselves at the corner of my eyes and mouth. I smacked my cheeks hard to force some colour into them. They rose red, but the enforced colour faded almost immediately. I straightened my jacket and my mind as I headed back outside.

'Hi, I'm Rachel, Rob's girlfriend. He's here having a session at the moment. I wondered if I could sit with him while he has it?' I queried as I approached Jenny on the desk.

'Hi, love. I'm so sorry, but you can't go in there during the treatment, as it is completely confidential. The doctor is with him at the moment. You can wait in the visitors' room at the end of the ward if you like – or there's a café on the ground floor if you'd like to get a coffee while you wait?' Jenny smiled.

'Are you sure I can't go in? Just for a bit? I think he would appreciate the moral support,' I suggested.

'No, I'm so sorry, dear. Those are the rules, I'm afraid.' Jenny turned back to her computer. The conversation was closed.

Tears pricked at the corners of my eyes, and I pursed my lips, nodding my tactic acceptance. I began to trudge up the corridor towards the visitors' room. I moved slowly, glancing into each room as I passed with the hope of glimpsing Rob. Most of the blinds were closed, but halfway along, the window in the door was open. I spotted Rob at the far end by the outside window, his back turned almost away from me. Catherine was seated opposite him, her notebook in her hand. Rob said something and she threw her head back laughing, revealing a set of perfect teeth as she thrusted her bountiful bosom towards him. She said something in reply and Rob's shoulders heaved up and down. They obviously shared a certain sense of humour. Catherine stood up to smooth her skirt, leaning towards Rob, her lab coat touching his arm. I wondered if she aroused him as he sat there. I wondered what secrets he told her. Did he tell Catherine his innermost thoughts and fears rather than sharing them with me, his partner?

'You can't go in there, Miss,' Jenny called, leaning over the edge of the nurses' station.

I looked down, surprised to see my fingers tight around the handle of the door, my knuckles white. I unfurled my grip and fled towards the lift, past Jenny and her colleague at the nurses' station. I pressed the lift button furiously, desperate to get off this floor of sickness and pass into the light.

Chapter 45

I had honestly thought that I had left the darkness of my youth behind. Having found Rob, I had almost believed in some form of angelic being, who had come to my rescue and led me down a new, contented path. But now I realised that this entity had been the devil, raising me up just high enough to smash me back down even further than I had fallen before. How stupid could I have been? Now, I finally understood that I had no right to be happy. Every relationship I had ever engaged in had been corrupted. I lay awake – now a permanent insomniac - retracing my wretched steps backward from Rob, to Doug, to Richard to Tim, all the way back to my long-lost parents. There had been a truly short time when I was happy - when I was extremely young - and there was one obvious event that had been the catalyst for change. BC and AC. That was the description of my life encapsulated in four letters. Of that, I was absolutely clear.

I had to stop this vicious cycle. If my life was going to plummet into despair yet again, then I must ensure that the agent of my fate would hold my hand as I fell.

Chapter 46

'So, there we have it, Dr Blake. You have the full story now – or the majority of it anyway.'

I was lying prone on the cold floor tiles, staring at the grey ceiling tiles, while Dr Blake perched on a hard chair at the other side of the room, hidden away in the shadows.

'Please tell me the rest of it, Rachel. We really need to finish this,' she implored me. Her voice echoed around the room, bare as it was of furniture to absorb any sound. 'Describe to me exactly how Catherine died.'

'For Christ sakes, you know all this already, my dear Doctor. Why do we have to go over it all again and again?' I whined, rolling onto my stomach, and banging my feet against the floor like a weary toddler. 'I'm so bloody tired of it all.'

'Just tell me this one last time,' Dr Blake implored. 'Please. Do it for me.'

'*Do it for me*,' I mimicked. 'Well, you asked for it, Doctor. So, let us begin at the end, shall we?

Chapter 47

Rob and I were barely on speaking terms. Whenever we did say anything to each other, it was barbed and unpleasant. Rob returned home from the office later and later every day. We both slept hanging off our own sides of our double bed to avoid touching each other. When Rob got up in the morning, I pretended to be asleep until he left. If we needed to communicate, we left each other post-it notes - *Read the gas meter. Put the bin out.* These were hardly our loving billets doux of old.

I was completely unable to lose the image of him with Catherine. Whenever I did touch him, it was Catherine's touch that I felt on his arm. When he laughed, I heard her giggle. I was certain that one day he would come home, sit me down and history would quite simply repeat itself.

'Rachel,' Rob would say, 'I've been seeing someone else.'

I would stare, unblinking, saying nothing.

'I thought it was a one-night stand – nothing more than that initially – but I find that I can't get her out of my head. I need to progress things with her - see what develops - or I'll never know whether it's important, or whether or not I can forget her. And as I say this, I know what I'm throwing away with you and how much I'm hurting you, especially when you find out…'

Rob would falter, his face scarlet. A small trickle of sweat would escape from his hairline and run over his eye. He would wipe it away.

'When I find out what?' I would gulp.

Rob would look down at his hands. 'When you find out who it is,' he would stammer.

'It's someone I know?'

Rob would nod.

'Christ, is it someone at work? I don't think I could bear the humiliation,' I would whisper, trying to hold back the lump of terror which threatened to force its way out of my chest.'

Rob would shake his head. 'No, no, it's not anyone from work, Rachel. I wouldn't, well, you know, I just wouldn't do that to you.' Rob's left hand would shake - and he would lunge at it with his right to make it stop.

'So who is it, Rob? Who the fuck have you been fucking?' I would ask.

And he would reply, 'Catherine.'

And I just could not go through all of that. Not again. Of course, the first time, I had been caught completely unawares, but this time, I knew exactly what was coming - and I had the chance to head it off at the pass. In fact, it was my duty to stop it.

I began to hang around outside the hospital on a daily basis, going into work late, leaving early, or simply taking days off sick. I kept myself hidden in the shadow of the trees across the road from the main building, lurking darkly like a private detective on a stakeout for any flash of a blonde ponytail. I learned Catherine's shift patterns off by heart - by day and by night. I noted carefully when she left with friends and when she was more likely to be alone. I hoped – and yet I did not hope– that I would catch her one of these days inflagrantio with Rob. I never actually did, but I remained convinced of their affair and of their regular clandestine meetings. Where else was Rob in the evenings?

Eventually, I decided that the moment had arrived to confront Catherine. I elected the time to strike with care. It was an ebony night with no moon in a lumpy, cloudy sky. The only fleeting light came once from a message flashing up on my mobile phone, which was Rob texting me to ask where I was. I ignored his questions, as these days he often ignored mine. It would not do him any harm to worry a little about my whereabouts for a change. The pavements were already turning white with a heavy frost, and I shivered as I waited, stamping my feet to keep them from going completely numb. I cursed myself for not remembering to wear my rubber-soled boots. I would never have survived undercover for long.

Finally, Catherine emerged from the rear door of the hospital. She was encased like a caterpillar in a long, black puffer coat with her hood pulled way up over her head, so that only a few blonde tendrils of hair were visible - but it was enough for me to identify her. She pulled on her gloves, slung her bag across her shoulder and began to walk, her shoulders hunched as she braced herself against the biting wind.

I followed from a distance, attempting to muffle my footsteps in case she heard me behind her. I knew her route well. She walked at a brisk pace up to Haverstock Hill, where she then veered left towards Belsize Park. Many lights still shone from the hospital windows, but The George pub was silent now, its patrons tucked up in bed long ago, no doubt snoring off their several pints of bitter. Catherine continued her short journey, turning left along the alleyway leading to Aspern Grove, which would take her home. I upped my pace to match hers.

The alley was silent, asleep, and unsuspecting. Catherine strode onwards, past the high wooden fencing on either side, covered in posters for ancient and forthcoming gigs in and around London. All the streetlights in the alley were broken, so that it was almost completely dark, save for a solitary lamp still fighting to stay alive, its bulb flashing intermittently, strobing the pavement. The air was fetid from the stench of the overflowing bins which lurked to one side of the wall. Catherine was not too far from her front door now. There was just a little more of the alley left to traverse, beyond which her house lights beckoned.

'Catherine,' I shouted, my voice croaky, splintering the icy air.

She stopped and jerked around, her movement nervy and unsteady.

I ambled towards her, my footsteps echoing on the concrete pavement.

'Who's there?' Catherine called. 'I have mace, so I'm warning you not to come any closer,' she called, fumbling unsuccessfully in her handbag, hampered by her heavy gloves.

'Oh, Catherine. Come on, that's not very friendly, is it? It's me. Rachel. You know, your sister? Long time, no see,' I drawled.

Catherine peered at me through the gloom, as if struggling to place me.

'Oh, come on, Catherine, don't play games. You can see it's me. Rachel. Your big sister. See. Ta da!' I yanked off my bobble hat. The vicious wind assaulted my ears.

'Rachel? Christ, I seriously didn't recognise you,' Catherine gasped.

'Well, I guess it's been a while, hasn't it, sis?' I laughed and replaced my hat, dragging it low over my forehead.

'Yes, it certainly has.' Catherine paused. 'What the fuck are you doing here in the middle of the night, Rachel? Are you following me?'

'Don't be so bloody paranoid, Catherine. Why would I be following you?'

Catherine took a step closer towards me. 'Well, there is no other explanation as to why we would suddenly bump into each other in the middle of the night, is there?' Catherine stared hard at me, trying to make me out in the dark. 'You look somehow different.'

'Well, perhaps I look a little better than the last time you saw me. Do you remember when that was?'

Catherine made no reply.

'Ah, Catherine. Of course, you remember. You know the time when I'd just been admitted to your hospital, and I was in the most dreadful state. You did that fucking weird, and frankly rather cruel thing where you pretended not to know me. You told everyone we weren't related. Catherine, you can't possibly have forgotten it.' I sidled closer to her, until we could almost touch each other.

Catherine shifted from foot to foot. 'Can you blame me? The time before that you'd tried to kill me.' Catherine took a step backward.

'That's a little over-exaggerated, isn't it? We merely had a little scrap, like when we were kids. And why did we fight anyway, do you reckon? Do you remember that at all, or have you completely lost your memory? Ah yes, that's it – I can see that you remember now.'

Catherine remained quiet, fiddling with the strap of her bag.

'So, let's recap, shall we, as you appear to have lost your tongue for once? We had a fight because you had slept with my boyfriend, Richard, and he had left me for you. So, a little rough and tumble was fair enough under the circumstances, wouldn't you agree?' I took a step closer towards her.

'Look, Rachel, it was a ridiculously long time ago, and I'm sure we've both made mistakes over the years, but we have moved on now, haven't we? It was years ago.'

'It's not exactly ancient history though, is it?'

'I'm not sure what you mean, but surely we are old enough now to be a little more civilised with each other.' Catherine hoisted her bag a little higher onto her shoulder, clutching the strap tightly as if I were about to mug her. 'Rachel, look, lovely as it is to see you, I've had an exceptionally long day. Much as I'd like to stand here reminiscing and all that shit, perhaps we can arrange to meet another time and talk things through then? Perhaps somewhere inside, where it's not pitch black and fucking freezing.' Catherine suggested.

'I really think we should talk now, Catherine. After all, who knows when we will have the opportunity to bump into each other again?' I smiled.

Catherine took a further step away from me. We were moving side to side, backward and forwards, like pieces in a strategic game of chess.

'For fuck's sake, Rachel. What are you doing here exactly? It's one in the sodding morning. What do you actually want? Do you need some money? Is that it?' Catherine glanced around, but we were still alone.

'Don't be so bloody patronising, Catherine. Do I look like I'm here for charity?'

'I have no sodding idea, Rachel, because I can't even see you properly. It's dark. Go home, will you - and let me do the same.'

'I will in a minute, but first of all, you have to answer just one question that I really need to know the answer to.'

'Go on then if it means that we can all go home,' sighed Catherine.

'OK, so my question is, have you fucked him yet?'

'Have I fucked who? Who the hell are you talking about?' Catherine asked, peeping over my head to see if anyone was approaching who might help her out.

'Rob, of course.'

'Rob who? Jesus, who the hell are you on about?'

'Don't play dumb with me, Catherine, because we both know you're not. Rob - my husband.'

'I still don't have the faintest idea who you're talking about, Rachel, you mad bint.'

'Rob, you know. He is around six foot two, blonde hair, unbelievably cute, got one ball, having chemo with you at The Royal Free. You're supposedly helping him to deal with the psychological side of things. Holding his hand - and probably a few other things as well. Ring any bells?'

'You mean, my patient, Rob?'

'Yes, your patient, my husband. He's called Rob, as you well know.'

Catherine burst out laughing. 'No, I'm not fucking him, Rachel. Now, are you happy? Are you satisfied? If we've cleared that up, can I go home now? I'm freezing my tits off here, Rachel.'

'No, no, Catherine, not quite yet' I answered, stepping right up to her, and grabbing the lapel of her coat.' 'Why the hell should I believe you? After all, you've done it before. You've got form, as they say,' I whispered into her ear.

'That was an exceptionally long time ago, Rachel. I was only a child when I went out with Richard. Rob is my patient, and I take my responsibilities as a doctor very seriously. I didn't even know he was your boyfriend. How could I have known?'

'He's my husband, not my boyfriend. Did Rob tell you he wasn't married?' I could feel sweat beading on my forehead despite the intense cold.

'No, I don't think so. I don't know, Rachel. I have so many patients. I can't be expected to remember every detail of the personal lives of everyone I treat without my notes in front of me.'

'Your memory's gone, has it, you poor, old dear. So, Catherine, I'll ask you one more time. Are sleeping with him?'

'No, I'm not sleeping with him, Rachel. Stop being so fucking paranoid. You've always been such a bloody weirdo.' Catherine straightened her hood. 'Anyway, what's a cute guy like him doing with you? He must need his head examining.'

'Isn't that what you're supposed to be doing? Talking him out of my bed and into yours?' I snarled.

'I've had enough of this shit, Rachel. I'm leaving now and I'm going home. Don't even think about following me.'

Catherine removed my hand from her coat and turned on her heel. She began to walk away, but I reached out and caught the back of her hood, yanking her backward. She stumbled and fell forwards onto the pavement.

'Ow. Jesus, Rachel. Look what you've done,' Catherine shrieked. I glanced down and the left leg of her jeans had torn. Blood oozed through the fraying gap.

'Oops, sorry,' I giggled.

Catherine remained sitting on the pavement, dabbing at her knee with her fingers. 'I've only just bought these jeans and they cost me a small fortune. You're still a complete fuckwit, Rachel, you know that?'

I pounced and straddled her. 'What did you say, Catherine?'

'Get off me, Rachel. You're not five anymore. Leave me alone.' She pushed at my chest, but I was stronger than her - and I was on top.

I grabbed her handbag, which had fallen off her shoulder as she hit the ground, and lobbed it behind me, scattering its contents across the concrete pavement.

'I'm sorry, Catherine, but I just can't let you do this to me again. I deserve to be happy at some point in my life and this is my time. But how can I be happy when you keep messing it all up for me? I remember the day Mum and Dad brought you home from the hospital. You changed them instantly with your defenceless little creature act. You demanded everything, yet despite that, you could never put a foot wrong as far as they were concerned. You've never cared about anyone except yourself, ever. You even murdered poor Lucy.'

'I did not murder Lucy, Rachel,' Catherine hissed. 'At the time, you gossiped to as many people as I did about her antics at the party, except you chose not to remember that part after she killed herself. You always did find it easier to change the narrative when it suited you.'

'That is a damned lie, Catherine,' I replied, pushing down hard on her ribcage.

'Is it, Rachel? Is it really?' Catherine panted.

I paused, slightly confused. Somehow or other, we had drifted off topic. 'Look, Catherine, I'm not here to talk about Lucy. I'm here to tell you to back off my husband.' I leaned back and sighed, relieved to have got that off my chest.

Catherine suddenly heaved and I fell backward. She jumped up and started to run, but as she did so, she tripped over her the strap of her own bag, which was lying unseen in the dark. She landed flat on her face. She made no sound after she fell. She just lay there.

'Catherine, are you OK?' I whispered, approaching her body carefully. I poked her in the back with my boot, but there was no response. Her puffer coat was so thick that I could not actually tell if she was still breathing. I bent down and rolled her onto her side. In the gloom, I could see that her nose was crushed on the righthand side and was pouring blood. There was a nasty gash on her forehead, the blood streaking her blonde tresses crimson.

'Catherine, are you OK?' I repeated, kneeling down to take a closer look.

Suddenly, Catherine opened her eyes wide and lunged forwards, wrapping her hands around my neck, and squeezing hard on my windpipe.

'I can't breathe,' I groaned, but Catherine maintained her vicelike grip, squeezing tighter. 'Catherine, stop,' I pleaded.

I grew extremely light-headed and thought I might pass out. Gasping for air, I fumbled in my coat pocket and felt for the paring knife. I had brought with me from my kitchen drawer, really very much as an afterthought as I was leaving the flat, just in case I felt the need to threaten or frighten Catherine a little. But now, in that moment, I knew that if I did not finish her off, she would have no hesitation in killing me. Struggling to breathe, I inched the blade out of my pocket. My lungs ached for oxygen. I had to act before I lost consciousness. I had to do something before Catherine made this story her own once again.

With the greatest of efforts, I raised my hand and plunged the knife deep into Catherine's chest, feeling it work against the resistance of muscle and bone as it pierced her body. She loosened her grip on my throat instantaneously, and I coughed. Catherine fell backward, her head crashing to the pavement. Her blonde ponytail lolled to one side, and her eyes stared upwards towards the streetlight at the end of the alleyway, her skin pale.

'Catherine, I'm sorry. You were hurting me, I coughed. 'I couldn't breathe. Come on, Catherine. Get up now. Don't start playing the dying swan.' I shook her. My hands came away covered in blood. 'Alright, Catherine, enough of the theatrics. Get up now, and I'll walk you to your house, and then we can talk again tomorrow when it's light. We can discuss this matter properly, like adults, without fighting. As you suggested. Agreed?'

Catherine made no reply. She merely lay there, defeated, with nothing further to add, which was frankly not like her at all. The bulb in the streetlight stopped blinking and went out.

Chapter 48

I sat in the dock and shivered. I was only wearing a cotton short-sleeved shirt and trousers fashioned from some cheap, thin, regulation material. The courtroom was icy cold, even though it was packed to the rafters with people. All my past favourites had come to see me - my darling mother and father, Richard, Rob. I think I even spotted Tim high up in the gallery one day - although if it was him, it was pleasing to see that he had lost most of his hair.

My trial appeared to have provoked some serious media attention. Details of the case had been discussed ad infinitum in the papers for months on end, and now that proceedings had begun, interest had revved up another notch. I found it fascinating to learn all about my motivations and deviant behaviour from every angle in the press, without anyone actually asking me anything about it. I had hoped that I would have the chance to give my side of the story, but my lawyer had already told me he would not be calling me to testify, due to what he delicately termed my sensitive state of mind.

The jury surveyed me coldly as they filed in. They seemed to have already decided that I was as guilty as sin. There was certainly no presumption of innocence on their faces, nor even a suggestion of reasonable doubt. I wondered if I could object to the judge about their obvious preconceptions, biased heavily against me by the gutter press, but he looked sterner than any of the jurors. His piggy, sunken eyes surveyed me with disdain as he perched aloft his bench, his three ample chins sagging southwards towards his gavel. My lawyer had advised me to stay silent, on the basis that I would only make matters worse if I spoke. I scratched at my sore wrists, asking him how I could possibly make things worse than they already were. He struggled to provide me with a satisfactory answer to my question.

My lawyer wanted to push for a plea of diminished responsibility. I quite liked that term. I thought it was a particularly apt description of the way I had led my life When I was asked how I pleaded, I stated quite clearly that I was not guilty, resolutely believing that to be the case. None of this – absolutely nothing – had been my fault.

A nervy policeman was the first to be called to the witness stand by the prosecution. He was extremely young and had the unfortunate flaw of blushing scarlet from the neck upwards the minute his name was called. If he had not been in uniform, you would have been forgiven for thinking that he was on trial, rather than myself. He promised to tell the truth, the whole truth and nothing but - the usual bollocks. Just once, it would have been refreshing to hear a witness swear to lie his head off. At least it might ring truer.

The barrister for the prosecution, Anne Hargreaves QC, was a sour-faced old bitch. She was extremely thin, so much so that her robes seemed to swallow her entire frame, the robe was wearing her, rather than vice versa. She sported cat-eyed reading glasses, which made her look like my old maths teacher from school, which did nothing to endear her to me any further. When she had no need of her reading glasses, they swung back and forth like a pendulum on an ostentatious gold chain around her neck.

'Constable Clarke, can you please tell the court what happened on the night of June 8 this year?'

'Yes, Ma'am.' He blushed like a ripe tomato, as he fiddled with the top pocket of his uniform. Retrieving a small notebook, he promptly dropped it. He scrambled around on the floor for a few moments to locate it. It was pure comedy gold. 'Sorry about that, Ma'am,' the constable muttered, straightening his jacket. 'I was, um, yes, well, I was on patrol with my colleague, Sergeant Barnes, when we received a call over the radio to proceed immediately to Aspern Grove, Belsize Park, London at 01.35,' the constable began, consulting his tiny black notebook. His hand was shaking.

'Did Control give you any information about what you might expect when you arrived at the scene?' asked Ms Hargreaves, adjusting her wig to the left, so that now sat slightly askew.

'We were told that someone had been stabbed, Ma'am. That was all the information we were given prior to reaching the scene.'

'And when did you arrive at the scene, Constable?'

'At exactly 01.57,' replied Constable Clarke, consulting his notebook again.

'And what did you find when you got there?'

'There was a small crowd gathered around two young women. One - the deceased - was lying on the pavement. She had been stabbed and was bleeding profusely. The other woman was kneeling next to her, and she had her head on the victim's chest. She appeared to be whispering to her.'

'Can you tell the court what she said?' Ms Hargreaves demanded.

'I couldn't hear what she was saying, Ma'am. She was just muttering. Sort of babbling, I suppose.'

'And do you see the woman in this court today?' asked Ms Hargreaves, glancing around the court as if she were in pantomime.

'Yes, Ma'am,' replied the constable.

'Can you point her out for the benefit of the jury, please?' asked Ms Hargreaves.

Constable Clarke raised his right arm and pointed directly at me. I was tempted to wave back to him, but I restrained myself.

'Please note for the record that Constable Clarke has identified the defendant,' Ms Hargreaves declared. The stenographer typed away. I must admit I admired her stamina. So many words per minute.

'What did you do then?' the QC demanded.

'My partner, Sergeant Barnes, approached the defendant and asked her to drop the knife.'

'She was holding the knife?' asked Ms Hargreaves, quite unnecessarily in my opinion.

'Yes,' replied Constable Clarke, who also looked at the QC as though it had been a strange question.

'And did she drop the knife?' Ms Hargreaves persisted.

'No, well, yes, I suppose she did in a manner of speaking. She stood up and handed the knife to Sergeant Barnes, saying,' – he stopped, opened his notebook again and flicked over a page. 'Here you go.' She said, 'I won't be needing this anymore.'

'Just like that?' queried Ms Hargreaves.

'Yes, just like that. She seemed completely calm.'

'And what happened then?'

'Sergeant Barnes took the knife, and I handcuffed the defendant. In the meantime, I checked the victim for a pulse, but found none. The paramedics arrived at that point and confirmed that the victim was deceased.'

'And the victim was Catherine, the defendant's sister?' asked Ms Hargreaves, her glasses swinging wildly across her chest as she became more animated.

An audible gasp was heard around the court, which surprised me, given they already knew all this detail from their reading of the in-depth media coverage.

'Yes, that is correct – although obviously, we didn't know that at the time of the arrest,' Constable Clarke elaborated.

'Thank you, Constable. That will be all,' Ms Hargreaves concluded with a smug smile.

Constable Clarke looked relieved, only to grow crimson again when my lawyer arose to cross-examine him. My lawyer was Mr Arnold Minchin – not a QC.

'Constable Clarke, when you arrived at the scene, what were your first actions?' asked Mr Minchin.

'Well, I, er, we assessed the scene and made it secure, I suppose.' Constable Clarke fidgeted in his seat.

'I see. And did you feel that you had done so successfully?' Mr Minchin scratched his right eyebrow.

'Yes, we did. The defendant surrendered the knife and we arrested her.' Constable Clarke seemed pleased with his achievements of that night.

'So, you assumed immediately that the defendant had stabbed her sister, rather than anyone else?' queried Mr Minchin.

'Well, yes. She was holding the knife and given what she said at the time, it seemed logical that…'

'Remind me what she said exactly, please,' requested Mr Minchin.

Constable Clarke flicked back through his notebook, a trickle of sweat running down from his temple. How could he not remember such a simple sentence? 'She said, 'I won't be needing this anymore.''

'And you took that to mean what?' Mr Minchin enquired.

'Well, that she had killed her sister with the knife, sir and that she no longer had further use for it - obviously, sir,' Constable Clarke stuttered.

'However, Constable, is it not possible that she could merely have been soothing her sister in her dying moments? Catherine could have been stabbed by someone else, and her sister might have been merely being compassionate in her dying moments – giving her permission to pass on, if you will?' Mr Minchin scratched his right eyebrow.

'Well, not really, sir' replied Constable Clarke. 'I mean, that could be one interpretation, I suppose, but it seems unlikely.' The constable smiled, pleased with his basic rationalisation of the situation.

'But equally, that could also be merely a statement of fact, could it not? Rachel may have merely meant that there was no longer a need for the knife, as it had already been used to kill her sister. It did not necessarily mean that she had used it herself to stab her sister. She may have picked it up after someone else had already attacked Catherine and dropped it at the scene.'

The constable opened his mouth to speak, but clearly thought better of it and closed it again.

Mr Minchin coughed. 'Excuse me, I have a tiny tickle in my throat. Now, constable, were there any witnesses to the attack?'

'No, not that we found. The crowd had gathered after the attack apparently, but no one actually saw what happened.'

'And did the defendant admit to killing her sister at the scene, or indeed did she admit to the killing subsequently?' Mr Minchin turned towards the jurors as he asked this question.

'No, she has always denied it. But the DNA evidence and other character witnesses suggest that...', Constable Clarke muttered.

'No doubt we will consider those individual testimonies later in trial, but for now, we can establish that there were no witnesses to the attack, and that the defendant has never pleaded guilty. Correct?'

'Correct,' stuttered Constable Clarke.

Mr Minchin turned and raised an eyebrow towards me. Clearly, his brows were an important part of his communications cannon. I must admit I was impressed. He had sowed a seed of doubt where none had seemed likely to exist. Who needed a QC anyhow?

Chapter 49

Richard was sweating in the witness box. He produced a large, white handkerchief from his pocket and dabbed at his forehead, before replacing it. What he had to do with my trial, I could not tell you, but Ms Hargreaves had clearly decided to dig out anyone from my past who might be able to prove that I was either a. psychotic, b. murderous or c. ideally both.

'Can you state your name for the record, please?' requested Ms Hargreaves.

'Richard Anderson,' Richard intoned. He looked older, obviously, but he was still handsome, his fine cheekbones standing out proudly from his face. His hair was still deep and dark, and he had lost none of it. I felt my heart crack open once again – even after all this time.

'And can you tell the court how you know the defendant, please?' demanded Ms Hargreaves.

'Well, I've not seen her for many years now, but originally we worked in the same advertising agency. Rachel worked in the creative department, and I was an account handler. We worked together on some projects.' Richard kept his eyes trained on the QC, never once glancing towards me. My gaze never left him.

'And was that the full extent of your relationship? You were merely work colleagues?' asked Ms Hargreaves, lowering her reading glasses having consulted her notes.

'No, we went out together for a while,' Richard replied, glancing down at his hands.

'You went out together for how long exactly?'

'For a couple of years, I guess.'

'So, it was a serious relationship, Mr Anderson?' pressed Ms Hargreaves.

'I suppose so. I mean, not as such. We didn't live together or anything. We hadn't made any real commitment to each other.'

I had to dig my nails into my hands to stop myself from standing up and screaming across the court, 'Lying sod. Cheating bastard.'

'And what happened with your relationship with the defendant in the end, Mr Anderson?' asked Ms Hargreaves, consulting her notes.

'I met someone else, and I broke it off,' Richard muttered.

'And who was it that you had met, Mr Anderson?' asked Ms Hargreaves, leaning in towards Richard as she prepared to land the killer blow. I wondered whose side she was really on. I was on the edge of my seat, as she moved in to expose him for the cad he truly was.

'It was Rachel's sister, Catherine.' Richard hung his head.

More oohs and aahs from the gallery. I drew blood on my palms with my nails.

'So, you began an affair with Catherine – the deceased and Rachel, your girlfriend's sister. Is that correct?' Ms Hargreaves clarified, just in case no one had quite got the point yet.

'Yes,' murmured Richard.

'Can you speak up, please, so that the jury can hear you?' the judge requested.

Richard raised his head and addressed the judge. 'Yes,' he repeated, slightly louder this time.

The judge made a note in his book. I wondered what it was: *Lucky bastard. He shagged them both. He's a braver man than me.*

'And what was Rachel's reaction when you told her that you were ending things in favour of her sister?' Ms Hargreaves continued.

Richard hung his head even lower, so that he was addressing his own chest. 'She was terribly upset, obviously - and extremely angry. Not unfairly, to be honest.'

Gee, that was big of him.

'And what happened after you broke up?' enquired Ms Hargreaves.

'I never saw Rachel again.' He still refused to make eye contact with me.

'And did Rachel see Catherine again after you told her about your relationship with her sister, do you know?' Ms Hargreaves continued to question.

'Yes, Rachel went to visit Catherine in Cambridge when she was still at university.'

'And how did that go? Do you know what happened?' asked Ms Hargreaves, smiling.

'Catherine said that Rachel attacked her in her rooms in college.'

'Rachel attacked Catherine in Cambridge?' Ms Hargreaves repeated.

'Yes. Catherine told me what happened at the time. She said that Rachel visited her room in college and wrestled her to the ground. She ripped her shirt. I remember because she showed me the shredded remains when I visited her afterwards.'

'And was Catherine hurt during this incident?'

'She banged her head on the floor and had a terrible bruise on her spine. She was pretty shaken up by it, as I recall,' Richard answered, seemingly regaining a little confidence. 'Rachel frightened her.'

Ms Hargreaves paused, allowing the jury to absorb this dramatic testimony.

'And did Catherine report this assault to the police?' Ms Hargreaves enquired, turning to face the jury.

'No, I don't think so. Catherine felt pretty awful about what had happened – you know, between me and her - and I think she wanted to give Rachel the benefit of the doubt.'

'The benefit of the doubt?', Ms Hargreaves echoed.

'Yes, I mean, she could understand why Rachel was so upset. Catherine was, after all, an extremely empathetic person.'

I let out an audible snort. I could not help myself. Every head turned towards me. Even Richard regarded me for the first time.

Moving the focus swiftly back to Richard so as not to lose momentum, Ms Hargreaves continued, 'Do you know if Catherine ever saw Rachel again?'

'No, not to my knowledge, but then again I couldn't say for certain. Catherine and I broke up shortly afterward. Neither of us ever felt completely comfortable with what we had done. I lost touch with them both.'

He meant that Catherine had dumped him, but sadly, Catherine was not here to give her version of events.

'Thank you, Mr Anderson,' concluded Ms Hargreaves, returning to her seat. She straightened her skirt as she sat down and smiled at her papers.

'Mr Anderson,' bellowed Mr Minchin, rising from his seat. 'So, you had an affair with Rachel's sister Catherine.'

All colour drained from Richard's face. 'Yes.'

'And how did that particular romance begin?' Mr Minchin asked, his face grim with disapproval.

'I met Catherine when I visited their family home in Manchester.'

'So, you went to visit Rachel's parents with Rachel, I assume, and began an affair with her sister? That's more than a little unethical, is it not?' The eyebrow was working up and down again.

Richard gulped. 'Well, not exactly. That's when I met Catherine for the first time, but we did not start seeing each other until a little later.'

'I see. So, you did not start to see Catherine until you had split up from Rachel?

Richard made no reply.

'Let me repeat the question, Mr Anderson. Did you start seeing Catherine before or after you split up with the defendant?'

'Before,' Richard whispered.

'Can you repeat your answer louder so that the jury can hear you properly, please?' demanded the judge.

'Before,' Richard repeated more loudly.

The judge made another note.

'So, let me get this straight. You were sleeping with both sisters at the same time?' Mr Minchin paused. 'You were an audacious chap, weren't you?'

'Objection,' shouted Ms Hargreaves.

'Sustained,' agreed the judge.

Richard stared down at his hands.

'Let me repeat the first part of my question. Were you conducting a sexual relationship with both sisters at the same time?' demanded Mr Minchin.

'For a short while, yes,' muttered Richard.

'And did you consider the potential repercussions of your actions at the time, Mr Anderson?' enquired my lawyer.

'Yes,' Richard replied, pulling at the skin on the top of his hands.

'But not enough to stop yourself?' Mr Minchin persisted.

Richard remained silent.

'Did it not occur to you that you might do irreparable harm to both girls – not to mention to the sisterly relationship they had with each other?'

No reply.

'I will give you the benefit of the doubt, Mr Anderson, and assume not. However, I think we might surmise that it would not have helped their sororal warmth towards each other. Would you not agree?'

Richard raised his head and addressed Mr Minchin. 'Probably not, no.'

'So, who broke it off with whom?' asked Mr Minchin.

'Excuse me?' Richard queried.

'You and Catherine. What happened? There were no more sisters, so I assume you moved on elsewhere.' The gallery tittered.

A low blow, I felt, but I enjoyed it, nonetheless. Even Ms Hargreaves did not raise an objection.

'I broke it off. Catherine was always comparing herself to Rachel and asking me to rank the two of them.'

What a liar.

'Rank them?'

'Yes, you know - sexually.'

'And did you?'

'No, of course I didn't,' barked Richard. 'I found Catherine's jealousy of Rachel intense and - in the end - unbearable.'

'So, Catherine was jealous of her sister, Rachel?'

'Yes, she seemed to be. She always seemed desperate to attract Rachel's attention, but Rachel was never that interested. In fact, I think Rachel found Catherine rather irritating.' Richard glanced over to me, and I looked down at my shoes.

'So, you are saying that Catherine may have gone out with you merely to get a reaction out of Rachel?'

'I think that it's possible, yes,' Richard admitted, looking somewhat feeble in his chair, 'although clearly, I didn't realise that at the time.'

But I told you that this was the case at the time didn't I, Richard. I told you that Catherine was playing you to get at me. But Richard did not mention any of my previous observations when giving evidence. He appeared to have a highly selective memory.

'So, is it possible that Catherine continued to try to provoke Rachel? Could it be that she became more and more aggressive over time towards her sister rather than vice versa?'

'I couldn't say,' answered Richard. 'As I say, I lost touch with both of them. It was a long time ago.'

'It's an interesting thought to mull over though, isn't it?' mused Mr Minchin, nodding to the jury.

Chapter 50

The parade of my ex-lovers continued for the titillation of the jurors. Now it was Rob's turn in the hot seat. I had heard that he had not been well again, but I was shocked to see how gaunt he appeared to have become since I last saw him. His lustrous yellow mane had thinned, his cheeks had imploded, and his muscles had wasted. As he stuttered through his oath, it was like watching a cadaver speak. I wondered whether his cancer had returned, or if his terrible appearance was purely down to the stress of our association.

'May I call you Rob?' asked Ms Hargreaves in a far more conciliatory tone than she had used with other witnesses. Even she appeared to appreciate Rob's fragility.

'Yes, that's fine,' Rob answered, his answer robust in contrast to his body.

'For the benefit of the jury, can you confirm your relationship with the defendant, please.'

'She is my wife,' Rob grimaced, as if he had tasted something sour. 'Was my wife. We are in the process of getting a divorce,' he added, unnecessarily in my opinion.

'And how long have you been married to the defendant?' continued Ms Hargreaves.

'Almost six years,' Rob replied, staring into the middle distance.

'And so I assume that you had also known her sister, Catherine, the murder victim, for a while too?'

'No, not at all. I never even knew that Rachel had a sister until all of this happened.' Rob gripped the edge of the wooden frame around the witness box, his knuckles transparent.

'You didn't know that Rachel had a sister, even though you were married to her?' Ms Hargreaves declared, seemingly shocked and looking up to the gallery for support. 'That seems rather odd, doesn't it?'

'No, no, I really didn't know. Rachel told me that her parents had died when she was a baby and that she had been brought up by an elderly aunt, who had also apparently died shortly before we met. As I understood it – as she told it to me, anyway - Rachel was an orphan and an only child.'

My mother, sitting a few rows back from the front, began to weep noisily. My father passed her a crisp, white handkerchief and she buried her face in it. Ms Hargreaves glanced towards them with clear irritation and then ploughed onwards.

'Why do you think that Rachel lied to you about her family?' asked Ms Hargreaves.

'I really don't know. I only found out the truth after Catherine was mur...after Catherine died. It was only then that I was told that they were sisters - and that her parents were still alive.' Rob craned his head to search my parents out and my father replied with a curt nod of his head. They had obviously become pals in my absence.

'But in actual fact, it appears that you had met Catherine before she died, as I understand it. Even if you were unaware that she was Rachel's sister at the time. How did that occur?'

'I met her without knowing the connection. It was genuinely a total fluke. I was being treated for cancer and Catherine was one of my doctors at The Royal Free Hospital. She worked in the psychiatric unit and was helping me to deal with the mental trauma of my illness.'

'And can you tell the court what Catherine was like?' questioned Ms Hargreaves.

'Well, she was an extremely competent doctor. She was very thorough and enormously encouraging.' Rob paused and swallowed, as if the memory of Catherine was painful to him 'She was always incredibly positive, which I found terribly reassuring.'

'Did Catherine ever meet Rachel during your treatment?' enquired Ms Hargreaves, turning towards the jurors. The jurors leaned forward in anticipation.

'No, I don't think so. I always went into the hospital for treatment alone and Rachel met me outside afterward. She wasn't allowed onto the ward while I was having treatment.' Rob shivered.

'Are you feeling well enough to continue, Rob?' asked Ms Hargreaves.

'Yes, I'm fine, thank you.' Rob straightened up in his chair.

'OK, well, if you are sure, I will carry on. So, the two sisters never actually met through you. But is it at all possible that Rachel saw - or even met - Catherine during your treatment outside the hospital?'

'Not that I was aware of at the time, but thinking back, I believe that she must have done, yes, because Rachel began to act very oddly all of a sudden.' Rob glanced at me again for a split second.

'She began acting oddly in what way? Can you be more specific, please?' Ms Hargreaves moved closer to Rob, egging him on.

'Well, I believe that, on one particular occasion, Rachel lied about the hospital calling to change an appointment, telling me that she never actually took the call. There was a mix-up when I went to the hospital and they said they had spoken to Rachel to ask me to change the date, but she completely denied it. I believed her at the time, but retrospectively, I don't think that she told me the truth. And then Rachel began asking me incessant questions about which individual doctors I had been seeing. She even suggested I moved my treatment elsewhere.'

'And did you ask her why?'

'No, not really. It was an incredibly stressful time for both of us, as I'm sure you can imagine. We had been trying for a baby for quite a while before I was diagnosed, and we had both undergone fertility tests. The results revealed that I had testicular cancer and I had to have an operation followed by radiation and chemotherapy. I thought Rachel was merely struggling to cope with the shock and the stress of it all – as I was.' Rob turned his head towards me for a brief moment and I smiled at him. He looked away.

'So, when exactly did you find out about the fact that Catherine was actually Rachel's sister?' Ms Hargreaves pressed.

'Not until after Catherine died. It was only then that I was told who she was – and that was when I realised that Rachel had lied to me about absolutely everything for the whole time that I had known her. Our whole marriage had been a total sham. She was - she is - a completely fictitious person.' Rob's voice faltered and he swallowed hard, shifting in his seat.

'Would you like some water?' asked Ms Hargreaves.

'Yes, please,' Rob croaked.

A clerk scurried out of the back of the courtroom and returned to provide Rob with a glass of water from the cooler, which he drank down in one, as if it were a vodka shot. In truth, that was probably what he would have preferred at this particular moment.

'So, your life with Rachel had, in actual fact, all been one hugely elaborate façade,' Ms Hargreaves summarised.

'Yes, you could say that,' whispered Rob. The judge did not ask him to speak up.

'No further questions, Your Honour,' stated Ms Hargreaves, turning her back on Rob, who seemed ever more withered by his testimony.

'Rob,' called Mr Minchin, rising from his seat. 'I won't keep you much longer, as I appreciate that you are unwell.'

'Thank you,' muttered Rob, his pallor whitening by the second.

'So, Catherine was your doctor?' Mr Minchin repeated.

'One of them, yes,' sighed Rob, somewhat exasperated by having to go back over the facts.

'And what was she like with you?' Another repeat question. Mr Minchin really was quite slow at getting to the point, whatever that was going to be.

'As I just said earlier, she was a good doctor - and she was extremely kind.'

'And did she flirt with you at all?' Mr Minchin enquired.

'No, not at all. We had a bit of a laugh and a joke on occasion. That was all. She was just being friendly. It was her job to cheer me up.' Rob's cheeks reddened.

'And did you find Catherine attractive?' smiled Mr Minchin.

'I suppose so. She was a pretty girl. But she was my doctor - and I was married to Rachel. I would never have acted on it. I was always faithful to Rachel.'

'But otherwise, you might have been tempted?' Mr Minchin pressed on.

'Objection,' cried Ms Hargreaves. 'This is pure speculation.'

'Sustained,' agreed the judge.

'Did you ever question Rachel as to why she was asking you so many questions about who you were seeing at the hospital?' Mr Minchin continued.

'No, as I've already stated, I thought Rachel was merely concerned and also quite stressed. I tried not to get into an argument with her about it. My treatment at the time had almost finished - and I was hoping we might be able to get back to normal.' Rob exhaled loudly.

I ached to console Rob, who looked so utterly defeated. I wanted to scream my apologies across the courtroom, but I had enough sense to stay silent.

'Rob, you stated earlier that you had no knowledge of Rachel's past life. Did it not strike you as odd that you had never met any of her family, or even any of her old friends?' Mr Minchin was standing right in front of the witness box now, staring Rob down. He was so tall that his back was bent into a permanent stoop from years of leaning down to converse with others as if he were a living question mark.

'I had absolutely no reason not to believe that Rachel was completely alone. If someone tells you that their whole family is dead, your first response is to feel sorry for them, rather than to assume that they are lying. I loved Rachel. I wanted to protect her.' Rob wiped a tear away from his left eye and sniffed.

'And you stated just now that you had always been faithful to Rachel?' smirked Mr Minchin.

Rob made no reply.

'Let me rephrase the question, Rob. Isn't it true that you had affairs with at least two of your work colleagues whilst you were married to the defendant, your wife?' Mr Minchin boomed.

Rob hung his head.

'Can you answer the question, please? I would remind you that you are under oath, Rob,' insisted Mr Minchin.

'I wouldn't classify them as affairs, no,' Rob murmured. 'They were merely one-off events.'

Someone in the gallery tittered.

'Merely one-off events. I think that still classifies as cheating, don't you?' Mr Minchin chuckled. 'So, when you stated earlier that you had always been faithful to Rachel, you were, in fact, lying?'

'No, yes, well it depends on your point of view, I suppose,' Rob whispered.

I leaped from my seat, all previous pity I felt for Rob vanquished by his confession. How dare Rob lie to me? 'You bloody, cheating bastard,' I screeched. 'You lousy fuck!'

'Silence, or I will have you removed from the court,' bellowed the judge.

The officer by my chair placed a steadying hand on my shoulder and I sank back down, panting. I started to concentrate on my breathing. Four breaths in, hold for two, out for six. My heart still raced.

'So, it is possible that you did have an affair with Catherine?' Mr Minchin suggested. 'Or at least, we could say that we cannot be certain that you did not have a one-off – as you put it - with her as well.'

'No. I told you - nothing happened with Catherine,' Rob stressed more loudly.

'Regardless, Rachel is an intelligent woman, and she may have detected some of your inclination towards infidelity, even if it was just what some might term female intuition.'

I clearly was not that intelligent, as I had never suspected Rob of cheating on me at any stage. I had only ever suspected Catherine. I was such a bloody idiot. My whole life everyone had lied to me and abused me. Why was I stupid enough to believe that Rob would be any different?

'I don't think Rachel was the jealous type – or at least, I didn't. Once I realised that Rachel's whole life was a lie, I genuinely didn't know what to believe anymore.' Rob peered at me, yet through me, as if he did not really see me, his head cocked to one side in wonder.

'It seems to me that you both lied rather effectively to each other,' Mr Minchin surmised. 'Wouldn't you agree, Rob?'

Chapter 51

Mr Minchin called one last witness.

'The defence calls Jenny Holmes,' stated my lawyer.

Jenny who? I knew no one of that name.

A small, stout woman stomped up to the witness box. She wore an ill-fitting jacket, which strained to hold together under the pull of her ample chest. Her lipstick was scarlet and had smudged onto her top front teeth.

'Please state your full name for the record,' asked the clerk.

'Jenny Daisy Holmes,' she boomed.

She was duly sworn in, and as she was, it dawned on me who she was. I had not recognised her out of uniform.

'Miss Holmes, can you please state your occupation?' asked Mr Minchin.

'I am a nurse on the psychiatric ward at the Royal Free Hospital,' she replied.

'And you worked with the deceased as I understand it?'

'Yes, you could say that. Catherine was one of our junior doctors on the ward.'

'And do you recognise the defendant?' asked Mr Minchin.

'Oh yes, I most certainly do,' Jenny confirmed. 'She came up to the ward a few months ago asking to sit in on one of her husband's therapy sessions with the doctor. With Catherine.'

'And did you allow her to do so?' enquired Mr Minchin, his left eyebrow lifting.

'Absolutely not,' Jenny announced. 'It is completely against hospital policy.'

'And did the defendant comply?'

'No, she did not. She wandered up the corridor as if she was just minding her own business on the way to the family room, where I told her she could wait – and the next thing I knew, she was attempting to get into the room where her husband was having his session.' Jenny crossed her arms and stared at me, still clearly annoyed about my infraction.

'And what happened then?' asked Mr Minchin.

'I told her she couldn't go into the room, so she beetled off downstairs, all embarrassed like. It was a bit odd, but I assumed at the time that she was just overly worried about her husband.' She paused. 'Mind you, if I were her, I would have been too!' Jenny smiled and burst into laughter.

'What do you mean by that, Miss Holmes?' asked Mr Minchin, glancing towards the jury.

Jenny leaned towards the judge, inviting him into her web of gossip. 'Well, Catherine was a terrible flirt. Honest to God, she really thought she was god's gift to all men. I wouldn't have wanted to leave her alone with my man, I can tell you!' She recrossed her arms and smirked.

'And did you feel that the defendant had any good reason to worry about Catherine having anything other than a professional relationship with her husband?' enquired Mr Minchin.

'I didn't feel that. I knew that. I'd seen Catherine snogging her husband - that man over there,' - Jenny pointed towards Rob, who was now seated once again next to my parents – 'on many, many occasions and not only that, sometimes, they locked the door and closed the blinds. He's a lying bastard. Those two were at it like rabbits,' Jenny cackled, looking straight at me.

'Are you sure about that?' asked Mr Minchin.

'I'm as sure as eggs is eggs. Catherine couldn't help boasting about it. It was like she had to prove that she could nab any man she pleased. She never stopped banging on about her conquests as if she was the most attractive woman in the world. I found her flirting with my other half once, but I soon put her right. I warned her that if she so much as looked in his direction again, I'd report her for unethical conduct with her patients. That soon shut the bitch up.'

'Indeed,' commented Mr Minchin, backing away from the witness box.

I knew it. I had been right about Catherine all along. I took one last look at Jenny's bright red lips before I fainted and fell off my chair.

Chapter 52

'All rise,' called the clerk of the court and we all rose on demand.

'Be seated,' instructed the judge, waving his hand downwards as if he were training a recalcitrant pack of dogs to sit.

'Ladies and Gentlemen, this has been a truly harrowing case and one of the most tragic over which I have ever had to preside. Sororicide is, fortunately, an uncommon crime, which makes it all the more horrific when it does actually occur.

Here we had two young woman, both of whom were given the best possible start in life, brought to mutual destruction. One of them has lost her life in a vicious attack on her by the other. The other sister has both lost her mind and, as a result, her liberty.

The jury has found the defendant guilty of manslaughter due to diminished responsibility and it is now my duty to pass sentence. Can the defendant please rise?' The judge peered at me over his half-moon glasses, his mouth a straight line of contempt.

I tried to stand, but my legs refused to obey my command. The two policewomen on either side of me hoisted me up under my armpits. I stood there wobbling, and almost fell down again, so I grabbed the rail in front of me to steady myself.

'Rachel Blake, I hereby sentence you to life imprisonment in a high-security psychiatric facility for the manslaughter of your sister, Dr Catherine Blake. My recommendation is that you should never be released, but this will inevitably be subject to regular medical review.'

I swayed slightly and the policewoman standing sentinel behind me held my elbow.

'I hope that you will be able to find the necessary help and support for your mental health problems in prison, which sadly you have not had help with previously, whilst also reflecting on the hideous crime you have committed. You have deprived a beautiful, intelligent young woman, an accomplished and extraordinarily successful doctor – not to mention your own flesh and blood - of the chance of living a fulfilling and happy life. For that, you must be punished. Whilst we can never bring Catherine back, I hope that in the fullness of time, you will comprehend the enormity of your actions and through that, that you can find some peace of mind of your own. Take her down. Court dismissed'

The gavel banged, its echo ringing in my ears as I was led away to my cell.

Chapter 53

'I had been assessed before the trial by some psychiatrist – not by you, Dr Blake, but by someone far more qualified – who diagnosed me as suffering from borderline personality disorder. You must have heard of it, Doctor?' I laughed, flipping onto my back on the cold, hard floor. I lay, staring at an old, grey watermark on the ceiling. It looked just like an elephant's head, with an uplifted trunk about to reach for an olive branch.

'Of course, I know all the symptoms of Borderline Personality Disorder, Rachel. And obviously, I recognised long, long ago that you fitted the profile exactly. You've always exhibited the classic symptoms for the whole time I've known you,' Dr Blake stated in a matter-of-fact monotone. She leant forward on her seat, so that I could just about make out her lips moving in the dusk.

'You've always been impulsive and unable to rationalise your own emotions. This led you to doubt not only everyone around you, but also to doubt yourself, hence the persistent self-harming from a young age. You felt disconnected from those around you most of the time - feeling somewhat other, if you will - which clearly fed your paranoia and made you question who you really were. That is why you've always found it so difficult to choose suitable partners, and to maintain good relationships with friends and family. It's all so glaringly simple.' Dr Blake slumped back into her chair, barely visible, pleased with her lucid analysis. 'It is similar to being bipolar, which is more of a mood disorder. I suspect that is what you were diagnosed as a child perhaps.'

'I was a polar bear,' I muttered.

'You were a polar bear,' echoed Dr Blake.

I jumped up. 'Enough with the psycho-babble. Anyone with half a brain can regurgitate that shit. You don't need a fucking degree to spout it - and I certainly don't need to hear it from a quack like you!' I yelled, banging the wall hard. My fists bounced off the soft surface. 'What I really want to know is, why did no one do anything about it at any point in my life? If you all knew I was suffering for all this time, why the hell didn't you do anything to help me? Why?'

A glut of tears stuck in my throat, choking me. I sank back down to the floor.

'People did try to help you, Rachel, but you refused to co-operate. You ran away from everyone who cared about you and preferred instead to trust those who never really gave a damn about you. Even now, I'm trying to help you, but you simply won't let me in.'

'But you can't help me now, can you, Catherine, even if you wanted to? It's far too late for that. Look at yourself – you've faded into the ether. You need as much help as I do – if not more. And if we are being completely honest here, my dear Dr Blake, you never really wanted to help me. You have done me more damage than anyone else ever has - if we are genuinely fessing up here. That's how we both ended up in this sodding mess. So don't start playing the part of saviour of the fucking universe with me now, when you've always been my arch-nemesis.'

Chapter 54

Someone was pounding away on my cell door. I locked my hands over my ears and pressed down hard, hoping that they will go away.

The intense banging came again, louder this time. 'Rachel Blake, shut up in there, will you? Stop gabbling to yourself and go to sleep. You're disturbing the whole block with your rantings. Do you want to go back to solitary? It can be arranged, you know.'

I just wanted them all to go away. I was so busy. I had another session to attend.

Chapter 55

I find it oddly ironic that having spent all our lives hating and hurting each other, or completely avoiding each other, Catherine and I have ended up bound together for good. There is no longer an escape route for either of us.

Like Sisyphus continually rolling his boulder up a hill in the depth of Hades, I spend each and every one of my waking days and insomniac nights in conference with my sister, the psychologist, Dr Catherine Blake. We spend hours thrashing out the minutiae of our lives, and discussing who did what to whom, where, when, and why. Catherine insists on asking me thousands of ridiculous questions again and again, to which she already knows almost all the answers. Neither of us will allow the other any respite to try to find true peace.

We talk in my cell, which morphs on occasion into Dr Blake's consulting room. At other times, we chat in our shared childhood bedroom at home, whispering to each other in the darkness, so that no one else can hear us, like we used to occasionally when we were small children.

Maybe, in time, Catherine and I can learn to forgive each other for our many trespasses and misdemeanours against each other, and also forgive those others who trespassed against us, as the old prayer goes. However, in the meantime, we are quite simply stuck with each other, whether we like it or not. We have the freedom to argue in perpetuity about which of us was the greater villain and the more aggrieved victim and to debate who deserved everything that came to them the most. We have the freedom to ask everything of each other and to continue to settle for nothing.

About the Author

Deborah Stone read English Literature at Durham University and lives in North London with her husband, two sons and gorgeous golden retriever, George.

Me and My Shadow is Deborah's second novel.

Her first novel, *What's Left Unsaid*, won The Chill With A Book Runner Up Prize for Best Book of 2018. www.whatsleftunsaid.co.uk

Her non-fiction book, *The Essential Family Guide to Caring for Older People*, is an important manual for any family looking after older relatives. It was published by Bloomsbury in 2019.

www.theessentialfamilyguidetocaringforolderpeople.com

Acknowledgments

With thanks to Gill Aldridge for her advice and support and to Vanessa Stone and Liv Christian for reading my early draft. Also, to Eva Myrick for her invaluable help bringing the book to the page.

Printed in Great Britain
by Amazon

82245481R00169